"I don't fall in love."

"Liar."

"Don't get your hopes up, girl."

She tried not to let his remark sting. She did know better than to fall in love with him. But it had happened so long ago she couldn't take it back now. A blatant lie seemed the best solution, considering the circumstances.

"How long have I known you, Jake?"

"Seems like forever."

"Exactly. So what makes you think I'd put any kind of thought in that direction?"

"I don't know. There's something in the way you kiss."

She grinned to throw him off the truth. "Maybe I'm just a good kisser."

"Maybe you're good at a lot of things." The corners of his mouth lifted suggestively.

"Oh. I am." She settled in the saddle a little more, which rearranged the short dress around her legs and lifted the fabric a little higher up her legs. Though hidden behind those sunglasses, she felt Jake's gaze follow the fabric up. "Too bad you'll never find out."

"We'll see."

We'll see?

By Candis Terry

TRULY SWEET
SWEET SURPRISE
SOMETHING SWEETER
SWEETEST MISTAKE
ANYTHING BUT SWEET
SOMEBODY LIKE YOU
ANY GIVEN CHRISTMAS
SECOND CHANCE AT THE SUGAR SHACK

Short Stories
SWEET COWBOY CHRISTMAS
SWEET FORTUNE
(appears in CONFESSIONS OF A SECRET ADMIRER)
HOME SWEET HOME
(appears in FOR LOVE AND HONOR
and CRAZY SWEET FINE)

CANDIS TERRY

Truly SWEET

AVONBOOKS

An Imprint of HarperCollinsPublishers

AVON BOOKS
An Imprint of HarperCollins*Publishers*
195 Broadway
New York, New York 10007

Copyright © 2015 by Candis Terry
ISBN 978-0-06-235115-9
www.avonromance.com

First Avon Books mass market printing: August 2015

Avon Trademark Reg. U.S. Pat. Off. and in Other Countries, Marca Registrada, Hecho en U.S.A.
HarperCollins® is a registered trademark of HarperCollins Publishers.

Printed in the U.S.A.

10 9 8 7 6 5 4 3 2 1

*It has been a joy to write and share the stories
of the six military heroes in my Sweet, Texas series.
And it is with much love and gratitude
that I dedicate this final book in the series
to our military heroes in the Marine Corps, Army, Navy,
Air Force, National Guard, and US Coast Guard.
Your love of country and your
selfless sacrifices know no bounds.
God bless.*

Acknowledgments

Special thanks to my publicist, Caroline Perny, who is not only the funnest, coolest chick, and not only does an amazing job, but she has such a love for Miss Giddy that she wanted to see Sweet, Texas's favorite farm animal get her own happily-ever-after. Your wish is granted, my dear. I hope you had fun with the name game.

As this series ends, I want to extend a very grateful thank-you to my amazing editor, Amanda Bergeron, for her constant support and encouragement, brilliant insight and ideas, and for bringing a sense of calm to my sometimes irrational e-mails. Thank you so much for helping me give life to Sweet, Texas, and the memorable Wilder family.

To my agent, Kevan Lyon, a huge thanks for always answering my crazy questions and for guiding me when I have no idea where I'm going.

Shout-out to Kelsi Copple for giving Reno and Charli's baby girl a very sweet name.

And, as always, thanks to my family for their love, support, and patience when I lock myself in my office for what seems like forever, and I often lose my smile when I'm under pressure to meet my deadlines. I love you oodles!

Truly
SWEET

Prologue

Under the scorching sun in the rocky terrain of an eastern province of Afghanistan, hell exploded in a firestorm of fury. In that hellhole, newly assigned Marine Second Lieutenant Jake Wilder and his twelve troops became the bull's-eye in a merciless path of destruction.

When the first crack of incoming mortar rounds screamed over their heads and exploded approximately one hundred meters behind them, Jake had no choice but to conclude that the confidential intel for their surveillance mission hadn't been faulty. They'd been betrayed.

Jake dropped to his knees, shook the ringing from his ears, blinked, then leveled his weapon.

"Fucking assholes!" This verbal eruption came from his best friend, Sergeant Eli Harris, as he dove behind a boulder barely big enough to cover his ass while rapid-fire and mortar rounds continued to discharge in their direction.

Any other time, Jake would have laughed at Eli's outburst. At the moment, he was too busy scoping the hills in front of them from behind his own meager refuge. Everything around them was drab—brown hills, brown sand, brown dust floating in the air. The enemy didn't fight in a uniform, and their garb was as colorless as the landscape, which made them hard to spot and twice as dangerous.

In his periphery, Jake caught the flash of sunlight against hard steel. "Contact north. Two hundred meters," he shouted to his team. "Additional small RPG west."

"Small RPG east. One hundred fifty meters and closing," Eli shouted in return while scoping the opposite ridge.

Muzzle flashes continued as Jake grabbed his radio to call in and report the three-sided ambush and request air support. A lack of response signaled the radio was either dead or off-line. He hoped it was only a momentary break in communication and not a sign that they were stranded out there without backup or communication while the enemy tried to turn them into Swiss cheese.

Not for the first time did he wonder if they were really brave or just plain crazy. A bullet pinged off a rock behind him. He hit the ground, then belly-crawled to a shelf of gravel that would give slightly better protection.

Crazy mothers, he decided. Just fucking crazy as hell.

Across the rocks and sand, flashes lit up the ridgeline. Jake again scoped the ridge and spotted a new cluster of insurgents in the bushes below.

Any minute, the new arrivals would engage, and he and his men would be in a damned dogfight.

In Afghanistan, the terrain was as much an enemy as anything else. They had to get to a safer location. Because sure as shit, these puny-ass rocks weren't going to protect them for long.

He grabbed his radio again and pushed out a call for backup. Not knowing if his request had been received, he ran the options he'd learned in training through his head. The only way to get everyone back home was to keep fighting. He'd promised Eli's pregnant wife he'd get her husband home in one piece. Which left Jake no choice but to retreat. In a split-second decision, as a mortar rocketed over their heads and exploded too close for comfort, he barked out the order to move.

Lifting their rifles, they fired as a safety cover and sprinted toward the larger outcropping of boulders to the south—away from the contact— and back in the direction from which they'd come. Private First Class Lieberman was the first to be hit. He went down like a stone. The silence and stillness from the young private sent a chill through Jake's heart. As he snapped out the order to keep going, he planned to grab Lieberman on the way to shelter.

Eli got to Lieberman first. He lowered his rifle and bent to grab the private by the vest. An RPG flew over their heads and detonated. Shrapnel flew, embedding in rock, skin, bones, and worse.

Jake flinched when the flash exploded. When

he opened his eyes, both Private Lieberman and
Eli were on the ground. Bodies torn and bleeding.
Both still as death.

The sounds of war rushed at Jake, and time
stopped.

A chill sliced up his spine. For a second, he could
hear nothing but the pounding of his own heart.
Then it all charged back like a speeding train. He
looked at the bodies strewn about the sand. He
couldn't hit PAUSE or REWIND. This shit was real.

No man left behind.

While bullets and mortars flew and shrapnel
dug into the soles of his boots and feet, Jake ran
to the fallen men and dragged them behind the
outcropping of boulders.

Crouched behind the rocks, Sergeant Bagley
looked down. "Lieutenant, I don't think—"

"Good. Don't think. Shoot." Jake looked down
to where his brothers in arms and in all ways
that mattered except blood lay looking up at him
through sightless eyes.

Eli was dead.

Lieberman was dead.

Anger tore through Jake and rattled his cage
hard. His chest constricted and caved as he closed
Eli's and Lieberman's eyes with his dirty fingers.
Jake made a silent promise to Eli that he'd get the
bastards that had done this to him and those who'd
killed his brother as well. Knowing his promises
didn't mean shit because he'd just broken the one
he'd made to Eli's wife, he got back to work.

He clicked on his radio and nearly howled with
relief when it came to life. He repeated the call

for air support and now, a medevac. He reported the casualties and injuries in a surprisingly calm voice. And then, wiping the sweat from his eyes and stifling the urge to scream, he came out from behind the protective wall of rock.

In that instant, he knew exactly what his brother had done on the day that he'd been killed. The desire to rescue lives became bigger than the fear of his own death.

He'd made it halfway back to the rocks—dragging a barely conscious and bloodied Private Stacks—when the impact and burn of a bullet to his thigh buckled his knee and stole his breath. Another soldier came out from cover to help, but Jake waved him off. Damned if he'd risk another soldier just to save his own sorry ass.

Once Jake got Private Stacks to safety, he dropped to the sand, ripped the bandana from around his neck, and tied it around his upper thigh to staunch the steady stream of blood while he shouted out orders probably no one wanted to heed.

Why should they?

He'd just gotten several men—including his best friend—killed.

The battle raged for hours in the blistering heat before night fell, and air support rocketed to their rescue, pushed the enemy back, and the dust settled. Under the cover of darkness, Jake assisted in helping to carry the fallen and injured to the medevac before he agreed to climb on board and accept aid for himself.

As the helicopter lifted off and spun sand like

Dorothy's tornado from *The Wizard of Oz*, Jake gave Bagley a salute and a silent prayer that the young sergeant would get the remaining men back to camp safely.

The blood of his friends on his hands and the chop-chop-chop whir of the helicopter blades beneath a starless night were the last things Jake remembered.

Chapter 1

Two months, three surgeries, and a stint in a military rehab hospital later, Jake kicked up gravel and dust in his black Chevy truck with the radio blasting Montgomery Gentry's "Hell Yeah." He flew down the proverbial long and winding road past the ranches that dotted the landscape with wide-open meadows and grazing longhorn cattle. Past the landmarks of Sweet, Texas, and the memories of his youth, where he and his brothers had raised more than a little hell while having the time of their lives.

In no hurry to be anywhere in particular, he turned the truck onto Main Street and cruised past the old water tower, where any high-school kid worth their weight in rebellion went to drink beer. At the stop sign while he waited for a young mother and her three small children to scurry across the street, he looked over to Sweet Surprise, the thriving cupcake and ice-cream shop his former sister-in-law Fiona owned. He thought about stopping in to sample his favorite flavor, but this morning his stomach rumbled for more than a sugary treat. Today, his taste buds hankered for the gut-bomb meal he'd craved all those months he'd eaten sand sandwiches in Afghanistan. Not to mention the bland fare called hospital food while they'd had his leg hijacked in some kind of futuristic contraption.

Maybe a burger dripping with cheese wasn't going to change the world or make him forget that the Marines had kicked him to the curb with what they'd politely termed an honorable discharge, but it would satisfy his hunger and momentarily get him away from the lovable hovercraft he called Mom.

His reentry into civilian life had taken place two days ago. During those forty-eight hours, he'd been overwhelmed by the surge of love and attention from family and friends. Not that he didn't appreciate it. But from the moment he'd walked through the front door of Wilder Ranch, the calls and visitors had been nonstop. The casseroles and desserts had piled up on the kitchen table until it looked like either someone had died, or they were preparing for one of the famous Wilder Family BBQ Blowouts.

All the while, his mother had barely taken her eyes off him. Though his healing and progress had been good, he still walked with a cane, which apparently communicated a distress signal to the woman who'd given him life. Mama Bear kept such a close eye on him, he figured any minute she'd put bumper guards on all the hard-surfaced furniture like she had when he'd been a kid.

Just this morning, he'd needed a moment of solitude and had gone into the barn to brush down Rocky, his favorite quarter horse. In two blinks, his mother rushed out to *check on him*. Jake had felt his throat tighten and a streak of panic grip his chest. While he appreciated the love and thoughtfulness, he was having a hard time adjusting to all the fuss.

He wasn't broken, he just needed a break.

A moment to forget the bad and remember the good. To find his way back into the rhythm of life—one that had nothing to do with military routines, high-powered weapons, and the enemies of mankind. To find the joy and laughter that had once been the foundation of his life.

Minutes later, he rolled the truck to a stop in the gravel lot beside Bud's Nothing Finer Diner. The exterior was little more than a yellow concrete box with a neon sign. But the interior overflowed with character and a patriotic red, white, and blue décor that shouted "Don't Mess With Texas" from every corner. No question he'd be walking into a bird's nest of gossip. Bud's was *the* place the townsfolk gathered to mourn, celebrate, discuss local politics or who was sleeping with whom.

From his open window, the aroma of grilled burgers and fresh apple pie made his mouth water. When he opened the truck door, he realized that getting down from the damn thing might not be as easy as getting up. He hadn't thought of that earlier when he'd climbed inside. His thigh muscles were healing in a way that made moving in one direction easy. The opposite direction, however, was like letting Freddy Krueger use him as a scratching post.

Thankful no one was in the parking lot to see him struggle, he maneuvered down to the ground, curled his fingers over the head of the cane, and controlled his uneven gait as he headed inside.

Bud's might be Sweet's breeding ground for chitchat, but he hadn't come looking for gossip, sympathy, or acknowledgment.

He'd just come for a burger and a milk shake.

Before he could reach for the door handle, the door swung outward. Holding it open from the other side was Chester Banks, Sweet's very own playboy octogenarian. The man had more nose than face these days, and his smile often displayed a set of false teeth that didn't always stay put, but he gave Jake a respectful nod as Jake maneuvered into the diner with as little detection as possible.

"No need to thank me," Chester said. "Been in about the same place as you. Got my scrawny ass shot up stormin' that damn beach in World War II. Sure puts a hitch in yer giddyup, but it coulda been worse, I guess."

"True that." Jake had no idea the old guy had ever served in the military, let alone one of the toughest wars ever battled. Of course, as a soldier himself, he knew there were two kinds of veterans; those who loved to tell war stories, and those who wanted to bury the memories deep. As easy as it was to poke fun at Chester's flirtatious ways, at least the old codger was still around to make it happen.

"Thanks just the same," he said, as Chester gave him another nod and left the diner.

While Jake made his way to a booth, he got a two-finger salute from Bill McBride, a Vietnam vet, and a chin lift from Ray Calhoun, both of whom were sitting at a table, playing a game of checkers. At the big round table in the back, the Digging Divas Garden Club looked up in surprise. Instead of their usual exuberance, most just smiled as though they realized he might need some space. The tear sliding down Arlene Potter's crinkly cheek could have been from allergies. Or it could have been because, even at her advanced age, Arlene loved a man in uniform. Not that he was wearing one. But that really didn't matter to Arlene. She had a vivid imagination.

Jake tried to relax. He hadn't known exactly what he'd be walking into here, but the silent acknowledgments worked just fine for him.

With his favorite booth vacant, he eased over to the middle of the red vinyl seat and stretched his leg. As he looked out the window at the passersby on their way through their daily routines, he took a breath to ease the ache slicing down his thigh. Moments later, a menu sailed onto the table in front of him, and a glass of ice water landed without a splash.

His head instantly came up.

Blue eyes focused, Annie Morgan stood there, weight balanced on one hip while she tapped the eraser of her pencil against the order pad.

In the past couple of years, the Wilder family had expanded with three of his brothers having said the I do's. Thanks to his brother, Jackson, and her sister, Abby, he and Annie were now related by marriage. Before that, they'd been adversaries for as long as Jake could remember. Always outspoken and not a stranger to butting in where she didn't belong, they'd gone head-to-head on many outlandish subjects. If he said the sky was blue, she'd argue it was turquoise. If he said a steak would take seven minutes to grill, she'd say five. If he said the Rangers would win by a home run, she'd bet they'd lose with a strikeout. It seemed like the girl just liked to argue. More often than not, he'd rise to the bait. Just as he always did with his brothers. One of these days, he'd learn to just sit back and smile.

Today probably wasn't that day.

"Forget something?" Her eyes narrowed just slightly, and the silky blond ponytail hanging down her back swung to the side as she tilted her head in a way that suggested she was primed for a challenge.

"Not that I'm aware."

"Uh-huh." She tucked the stub of a standard yellow pencil behind her ear. "Guess you've been away too long to remember that most folks walk in here wearing a smile. Looks like you left yours at home."

"Guess I'm just not much in the mood."

"Seriously?" Her eyes narrowed a bit more, yet somehow a shower of silver sparks still managed to flash. "Why?"

He hated to use the word *Duh*, but it seemed so apropos.

"So . . ." Her shoulders lifted and dropped. "What? You're going to let that walking cane snuff out the eternally grinning smart-ass that lives inside you?"

Her comment hit its mark with stinging success.

Jake clenched his teeth and lowered his gaze to the laminated menu he'd been able to recite by heart since he'd been twelve. "Annabelle, how about you go away and give me a minute to look over the menu?"

"Because that would be a total waste of time, *Jacob.*"

His gaze jerked up again just as she shifted her weight to a position she probably intended as a show of obstinacy. Yet all it really managed to do was push her full breasts against that snug white *Bud's Diner* T-shirt. Instinctively, his gaze dropped lower to the little black skirt hugging nicely rounded hips and the pair of tanned, shapely legs that ended with the sparkly blue sneakers on her feet. Liking what he saw, his gaze took that same slow ride back up her body.

When the hell had little Annie Morgan grown up and gotten so curvy?

"You can stare at that menu all day long," she said through lips that were pink, plump, and glossy. Lips that looked like they needed to be kissed.

The unexpected and unwanted thought was like a splash of ice water in his face. Annie had been a pain in his backside for as long as he could remember. The last thing he should be doing was thinking about her damned mouth. Or her curvy body. To his dismay and against his commands, awareness tightened his body below the belt.

"In the end," Annie continued, "you're going to choose a double Diablo burger with extra peppers, a side of sweet-potato fries—extra crispy, and a chocolate-banana shake."

Challenged, he leaned forward and met her glare. "How do you know what I want?"

"Because." She planted her palm down on the table and leaned in till they were nearly nose to nose. "While you and your football buddies parked your cocky behinds in the booth by the door so all your minions could see you and come in to fawn all over you, some of us were slinging hash and cleaning up your mess after you left."

He leaned back. "I don't remember your working here."

"Why would you?" She shifted her weight again, and he'd have to be dead not to notice that somewhere between his last visit home and now, Annie had become quite a knockout. "In those days, you could barely see beyond Jessica Holt's big brown eyes and bodacious ta-tas. I, Annie of the flat-as-a-surfboard chest and metal mouth, deterred your hormonal-teenage-boy scrutiny."

She certainly wasn't flat-chested anymore.

He could argue about the hormonal part, but why bother. In high school, he'd been interested in three things; having fun, getting laid, and getting laid.

Some things were important enough to be counted twice.

"You make me sound like such a jackass."

One corner of her luscious pink lips kicked upward. "You were."

Yeah. He probably had been. And he wasn't really sure he appreciated the reminder.

"So why are you working here now?" he asked, deftly changing the subject. "Didn't you get enough slinging hash the first time around?"

"A girl's got to earn a living somehow. Slinging hash is all I've ever really done. My hand-dipped chocolates haven't exactly taken off like wildfire. And since Sweet's street corners are already occupied with whiskey barrels and petunias, there isn't any room for me to hang around waiting for customers."

"Always the smart-ass," he said.

"Takes one to know one."

Before he could protest, she lifted her hand off the table and stepped back with a serious look.

"When you're a single mom with a baby, you have to earn a living somewhere that will understand your child is your first priority. And that if they're sick, you might not be able to make it to work that day. Bud's a dad and a grandfather, so he understands. He also knows I'd never take his generosity for granted."

Shit. How could he have gotten so tangled up in his own troubles that he'd forgotten Annie was a single mom now after having been abandoned by her baby's slimeball father?

"How's Max doing?"

"Growing like the cutest weed in the garden

of life." Pride burst across her pretty face. "He's walking now. Gets into everything. Izzy's trying to teach him to talk in sentences. But his favorite word is still *Mamamamamama*."

He chuckled, and the sensation that pushed through his chest felt as warm as sunshine. Then just as quick, regret that he'd missed so much kicked in. "It seems like I was gone for an eternity. I can't believe Max is walking. Reno and Charli have a baby. Jackson and Abby have one on the way. And Izzy's already started kindergarten."

"Your brother can't believe it either. I think it's hard for Jackson not seeing Izzy all the time because of the shared custody with Fiona. Even though Fiona's an amazing mom and they have such a wonderful relationship. Mostly he complains that Izzy's growing up so fast makes him feel old."

Jake got that. He felt ancient, and he'd just barely turned thirty-one. "So I guess you'll be at this get-together my mom is planning?"

"Wouldn't miss it for the world."

"I don't suppose you could talk her out of it."

Eyes wide, she exhaled a little puff of exasperation. "Are you kidding me?"

"Nope."

"Pardon me for being blunt, but why would you want to take that away from her?" She sighed, then glanced away when a customer called her name. With a nod in their direction, she brought her eyes back around to him, sharp and focused. "I know I can't imagine what you went through over there. And I know when you guys come back you don't always like to talk about it. But I was here with your mom when she got the call about what happened. I saw the absolute devastation and the fear on her face when she realized that not only had she lost her firstborn son and the husband she loved with all her heart, but that she'd also come very close to losing her baby boy. She's so damned happy you made it home, there's no way I'd try to talk her out of celebrating the fact that you're alive."

Rendered speechless for maybe the first time in his life, Jake lifted the glass of water to his mouth and sipped.

"You should be happy too, Jake."

With a thud, he set his glass down on the table. For a long, awkward, silent moment, he watched the condensation slide down the side of the glass pitted by many trips through the dishwasher. When he composed himself, he looked up and pushed the menu in her direction.

He wasn't happy.

And the constant ache in his chest made him realize he might never be happy again.

"So . . ." Annie tossed him a know-it-all glare. "Double Diablo burger with extra peppers, a side of sweet-potato fries—extra crispy, and a chocolate-banana shake?"

"Sure." Dammit. He hated to let her win.

One purple-polished fingernail dragged the menu across the table. Jake held his breath and willed her to leave. But, of course, this was Annie, and God knew the girl did things in her own damned way and in her own damned time.

"Well, even if *you* aren't happy . . ." She snatched up the menu. "*I'm* really glad you made it back."

$\mathcal{S}$eeking a much-needed break, Annie tossed Jake's menu on the stack of others near the cash register, gave Bud a finger-across-the-throat indication that she was momentarily frazzled, and headed toward the back door. The screen door slammed with a shotgun bang behind her as she leaned against the old yellow building and sucked in a calming lungful of warm air.

The relief of seeing Jake alive and back on home turf filled her heart with so much joy, it was hard to breathe. The moment he'd walked through the door, she'd wanted to reach out and touch him to make sure he was real and not just another one of her highly imaginative dreams. But touching Jake had never been a part of her reality. And that's just one of the many things that sucked about worshipping from afar.

If she'd been a smoker, now would be the time she'd light one up to calm her nerves. Instead, she reached into the pocket of her apron, took out a watermelon-flavored Jolly Rancher, unwrapped it, and popped it into her mouth. The sugary tartness rolled over her tongue, and she closed her eyes to ward off the memories that nipped at her heels.

Closing her eyes only made those memories more powerful.

Why men had a habit of either rewriting history or dismissing it altogether, Annie didn't know. But it seemed Jake had fallen down the rabbit hole and forgotten how, once upon a time, they'd spent hours together having heart-to-heart discussions about everything from why girls spent so many hours in front of the mirror trying to perfect what God had given them to why guys had such a crazy need to be so rough-and-tumble. They'd discussed how difficult it had often been for him to keep up with his brothers when sometimes all he really wanted to do was go out and dig a garden or move some rocks to form a nice landscape. They'd talked about how she felt every time her parents left her and her sister alone to go party for days on end.

Back in the day, they'd been each other's confidants. Then Jake had gone away to college and subsequently joined the Marines. And he'd forgotten about her. She couldn't help feeling a little lost after he'd walked out of her life. Sure, she'd had her sister to talk to. But Jake had been closer to her own age—only two years older—and he'd become the objective voice she'd needed when her demons tried to drag her down. Her personal testosterone-packed voice of reason.

She'd trusted him.

Completely.

When he was no longer there, she found, once again, she'd been left behind. Forgotten as though she didn't matter. Her response had been to make a string of really bad decisions.

Now it appeared Jake had forgotten—or dismissed—all those times they'd sat on a stack of hay bales in the barn, or ridden out over Wilder Ranch on horseback while they deliberated deep and sometimes dark matters of the heart. Now, it seemed like all he could remember about her was . . . well, nothing really. And that hurt. No matter how hard she tried not to let it.

Still, he was alive.

Thank God.

Beside her, the screen door creaked open, and a very pregnant Paige Marshall stepped out and joined her in the shade. For a moment, her friend and coworker said nothing, just rubbed her hands over her ever-increasing belly.

"Jake's hurting," Paige said with a little sigh. "I know because he's got that same haunted look in his eye that Aiden had when he came back from the war."

"Did he ever tell you what happened over there?"

"A little. Not all." Paige held out her hand. "Got another Jolly Rancher you can spare? This baby craves sweets, and I left my cinnamon bears at home."

Annie plopped an apple-flavored candy into Paige's hand and watched as her friend unwrapped it and stuck it in her mouth.

"Aiden thinks he's protecting me by not telling me," Paige explained. "But all he's really doing is trying to keep the pain from rising to the surface. Sometimes that makes things worse. But I guess until they're ready to tell the story, they'll continue to try to find a way to cope."

"Or realize they can't?" Annie asked.

"Yeah. But Jake has his brothers. They've all been in his shoes. They've all suffered in some way, shape, or form. They all lost their big brother.

They know the pain. So, hopefully they'll be able to get him to talk."

"What if he doesn't?"

Paige turned her shoulder to the wall and looked into Annie's face. "Then you'll be there to catch him when he falls."

"Me?" A cynical laugh pushed through Annie's lips as her heart stumbled. "I'd *never* be the one Jake would turn to if he needed someone. Not as a friend or anything else." At least not anymore.

"But you want to be?"

She blew out a sigh. "Guess there's no denying I've always had a crazy thing for him."

"Crazy as in he's so gorgeous you want to jump his bones? Or crazy as in you could see yourself spending the rest of your life with him?"

"Both. But he never really noticed me." In *that* way. Annie shook her head. "Still doesn't."

"Have you ever told him how you feel?"

Annie scoffed.

"That's a lot of time to be thinking about a man and never letting him know."

"Yep. A lonnnnng time." Annie sighed and rested the back of her head against the side of the building. "But for some reason, whenever I get around him, my emotions tangle up my words, and we end up arguing. So I never opened that door. At first I didn't because I didn't want him to laugh at me. Then . . ." She shrugged. "I don't know. I guess I just didn't ever want to hear him verify that he'd never feel the same about me."

"I totally get that. I told Aiden how I felt right

after he came back, and he basically threw my words in my face."

"And yet, now you're married and have a baby on the way."

"Which wouldn't have happened if I'd let the stubborn and clueless man have his own way."

"I think about that. Jake almost died, and I never told him how I feel. Not that he'd care."

"Don't try to second-guess a Wilder, Annie. You won't win. And I'm willing to give Jake a lot more credit. He's a smart man."

"I know."

"Then why waste any more time? Why tempt fate?" Paige rubbed her hand over her belly again. "And just in case you were wondering, there's a remedy for that arguing thing you two frequently do."

"What's that? Duct-tape my mouth?"

After Paige quit laughing, she cupped her hands over Annie's shoulders. "No need for that. You just play it straight. Give him the business side of that mouth."

"Which is?"

"You just kiss the poor guy, Annie. If the words don't come out right, you let him know how you feel in a different way."

"That's what worked for Aiden?"

"That and a little moonlight."

"What if Jake's really *not* interested?"

"Then you get him to change his mind." Paige grinned. "You want proof that technique works? Look no further than your own sister. Abby was in love with Jackson forever. For years, he refused to move her out of the *friend* zone. And even though for a while they went their own ways, she finally found a way to sneak past that stubborn, locked-down heart of his." The hard candy clacked against Paige's teeth.

"And look at Charli," she continued. "Reno put up every barrier he could invent and then some to keep her away. But she still managed to get him to see reason. Although I suppose mentioning to him that she'd forgotten to put on panties while they were at the Wilder Barbecue Blowout might have helped a little."

They both giggled at that.

"And if you want to talk about accomplishing the impossible, look at Allison. She had the challenge of turning Sweet's most infamous playboy into a happily married man."

"I think it was the other way around with Allison and Jesse. Seems to me *he* was the one who had to do all the sweet-talking."

"An even better example of the endless possibilities." Paige gave Annie's shoulder a sympathetic pat. "Jake is a Wilder brother, Annie. He's not going to make it easy. But if you really do have strong feelings for him, I guarantee he'll be worth the trouble."

There had been a time in Annie's life when she'd have jumped through hoops, stuffed her bra with tissue, or learned the Victoria's Secret angels *slinky* walk to get Jake's attention. The fear of rejection and humiliation had always stopped her from going after what she'd wanted. Back in the day, he hadn't even put her in the friend zone, at least not when they'd been out in public. In private, he treated her completely different than he did in front of his family and friends. Those private moments they shared were few and far between. But they were precious. And she was pretty sure they meant a whole lot more to her than they ever did him.

Once he'd enlisted in the Marines, she knew he'd never come back and see her any different. He'd be too worldly. To him, she'd always be Annie Morgan, royal pain in the backside. She'd never be, Annie, the love of his life. So she'd moved on and away— almost two thousand miles—to try to find a life that would fill her soul with all the love and emotion she craved. Unfortunately, all she'd found was a low-paying job, loneliness, and heartache.

So much for grand ideas.

In Seattle, she thought she'd found love—her very own Prince Charming. Doug had been a hot musician with plenty of edge to keep him interesting. His music had been reflective and romantic. He'd had dark curly hair and seductive eyes like Jim Morrison from The Doors.

It had taken her almost two long years after Doug had moved into her apartment to realize he'd been too focused on his career to pay her much mind. On the other hand, for him she'd been a passionate supporter of his music. A financial support so he could focus on his career. And doormat for him to wipe his feet on when he learned she was pregnant with his child.

Beneath Doug's stimulating rock-and-roll exterior, he hadn't been charming at all. What she'd really found beneath all that hair and songwriting genius was a toad who proved there was no room in his life for her or their child.

As Paige opened the screen door for them to go

back inside the diner, Annie admitted she'd made plenty of mistakes in her life. Having her little boy wasn't one of them. But never letting Jake Wilder know how much she really cared might have been her most monumental.

Times had changed.

She was older, wiser, and she'd learned to never back down from what meant the most.

Jake meant something to her.

He always had.

He was far from perfect although he was perfect to look at. But she knew that deep down, beneath the shell of that gorgeous exterior; he was a man with heart, honor, and loyalty. He'd been raised to respect family and community. And she knew that just like his brothers, when he fell in love, he'd be a forever kind of guy.

The question now was . . . could he ever fall in love with *her*?

Maybe Paige was right. Maybe it was time to step up and find out. Wondering wouldn't ever give her an answer.

Determined, she smoothed her hands over her hair and down her skirt. At the window, she grabbed up Jake's order and headed toward his booth. As professionally as possible, she set his Diablo burger, fries, and milk shake in front of him. He looked up at her, eyes dark, blue, and intense.

"If there's anything else you want, anything at all, just let me know," she said. Then she gave him a "Brace yourself, cowboy" smile and walked away.

When she glanced back, he was still looking.

Chapter 2

Annie glanced in the hallway mirror for the umpteenth time to check out her backside. There were no two ways about it, jeans fit differently after you had a baby. She might only weigh one pound more postbaby than she did prebaby, but hips didn't lie. Neither did butts. And hers were definitely a smidge wider. Not that she had to go the whole lying down on the bed and sucking in so she could raise the zipper thing, but body parts south of her belly button no longer captured that youthful vibe. She wasn't even going to think about what breast-feeding had done to her boobs. Although there was no question a good push-up bra had become her best fashion accessory.

Call her crazy, but tonight she wished she still had that fresh and innocent thing going on. The one that turned a guy's head and brought him to his knees. She would never take back having Max for one second. But even though she'd worked hard to get back in shape, she was now a mom, and things had just . . . shifted. Enough, at least, to make her wonder if now she'd even appeal to a man.

Or, one man in particular.

A snorted laugh jumped from her mouth. Max giggled as he slapped his chubby little hands on the mirror, then stuck his tongue out and licked his own reflection. Oh to be young and oblivious to the often unfair ways of the world.

With one more turn to the mirror, Annie knew she'd have to be satisfied with her appearance. She'd washed and blow-dried her hair, then styled it with a wild array of soft curls. She'd applied her makeup as perfectly as watching an active one-year-old would allow. She'd spritzed on her favorite strawberries-and-cream body mist and applied a swipe of strawberry-tinted gloss to her lips. Though why she bothered with any of it seemed to be the question of the day.

Jake Wilder had never paid her any real attention before. Why would that change now just because she'd gussied up a little?

Could it be too much to hope change was in the air?

The moment he'd come through the door of Bud's Diner yesterday, she'd noticed the huge difference in him. The laughter in his dark blue eyes had dimmed. The quick comebacks he'd tossed with the speed of the football he'd once thrown had dive-bombed into quiet consternation. And one would need a ladder and an axe to knock that *Titanic*-sized chip off his broad shoulder.

A casual observer would probably figure the

wooden cane he now depended on was the cause of all that alpha-male angst. But Annie had known him long enough to sense there was far more smoldering beneath the surface. He might not agree, stubborn as he was. But Annie knew him. She'd been around him, watching him, studying him for years. She knew that when he tipped his head back and laughed, the amusement was all for show. But when he leaned forward and slapped his knee or curled a long, muscular arm around his washboard stomach, the laughter came from his heart.

Besides knowing his favorite meal at Bud's Diner, she also knew he preferred fresh strawberry pie over apple. That his favorite type of movie was not action-adventure or the sophomoric humor someone like Adam Sandler might deliver. He preferred dramas that made him think, or romantic comedies that made him feel good long after he left the theater.

She knew he was highly competitive, drank milk from the carton, and that he slept in the buff. This she learned years ago during one of her parents' frequent party trips that took them away from home for a number of days.

It hadn't mattered to her mom and dad that it had been her sixteenth birthday. Thankfully, Jana and Joe Wilder had known and cared, and they'd invited her and Abby over for a barbecue and birthday cake. The festivities ran late into the night after they'd all gathered around the kitchen table for a game of Monopoly and extra servings of cake and ice cream. Jana had insisted she and Abby stay the night. Not only because it had been late but because their parents weren't at home. Again. Abby had fallen asleep on the sofa while Annie had lain on the love seat, wide-awake and savoring the Wilder's generosity beneath a warm blanket that smelled like mountain wildflowers.

Sometime in the middle of the night, Jake had wandered through the living room and into the kitchen. She'd squeezed her eyes shut, feigning sleep until the light from the refrigerator blinked on. Then she'd peeked through her lashes at a very young, very healthy, and very naked Jake Wilder as he guzzled what had been left in the jug of milk.

Their eyes locked—long enough for him to ac-knowledge the free show he knew he was giving her with a nod—before he tossed the empty carton in the trash and casually strolled back through the living room as though she hadn't just witnessed him in his birthday suit.

He'd been the first naked man she'd ever seen.

True, he'd only been eighteen at the time— barely a man—but she couldn't help wonder if the years and maturity between now and then had lavished their generosity on a guy who'd already started out in a *big* way.

Sleep had been impossible for the rest of that night. Her imagination had taken flight, and she'd fallen even more in love. Maybe at the age of six-teen one could argue that it had been a simple case of lust, but she was now twenty- nine, and nothing had changed.

Except Jake.

Unable to avoid the inevitable any longer, she reached down and swept Max up into her arms.

For a moment, he protested. Loudly. Then she turned on her "be a good boy and Mommy will give you a treat" tone and he became all blabbering giggles.

She buried her nose in his blond curls and inhaled the sweet scent of baby shampoo. "Are you ready to go watch Mommy make a big ol' crazy fool of herself?"

"Eeeee! Mamamamamama!"

"I'll take that as a yes." Annie chuckled while the warmth of his pure-and-joyful baby love rushed through her heart. She bent her head and rubbed their noses together. "And for what it's worth, young man, it would help tremendously if y'all didn't upchuck your dinner on anyone tonight. Just sayin'. Mrs. Lewis is still trying to get your blackberry applesauce out of her favorite yellow muumuu."

Max guffawed as though he knew Gladys Lewis's loud yellow muumuu was atrocious even without the stain she received from bouncing a one-year-old just after he ate.

"Come on, bubba. We've got to go get our flirt on with big bad Jake Wilder. Is that completely crazy or what?"

"Geeeeeee!"

"My thoughts exactly."

The warm September night drew a large crowd to Wilder Ranch for Jake's homecoming party. It didn't go unnoticed that his mother, brothers, and their wives had gone out of their way for the celebration to compete with their huge summer barbecue blowout, which a majority of the community attended.

The military-tank-sized grill he and his brothers had constructed way back when was cooking brisket and ribs at full capacity. Picnic tables had been brought out and set up beneath the large oaks that filtered the setting sun and also served as holders for the Mason-jar candles that hung from the branches. Tablecloths in patriotic colors covered the rough wood surfaces of the tables so a display of salads, side dishes, and desserts could be set out in a spread hearty enough to feed an army.

A full bar had been constructed inside the barn, where galvanized buckets were stocked with chilled bottles of Shiner Bock Ale and assorted sodas for the nondrinking younger set. On the makeshift bar sat beverage dispensers filled with sweet tea. Bales of hay were placed everywhere as seating for those who preferred not to stand or for those who liked to sit in groups to chat. Banners of WELCOME HOME JAKE hung above the barn doors and across the veranda of the house. And from the flatbed hay trailer, a local cover band played Luke Bryan's "Country Girl."

The air was bursting with music, conversation, and laughter. But Jake didn't feel much like partying. Didn't mean he'd ruin the party, either. His mother had worked too hard putting everything together. Friends and family had gone out of their way to come by and welcome him home. He might be a hard-ass, but he wasn't an asshole. He appreciated the love, but all the fuss made him feel awkward and a little edgy.

Standing beneath the oaks talking with Hazel Calhoun and Gertie West about their chances of winning a blue ribbon at next year's Sweet Apple Butter Festival hadn't exactly been on his radar. Still, he smiled and nodded at appropriate times, and even managed an "Ahhh" when Gertie mentioned that adding a fresh peach to the recipe was her secret ingredient.

"Well, if that isn't just about the cutest thing," Mrs. Calhoun said with a hand settled on her ample bosom. "Bless her heart."

Jake lifted his head to look in the direction of Mrs. Calhoun's attention. He hadn't needed to search far for the recipient of the comment.

In the middle of the large open area currently being used as a dance floor, Annie held her chubby baby boy in her arms as they danced to the lively tune. The baby threw his head back in a fit of giggles that sent a grin to his mother's pretty face. Annie had been dealt a shitty deal by the musician she'd gotten tangled up with in Seattle. Initially, when he'd heard the news, Jake had considered hunting the guy down and rearranging his face. Distance had cooled his temper. Still, knowing someone treated a person he considered almost family so poorly made him madder than hell. Later, when he'd come home for Jackson and Abby's wedding and seen Annie with her baby, he'd realized, though it hadn't been planned, and Annie might have preferred the father stuck around, she certainly was happy about having that little boy.

"Dancing with her baby. Isn't that just the sweetest thing?" Hazel Calhoun said. "Although if you ask me, someone should have taken a bat to that ex-boyfriend of hers. Imagine deserting her like that. Such a shame."

"Don't you worry, she'll find herself a good man now that's she's back home in Texas," Gertie proclaimed. "We raise more responsible young men here."

Jake wasn't so sure Texas had a corner on that market.

Watching the single mother and fatherless child sent a fresh wave of guilt through his heart. That's exactly how Eli's wife Rebecca would be now. Alone. With people talking behind her back about her having to find a man to replace Eli.

As the result of a factory explosion where his father had worked, Eli had grown up fatherless. He'd confided in Jake that when he'd enlisted in the Marines, his greatest fear was leaving his own child fatherless, too.

Eli's anxieties had become a reality.

The wooden cane beneath Jake's palm burned like the mortars that had been fired that fateful day. His stomach rolled with the same nausea that had clogged his throat as he'd helped load Eli's breathless body into the medevac. Jake couldn't stop the memories any better than he'd been able to stop that lethal bullet that had taken his friend's life. The bullet that had made his friend's wife a widow and their child fatherless.

Diversions had been suggested by the team of counselors Jake had been assigned to while he'd been recuperating.

Pleasant diversions.

Things that made him happy. Feel a sense of accomplishment. Distractions that would help him to put one foot in front of the other and move toward the future instead of constantly stepping back into the past.

But the task seemed insurmountable.

Jake had broken promises.

First to Eli's wife, when he'd promised that her husband would return home to her, alive. The second to Eli, when he'd promised that if anything *did* happen, Jake would be there to support Rebecca.

He'd yet to do his duty.

He'd faced battle, but couldn't seem to find the courage to face his friend's widow.

Jake knew he couldn't change history. Couldn't change the way he felt. Maybe at this point, all he could do—needed to do—was as the counselors suggested. Find a pleasant diversion from the guilt that burned white-hot and deep in his soul.

Watching Annie's boots kick up a little dirt and the sexy way her body moved was as satisfying as things were likely to get. Even if he didn't already know he could never again take pleasure in life as he once had, this was Annie. She was like family. He could look but not touch.

All he could do now was sit back and appreciate the snug jeans that molded nicely over her shapely hips and rear end. The way the slinky blouse floated over her full breasts and gave him just enough view of her cleavage to raise his eyebrows. Even if looking at her caused things in his body to stir to life, all he could do was lift the bottle of

Shiner to his mouth and take a drink to drown the nightmare that haunted him day and night.

"Stirring up trouble again, little brother?" Jackson and his very pregnant wife crowded in between him and the senior ladies.

"Jake's too sweet to stir up trouble."

Jake smiled when Abby came to his defense. Having sisters-in-laws who head-butted his ornery brothers was a plus he was just beginning to appreciate.

His eyes lowered, and his heart clenched as Abby rubbed her hand over her big belly. Everything that made him the son of Joe and Jana Wilder wanted to feel that rush of celebration for his brother's soon-to-be-born baby instead of the wave of guilt for another man's child who would never look up and see his father smiling back.

"Sweet?" Jackson barked out a laugh. "The boy's had the devil in him since he learned to walk."

"For your information, young man"—Gertie West gave Jackson the stink-eye—"he's not half the dickens you are."

Jackson had the audacity to look surprised, which made Jake laugh. He'd need more hands than two to point out how many times his older brother had led him astray. Jackson might be married, a father, and captain of his own fire station now, but Jake didn't see him changing his errant ways anytime soon.

"Yeah." Jake looked slightly down at his older sibling. Because even though he was the baby of the family, at six-four, Jake was also the tallest. A fact he never let the brothers live down.

"Ooh. Nifty comeback." Then Jackson grinned, pulled Jake into a hug, and did the good-buddy-backslap thing. "Damn it's good to see you."

"Me next." Abby held out her arms, then laughed when he couldn't get close enough for a real hug. "Apparently, I'll have to claim that hug after the baby's born."

"When's she due?" Jake asked.

"*She?*" Abby's eyes narrowed accusingly at Jackson. "How did you know it's a girl? We haven't told anybody."

He shrugged. "A long time ago, I heard that God gave baby girls to fathers who were nothing but trouble when they were boys. Jackson wrote the book on nothing but trouble."

Everyone laughed because it was true. Then, before Gertie West walked away, she told Jake to make sure he tasted the turtle-thumbprint cookies she'd made just for him.

"I'll sure do that, Mrs. West." His stomach rumbled, and he thought about going in search of those cookies now before they were all gone. "And thank you."

"Speaking of girls, looks like someone has their eye on our Annie." Obnoxious as ever, Jackson grinned and poked Jake in the biceps with a half-empty bottle of Shiner. "Sorry, little brother. You snooze. You lose."

Despite the dark glares she was getting from Jake, who stood beneath the canopy of oaks with several ladies from Sweet's Senior Center, Annie focused on Max and his belly laughs. The more he laughed, the more she swung him into the dance. With her luck, he'd end up being a total adrenaline junkie. He'd already proven himself to be quite the daredevil and added to his bumps and bruises daily as he gave up the baby Army crawl and mastered the art of walking.

"Mind if I join you?"

Annie looked up to find Bo Jennings with his hands out, ready to take Max into his arms. Bo was a great-looking guy whose parents owned one of the largest cattle ranches in the area. Bo had sought independence by forsaking the family business and becoming an ER doctor. Annie figured the Jennings family could hardly hold a grudge when their son's intent was to help others and save lives.

"You mean you want to dance with us?" Annie asked.

"You bet." He tipped back the brim of his straw hat. "One thing I learned long ago, never let an opportunity pass that you'll later regret."

Her son wasn't too sure about the stranger who was lifting him into his arms. His giggles ceased and his little brows pulled together over his big blue eyes. "Ummm. Max doesn't seem too eager."

"No worries. I'm pretty good with kids." He grinned and pulled her into his unoccupied arm. While the music played, they struggled to manage an awkward two-step.

Once they started moving, she expected Max to start giggling again. He didn't. Instead, he puffed out his bottom lip, then reached out his arms, wanting to be back in a familiar embrace. Her son was great with those he knew, but he shied from strangers. Even nice ones like Bo.

"I'm sorry," she said over the music. "He's just not that open to—"

"Don't you worry. I've got him." Out of nowhere, Jana Wilder appeared. "Gimme that precious little boy."

Max let go a drooly squeal of glee at the sight of the woman who was more of a grandmother to him than Annie's own mom, who'd never even bothered to come see her grandson since he'd been born.

Though a year had passed since Max came into the world, Annie had never even received a card from her parents that acknowledged her little boy's existence. The snub hurt more than Annie would ever admit. Now, with Abby expecting her own child, the hurt doubled. Because they weren't acknowledging Abby's baby, either. And though their parents had been personally invited via telephone as well as a formal invitation, neither of their parents had bothered to attend Abby and Jackson's wedding. Annie had been surprised how well Abby had handled the situation.

"Why bother packing up and flying halfway across the country for a second marriage that would most likely end up like the first—without the big payoff at the end?" their mother had asked.

Annie had bitten her tongue to keep from arguing that her big sister's first marriage had ended because her first husband was a complete and total dick. And that Abby should have married Jackson the first time around anyway. Her argument would have been a big waste of time. Simply put, their parents only cared about themselves. Always had. Always would. The lack of interest, love, and support from her own flesh and blood made Annie appreciate Jana even more.

Jana took Max into her arms and smothered his face with squeaky kisses. "You just keep on dancing, sugarplum," she told Annie. "Have some fun."

"Are you sure?"

"As sure as this little dickens has a wet diaper. I'll go take care of that right now before he notices." Jana grinned like she'd been awarded a million-dollar prize.

"Nice lady," Bo said, once Jana walked away. Then he took Annie's hand and drew her into his arms to finish the two-step they'd started.

Tall, dark, and handsome, with a smile that reached all the way up to the flecks of gold in his jade green eyes and a lean physique that spoke of more hours working out than snogging down Big Macs, Bo was everything a sane woman looked for in a man. Smart. Strong. Handsome. Responsible. And yet she couldn't muster up the interest. Not one single tingle rippled up her spine or through her heart.

The lack of awareness was disappointing to say the least.

As they twirled around the dance floor with the other couples, she caught Jake in her periphery. She'd noticed him the moment she and Max had arrived. Well, it was hard not to notice someone you'd actually been looking for.

But what she noticed gave her great concern.

The brittleness on his face and the way he tried to lean into the cane without anyone's noticing the grimace of pain in his blue eyes turned her stomach. Throughout the evening, she'd recognized his attempts at reincarnating the old Jake, the good-time guy who flirted with the ladies both young and old. The old Jake, who could tell a knee-slapping joke with the best of them and dance the night away until the band finally gave up and went home.

Watching him, one thing became crystal clear.

Jake was struggling to find himself.

She could use the excuse that since she'd known him most of her life, she'd be happy to help him. The truth was, she cared. Deeply. The stubborn set to his jaw told her that if she even mentioned it, he'd only narrow those deep blue eyes and tell her he was just fine.

He wasn't.

When the song ended, Bo kept hold of her hand as he walked her off the impromptu dance floor. "It's still pretty warm out," he said. "Can I get you something to drink?"

"I'd love—"

"I've got that covered," said a deep voice that sent a tingle of awareness up her spine.

She sighed. Why couldn't that have happened with Bo?

Annie didn't need to turn around to know to whom the voice belonged. And she tried really hard not to smile at the slight testiness to his tone. Before she could blink, his large hand came around and handed her—of all things—a bottle of her favorite raspberry iced tea.

Did he remember? Or had it just been a fluke?

To accept the bottle, she had to let go of Bo's hand, which she hoped was Jake's intent. Then again, she'd always been a big dreamer. Jake had never shown signs of interest in her. At all. In fact, if she carefully considered their most recent discussion at the diner, Jake spoke to her with a persistent twitch to his jaw. As if he were hovering on the edge of using that squared jawline to snap her head off.

"Thank you." She accepted the iced tea. "Very perceptive of you to realize I was thirsty." She noticed he didn't bring anything for Bo, who was likely just as parched.

"How's the leg?" Bo asked. Annie was positive he wasn't trying to point out Jake's weakness. After all, he was a doctor. And wasn't there some kind of Hippocratic oath to be kind to the sick and wounded?

"Doing great." Yep. The muscles in Jake's jaw twitched. "Couple more weeks of walking with this thing, then I'm good."

Annie frowned at Jake's delivery of the well-practiced line of BS. She knew the extent of his injury. Knew how he'd been shot. Knew everything about that horrible day. At least what the Marines had relayed to Jana. Jake, so far, had said nothing. Like that day had never happened and he'd gotten the injury from something as simple as falling off his horse. From what she'd read about soldiers who returned home either with injuries or PTSD, a lot of them didn't want to talk about it.

Even if talking was what they really needed to do.

"That's great to hear." Bo took a breath, turned

away from Jake, and gave Annie a smile. "Maybe I can call you sometime?"

Had they been alone, she wouldn't have dreamed of leading him on. But when Jake's dark slash of brows jacked up his forehead, she found herself saying, "I'd really like that."

With a nod and two fingers to the brim of his hat, Bo bid them good night.

When he was out of hearing distance, Annie turned and looked up at Jake. "What was that?"

He tilted his head. "What was what?"

"Bringing me something to drink." She lifted the bottle of iced tea as a point of reference. "Butting in. Acting like you were staking a claim or something."

His head snapped back, and he looked at her like she'd taken too many spins on the crazy train. She knew it was too much to hope he'd been doing exactly that, but she'd already stuck her entire boot in her mouth. No backing down now.

"Bringing you an iced tea is staking a claim?"

"Maybe."

"It wasn't."

"Felt like it."

"There you go, being all delusional again."

"There you go, being all stubborn again."

His eyes flashed. Annie waited for his jaw muscles to twitch again. Instead, his sexy man lips curved upward.

"And what's *that*?" She pointed to his mouth. "You're *smiling*? We're arguing, and you're *smiling*?"

"Guess so."

"Why?"

"Maybe I just realized something."

She crossed her arms. "And what's that?"

"I don't know. Maybe I like arguing with you." His broad shoulders came up in a shrug that made his chest look even broader if that were possible. "More than anyone else in the world, more than my pain-in-the-ass brothers, you make my blood boil. In fact, over the years, I've often envisioned wrapping my hands around your pretty little throat and squeezing ever so gently. But when it comes right down to it, I guess I might have missed our squabbles while I was away."

He missed her?

"You're crazy," she said.

Correction.

She was crazy.

He'd said he *might* have missed their *squabbles*. Not that he'd missed *her*.

"So I've been told," he said. "Often."

His gaze dropped down to the front of her blouse and the cleavage she'd been only too happy to expose tonight—just enough to maybe grab his interest. If only for a moment.

Desperate move, she knew.

But she figured she'd waited long enough for Jake to finally notice her and realize they could be good for each other. In order for him to see things the way she did, he had to stop looking at her as little Annie, proverbial pain in the ass.

"Well, sorry to disappoint you, but I didn't come here to argue." Planting a hand on her hip got her point across. It also managed to thrust her top half out just a bit farther.

Judging by the flash in his eyes, he noticed.

"I came here to have a good time," she said. "To welcome you home. And to sample as many of those delicious desserts as I can before my jeans get too tight." To her delight, he dropped his gaze again, then looked back up at her with another hint of interest. She lifted her bottle of raspberry iced tea and gave him a little salute. "So thank you for the drink. But if you'll excuse me, I'm going to go find someone who's interested in having a little fun."

As she spun an about-face, the heels of her boots ground in the dirt, and she could feel the heat of Jake's eyes on her backside. With any luck, he'd be looking at the sway of her hips and not the fact that her hips were now a smidge wider.

"Hey," he called out.

She turned. "What?"

"You really going to go out with that guy?"

A distinct pucker pulled his dark brows together over his narrowed eyes. Always a good sign.

"*That guy* is an ER doctor. An outstanding citizen of Sweet. And someone who would help a little old lady cross the street. So why wouldn't I go out with him?"

One corner of his mouth kicked upward. "Because you're not a little old lady?"

"Nice to see your smart-ass side back again." She pointed. "Hope it sticks around for a while."

As she walked away, she heard him mutter, "Damned crazy woman."

That's all it took to put a little more sass in her sway.

Yes. She was a woman. Crazy, no doubt.

And hallelujah that Jake had finally opened his eyes and noticed.

$\mathcal{T}$wo things Jake was pretty damn sure of as Annie walked away. One, his leg was killing him from standing for so long, and, two, since he'd forgone the use of painkillers, the bottle of Shiner in his hand wasn't helping. Surprisingly, there was a third note in his little pack of woes, and she'd just walked away.

The fact that he was actually watching Annie walk away was bizarre. She'd been right about what she'd said in the diner the other day. He'd never really noticed her other than she was kind of a permanent fixture around the ranch. Sure, they'd had some good arguments and plenty of lively discussions back in the day, but when he heard she'd taken off for Seattle, he hadn't given her another thought.

So why now?

Had his mind flipped some kind of pathetic switch where because he wasn't as whole as he used to be, he'd suddenly become needy, and she was just within reach? Hell no. He slugged down another drink of ale. He wasn't needy. He was on the mend. He'd be back to a hundred percent in no time.

So why was he checking out Annie's curvaceous behind in those tight jeans?

There were numbers a mile long in his contact list. Women he could call to relieve a long sexual dry spell. Maybe that's all he needed now. Maybe he just needed to get laid. It had been a really long time. First, he'd been stuck in the sands of hell for over eight months, then he'd been in the hospital and rehab for eight endless weeks. Shit, he'd been so busy and banged up, he and his own hand hadn't even connected.

Yep, he concluded, that's all it was.

The need for sexual release.

That explained his sudden attention to Annie. Not that she wasn't pretty or didn't have a great body, he'd just never *realized* she was pretty and had a great body.

Until now.

Not to be outdone by any two-legged party attendees, Miss Giddy, his mother's pet goat, trotted over and looked up at him with her big brown eyes.

"Meh-eh-eh."

"Missed you too, you crazy old goat." He stroked her head between the horns. Tonight, the fashion-minded farm animal sported a red-white-and-blue silk ribbon around her long neck. Why his mother had chosen a goat instead of a normal animal like a dog or cat to pamper was anyone's guess. But over the years, Miss Giddy had become a part of the family. "You're looking a little pudgy these days, old girl."

"Meh-eh-eh."

"No insult intended. Just making note."

Miss Giddy tossed her head and trotted away as if the comment had hurt her feelings.

"You look like you either need a stronger drink or a place to sit."

Jake turned as Reno, Charli, and their adorable

three-month-old baby, Adeline, strolled up. Jake was sad he'd missed the baby's birth, but it was good to see his big brother happily married and now a doting father. Reno deserved all the good things life could deliver. He'd suffered some serious shit when he'd been a kid. And though he wasn't a brother by the same parents, he was a brother by blood and heart.

"Probably both." Jake laughed to cover the sting of the truth.

"I can make that happen," Reno said. "You want to hold Addie while we go get them?"

From inside the carefully swaddled pink blanket, his tiny niece looked up at Jake and blinked her blue eyes. Then, that perfect little pink Cupid's bow of a mouth opened in a smile, and it was all he could do not to grab her up and bury his face against her sweet little head.

"I'd better not," he said. "I'm afraid I might drop her."

Adeline had the nerve to coo at him, which was basically like her reaching out and grabbing hold of his heart with her pudgy little hand.

"Sorry." Reno glanced down at the cane. "Not like me to be so insensitive."

"Really?" Jake yanked his gaze away from the adorableness Charli held in her arms. "Just because I was stupid enough to get hit with a bullet, you're going to go all girly on me?"

"Fuck you." Reno grinned. "I'm not going all girly."

"Yes, you are," Charli said. "And please start practicing now to say things like *frig* instead of the F word. Or *shut the front door* instead of—"

"Shit. I get it." Reno grimaced. "I mean shoot."

Charli leaned in and kissed his cheek. "Go get your brother a chair and a beer. I'll stay here and make sure he remembers there are now two sets of little ears to protect."

"Yeah. And Izzy's getting old enough to reprimand you herself." Reno lifted his chin. Before he walked away, he lightly punched Jake's arm. "And by the way, you *are* stupid."

"Fuck you."

"Boys." Charli admonished, as Reno disappeared.

"Sorry. Guess we're going to take some work," Jake apologized. Although he was pretty sure the grin he wore negated his good intention.

"I'm going to hold out hope that it will sink in eventually. Maybe all you need is to be around the little ones more often."

"Ha. Then you'll be able to blame me for everything."

"Not everything. There's plenty of blame to throw on Jackson and Jesse too."

"I like that idea. Blame them first. It's what I always do. Kept me off restriction for years."

Charli laughed. "I can imagine you all kept your mom and dad guessing and hopping."

"That's why mom has to dye away the gray now. Dad? He was always onto us, but he was selective for the reasons he'd give us *the lecture*." Thinking about his dad rendered him silent for a moment as the grief from his father's death swamped him with renewed emotion. Jared had been the first-born brother, and though neither of their parents admitted it or even showed it, there was something special about him. He'd been the best big brother anyone could ask for. He'd been a model son, student, and Marine. He upheld the name Wilder like none of the rest of them had ever been able to.

As a result of Jared's having been killed in Afghanistan, their father fell into a heartache and depression that stole the life from him. One morning, Reno had found him slumped over the desk at the family hardware store that now solely belonged to Reno. Little had they known at the time that their father, along with Jesse, harbored Jared's secret that he was gay. Jake understood the military's take on homosexuality though he didn't agree with it. And the fact that his brother had found the love of his life in another man mattered only that his brother had found the love of his life.

Jake missed his dad and brother more than he could ever measure.

And that thought led him right back to his friend Eli, who would never see his child be born or hold him. He'd never watch him grow, play ball, lose his first tooth, or become a man.

"Are you sure you don't want to hold her?" Charli asked.

Jake's head came up. "What?"

"The way you were looking at Addie. It looked like you really want to hold her."

"I do." He gestured toward the cane. "But I'd better wait."

Emotion stirred in the depths of Charli's deep brown eyes. "That cane really isn't the issue, is it?"

Damn. His sister-in-law was too perceptive for her own good.

"I don't know what you mean."

"Yeah. You do." Her shoulders lifted on a sigh. "But I've already pushed one Wilder brother further than he ever intended to go. I'll let someone else push you."

Charli's compassion was heartfelt and, for him, hard to take. So he glanced away. Unfortunately, the direction of his gaze landed on Annie, who was once again dancing with Bo Jennings. This time to a much slower tune. In Jake's opinion, Bo was holding her way too close.

"She'd be the perfect choice."

Jake snapped his head around to find Charli now smiling. "Who?"

"Annie."

"Are you kidding me?" Jake barked out a laugh. "We'd tear each other's throats out."

"Or each other's clothes off. Which sounds like a much better solution to me." Charli flashed him a wink, then she and baby Addie strolled off.

The frown tightening Jake's forehead gave him an instant headache. He hated to be the one to tell his brother he'd married a crazy woman. But the possibility was there. Because for her to even put him and Annie together in the same thought made no sense at all.

Chapter 3

The morning after the party, the delicious aroma of bacon, eggs, and sweet-potato hash filled the air while Jake sat at his mother's kitchen table sipping a steaming cup of coffee. She, on the other hand, darted around the room, putting breakfast together for him.

"Are you sure you don't want me to help?" he asked for the hundredth time.

"Don't you be silly, sugarplum. I've been waiting for you to get home just so I can do exactly this."

"But, Mom. I'm an adult. You don't have to take care of me anymore. Let me do something for you after all the work you put into the party."

She turned with a spatula in one hand and a grin on her face. "It really was a wonderful party, wasn't it?"

"It was great." Even though he hadn't been in a celebratory mood, it had been really good to be surrounded by family and friends after spending so much time looking at the desolate mountain ranges of Afghanistan and subsequent bland hospital walls. Nothing compared to being home in the Texas Hill Country and being able to see the faces of his loved ones any damn time he wanted.

"It does my old heart good to see everyone together again."

"Mom. You're not that old."

"Tell that to the gray hairs on my head."

"You had those a long time ago. Comes from being the mother of five hell-raising sons."

"True." She flipped the hash with the expertise of someone who'd done it many times. "But I'd do it all over again. As much as y'all drove me crazy, you also made up for it with love."

"Perhaps you're forgetting the time Jackson got himself banged up in that Oklahoma rodeo and spent weeks on the sofa with the little bell you gave him to ring when he needed something."

"Oh, God." She sighed a little laugh. "He did abuse the use of that bell, didn't he?"

"Until Jared got sick of hearing it and stomped it with his big-ass boot."

"Good thing it wasn't a family heirloom."

Jake laughed, then shook his head. "I really miss Jared."

"Me too, son. Me too."

"You think his partner will ever get in touch with us?"

His mother flipped a perfectly cooked sunny-side-up egg onto the sweet potatoes and set the plate in front of him.

"I don't know. It's been so long now that I've kind of lost hope."

"He probably thinks we're a bunch of back-woods yahoos who'd judge him for being gay."

"I can't imagine Jared would present us like that to anyone. Even if he'd been hesitant to tell us about his homosexuality."

"Guess you're right." Jake popped a forkful of egg and potato in his mouth and moaned.

"Good?"

Busy chewing, Jake just nodded. No one could cook like his mom. He and his brothers could grill and barbecue like nobody's business, but when it came to the full-on meal, his mom was magic.

"Martin will be stopping by shortly." His mom set her plate down on the table, then scooted onto the chair next him. "He's going to bring down some items from the barn loft, so I can take them to the shop to sell. Guess that's a sign that business is good."

"You still only open three days a week?" The antique-and-design store she and Charli opened in the old Victorian house on Main Street just as you came into town seemed to be thriving. It was filled with the items his mom had picked for years from flea markets, yard sales, and dilapidated barns. She and Charli had decided their styles meshed and that going into business together would be a good idea. But both women were now so busy with other things, like a baby and wedding plans, that Jake wondered if the shop was more hobby than livelihood.

"If it ain't broke, why fix it? The schedule gives

Charli plenty of time to be with Addie. Besides, we didn't really open it to get rich."

"Most people would question if not for riches, why bother?"

"Because passion can't be ignored." She took a thoughtful sip of coffee, then looked up at him with the blue eyes that were dominant within the brothers. "Your daddy and I were just kids when we fell in love and got married. Just kids, really, when we had Jared. We worked hard for everything we had. For everything we put on the table. During all those years, it was my passion to make a warm and welcoming home for y'all. Even as time went on and things became easier, we hoped to teach you boys that happiness can't be found in things that can be bought. Happiness comes from the heart. Family, peace, giving to the community, finding your passion, finding love . . . those are the things that make you rich."

Jake knew he might be having a little trouble with the whole being-happy thing right now, but he also knew his parents had worked hard to teach him and his brothers about the most important things in life. Which was just one reason why they'd all joined the Marines after 9-11. Serve your community. Serve your country. They all had, and they'd paid the price. Yet Jake knew if you asked his mother if she'd change anything, she'd tell you no.

He settled his hand over the top of his mother's. "You and Dad were always the best."

She turned her hand over and gave his a squeeze. "Your daddy and I were very proud of you boys and the men you've become. All of you."

The compliment felt good, and Jake smiled. "Need some help bringing those items down from the loft?"

She gave him a look that reminded him he was still using a cane to get around.

"I'm just a little gimpy at the moment, Mom. I'm not an invalid."

"Just don't want you taking any tumbles down the stairs." Her brows knitted together in the way they always did when she sensed trouble brewing. "Those hay bales really don't make all that soft of a landing."

Tell him about it. He'd picked sticks from his hair for days after one particular hayloft rendezvous with Jessica Holt back when they'd been seniors in high school. He'd spent a lot of time with Jessica over the years, even as recently as the last time he'd been home on leave. She'd provided the *yee* and he'd supplied the *ha*. Jessica offered a short-term kind of happiness he'd been only too happy to take advantage of. And with the way he'd been checking out Annie at last night's party, maybe he should consider giving Jessica a call. Relieve that sexual frustration that had been building up inside him for months.

Yes, he decided while shoving the last bite of bacon into his mouth, all he needed was a good bit of sexual release, then he'd be back on track, thinking about important things. Like what the hell he planned to do with the rest of his life now that the Marines didn't want him anymore, and not about Annie and her curves, or that smart mouth that suddenly looked so tempting.

Annie parked her car in the shade of the barn at Wilder Ranch and near the canopy of oaks that sheltered the area where last night there had been one heck of a homecoming party. As the evening had rolled on, it even seemed like Jake had loosened up a little. He hadn't exactly moved onto the dance floor as he would have before his injury, but he'd kicked back with a beer in one of the Adirondack chairs and held court among his brothers and friends.

She hadn't meant to watch him so often, yet every time her gaze wandered his way, his seemed to do the same. True to form, he hadn't missed a beat in his storytelling. Had she not known him so well and caught either the narrowing of his eyes or the lift of his brow, she would never have known he'd been looking back. But if there was one thing she knew well in this world, it was Jake Wilder.

Or, at least she thought she did.

Every now and then, he'd do something that completely surprised her. Like the time he'd volunteered to set up the church carnival without being prodded to do so by his parents, or when he'd been home on leave and worked the entire time helping rebuild the Miller family barn that had burned after their hay bales caught fire. Not that Jake wasn't generous, he was just usually a bit more selective as to where he spent his time than the rest of the brothers.

She unbuckled Max from his car seat and swung him up into her arms. "Come on, little man. Grandma Jana is going to watch you while Mommy tries to earn some Christmas money."

"Mamamamamama. Dote!" Gleefully, he pointed down to Miss Giddy, who'd trotted up to say hello.

Sporting the same ribbon she'd worn last night to the party, Miss Giddy nodded. "Meh-eh-eh."

Annie laughed and held Max down so he could give the goat a pat or two between the horns. "Looks like Miss Giddy had a little too much celebration hay at the party." She petted the goat too. "You're getting a little puffy around the waistline, Miss Giddy. What's up with that?"

Miss Giddy took off, kicking up her back feet like she'd been insulted.

"Sorry about that," Annie apologized, then laughed at herself for doing so.

Pushing open the back door to Jana's house with her hip, Annie struggled to get the diaper bag, her wiggly little boy, and herself inside. A pair of large hands appeared and took the overpacked bag. When she looked up, Jake was there. The thick slash of his brows was drawn down over eyes that appeared a little bloodshot this morning.

The air smelled delicious although she wasn't sure whether the source was the freshly showered man in front of her or the lingering scent of bacon. Maybe both. Either way, she realized she was hungry.

For both.

"Good morning." Jana clapped her hands together, then held them out for Max. "And how's my little sugarplum today?"

It did Annie's heart good that Max practically jumped into Jana's arms. While baby talk and baby blabber went on between the two, Annie looked back at Jake and held out her hand for the diaper bag.

"Thanks for the help," she said, snatching the green-and-gray bag and trying not to study him like a bug under a microscope.

For what it was worth, Jake somehow always made her feel safe. And horny. Very horny. No doubt his military skills gave her the false security of someone who could take care of any situation. Because there was also no doubt that Jake Wilder was a complete wild card. Besides Jackson, Jake was the one who always jumped into trouble feet-first. Just the look of him, tall, tousled, and muscular, with a smile that surely made angels sing, said he could sweet-talk you right out of your lacy underwear before you even knew his name. He had a magnetic personality that right now seemed to be struggling to surface.

"No problem." He stood there with his hand still out as though waiting for something more than a verbal acknowledgment. Confused, her eyes shot to his. But the mystery behind those incredible blue depths didn't give her any clue.

"Don't you worry about hurrying up today, Annie," Jana said, unknowingly rescuing Annie from doing something dumb like grabbing Jake's hand and pulling him against her. "Me and this little dickens are going to have us some fun."

While Jana bounced giggling Max on her hip, Jake finally tore his gaze away from Annie and shot it toward his mother. "I thought Martin was coming over, and you were going to bring down some stuff from the loft."

Jana's fiancé was a wonderful and patient man who had been trying his very best to fit in with the Wilder family. Everyone loved him, but all the boys were still reserving the right to change their minds at any second. Though Martin had made it clear he wasn't trying to take the place of their father, the brothers wanted to make sure he'd take good care of their mother just the same.

Apparently, in their minds, the jury was still out.

"He is," Jana said while rubbing noses with Max. "And we are. Son, have you been away so long you've forgotten that your mama is the queen of multitasking? I raised all five of you boys while helping your daddy run this ranch, aiding the community, and serving at church. And I managed to win several blue ribbons at the fair and the Apple Butter Festival too."

"Which begs the question, if *you* can do all that, why does Annie need a babysitter?"

"Jacob Wesley Wilder! Mind your manners."

When Jake cringed at his mother's sharp tone, Annie laughed. "It's okay, Jana. It's a valid question."

"I didn't mean it as an insult," he explained.

"You've been insulting me for so long, it doesn't matter anymore," she said.

He flinched again, and Annie almost felt sorry for him.

Almost.

"Besides, it's not that I can't do it all," she said. "It's that your mother knows I'll be working with hot liquids, and with Max walking now, it can be dangerous. Your mom has generously offered to watch him this afternoon for a few hours so I can get some things accomplished."

"What kind of hot liquids?"

"Chocolate."

Curiosity lifted his brows.

"You don't have anything to do today, son," Jana said. "Why don't you go over and give her a hand?"

"Who said I didn't have anything to do?" he said to his mother. Then he turned back to Annie. "What are you making?"

"Hand-dipped chocolates." Not liking his grilling, she folded her arms. "I sell them at Fiona's cupcake shop and some other shops as well as to the bed-and-breakfasts in the area. I'm making a bigger batch this time to try and earn some Christmas money."

"Christmas is three months away."

"And as a single parent, I have to plan ahead."

"That's a lot of ahead."

"When you went out on a mission, didn't you have to plan as far in advance as possible?"

"Of course."

"Well, consider it my mission to give my son a great Christmas."

"She could use some help getting things done," Jana said, stroking her hand down Max's back while he played with the gold chain around her neck.

Jake scoffed. "I don't wear aprons."

"Chauvinist."

His brows lifted again. "Seriously?"

"If an apron is good enough for Bobby Flay, it's good enough for you," Jana said.

Annie watched his lips flatten and his eyes narrow. One thing Annie knew about Jake, he didn't like to be cornered. And because he was still on the mend and obviously struggling with matters of the heart, she took pity on him. Even though she thought he'd look pretty darned cute in one of her frilly pink aprons.

"No worries, buddy." She patted him on that solid, muscular chest, and her fingertips tingled. "I don't need your help. I've got it covered."

Relief washed over his handsome face.

Defeated, Jana let go a frustrated sigh and disappeared with Max into the living room.

"Thanks for getting me off the hook," he said.

"Like I said, no worries. It didn't take me long to learn that men really aren't a necessary element in a woman's life."

"What the hell do you mean by that?" His hands went to his hips. "What about sex?"

"Really, Jake? You're going to reduce your kind to what happens between the sheets?"

"Between the sheets." He took a step closer. "Against the wall. On the kitchen table. Wherever and whatever makes you moan the loudest."

Annie opened her mouth to return fire. After all, there were so many products on the market these days, a single woman could have whatever kind of sex she wanted. But the sudden darkening of Jake's eyes warned her that while she could buy all the battery-operated products she wanted, she'd never find the kind of sexual satisfaction he could deliver.

Chapter 4

"Anybody home?" Jake wandered into the backyard of Jesse's house, eventually finding his brother stretched out on a lounge beneath the pergola beside the pool. Condensation dripped from the amber bottle of Shiner Bock he lifted in welcome.

"Hey, little brother," Jesse called. "Come on over and sit your ass down."

Jake gave him a nod, then made his way around the pool and through the extravagant backyard Jesse had custom-designed and built himself.

Looking around, Jake tamped down the desire to get his hands dirty. To create special places just like this. Before he'd gone into the Marines he'd been studying business, horticulture, and landscape in college. Working with what Mother Earth provided had always been what brought him a sense of calm and accomplishment. Could getting back into that be the diversion the counselors had recommended? Maybe. Could he turn it into more than a diversion, maybe even a future? Might be worth some consideration. Trouble was, at this point in time, he didn't really have anywhere to practice his skills. Jake had land available, but it was pretty barren, and he'd yet to envision the dream to develop it as had his brothers.

Jesse had taken the section of land given to him by their father and created paradise.

Surrounded by oaks and shrubs and a stone-enhanced back patio that served their entire family well, the place was a luxurious retreat by day. At night, it became part enchanted forest, part whimsical fairy garden, and Partytown USA.

Before he'd married Allison, Jesse had been only too happy to host spontaneous pool parties with friends and family. The waterfall that flowed into the pool and formed a secret grotto was what Jake had always imagined the Playboy mansion would be like. Minus the bunnies and Playmates of the Month. Then again, he'd always had an overactive imagination. Since he'd settled down, Jesse had proven he'd never been quite the playboy everyone assumed. No one had been more surprised at this revelation than Jake.

"Where's your wife?" Jake asked as he snagged a Shiner for himself from the outdoor refrigerator.

"At school. I swear, once she gets her psych degree, she's going to be able to figure me out, then there'll be real trouble."

Jake popped the cap to the ale and took a refreshing drink.

"No cane today?" Jesse asked.

"Left it in the truck. Don't really need it anymore."

Jesse squinted against the bright sunlight. "That what your doctor says?"

"Don't give a shit what the doctor says."

"You will if you do further damage."

"No worries, *Mom*. I only have about a week and a half left of using it anyway. Just trying to wean myself off a little sooner."

"Because it makes you feel weak?"

"Because it makes me *look* weak. I can still kick your ass anytime you're ready."

Jesse laughed and ran a hand through the much shorter hairstyle than he'd had the last time Jake had been home. "Guess I have no room to talk. I've disregarded good advice a time or two myself."

Jake eased down in a comfortable rattan chair next to the lounge. Though the shade gave a cool respite from the unforgivable Texas sun, his brother had gone above and beyond with a misting cooling system.

"I'm not saying anything against Allie because I think you were damn lucky to get a woman like her." Jake leaned back and crossed his ankles. "But you really did set yourself up with a nice bachelor pad here."

For years, Jesse had a reputation a mile long, and he'd been labeled with various titles like *most eligible bachelor* or *Sweet's favorite playboy.* So the eye roll and groan he gave really didn't surprise Jake.

"I set myself up with an excellent place to enjoy private time with my wife," he explained. "Which also allows us enough space to entertain family and friends. If Dad hadn't willed us all these huge pieces of land on Wilder Ranch, I'd have been living in some little house in town all this time."

"Right." Jake had been given the same amount of acreage as his brothers, and it sat nicely between Reno's and Jackson's homes. Someday, he'd figure his shit out and build a place for himself. But for now . . . yeah. For now he really did have to figure his shit out. Otherwise, he wasn't any better than a dog chasing its own tail.

On cue, Jesse's black Lab charged toward them from across the lawn with a slobbery yellow tennis ball clenched between his teeth. When he reached the pergola, he dropped the ball and got down on his front legs. His back end wiggled in anticipation of the game. Jesse reached down, grabbed the ball, and sailed it across the yard. It took a bounce into the pool and Dinks leaped in after it without hesitation.

Jake chuckled. "Dinks is pretty good entertainment."

"You should get yourself a dog. They're great companions. I'm sure Abby would be happy to pick the perfect one out for you from her rescue center."

"I hardly think I need to add the care of a dog to the list of my screwups."

Jesse cocked his head as though Jake had spoken gibberish. "You love dogs."

"I know. But you can't honestly think I'd be a good dog parent. Not right now."

"What's holding you back, little bro? So you've got a bum leg at the moment. Who the fuck cares? It'll heal."

Jake slugged down the remains of his Shiner. "It's not the leg."

"Yeah." Eyes dark with understanding, Jesse nodded. "I get it. The war fucked up a lot of shit for a lot of people."

Jake pushed out a harsh breath. "A lot."

"Want to talk about it?"

"Talking about it means I have to face it."

"Might be time."

"Might not." Jake lifted the empty bottle.

"Got news for you, little bro. Eventually, it's going to catch up with you—ready or not."

"It already has. Which is why I'm taking a step back."

"You sleeping at night?"

"Not much."

"Might sleep better if you work it out."

"Probably."

"Don't for one minute think you're alone in this, Jake." Jesse swung his eyes, sharp and focused, in Jake's direction. "We might not have been there beside you that day, but we all understand. Each of us has had some kind of cross to bear. Reno suffered a triple loss in quick succession with Jared's, Dad's, and his fiancée's deaths. Jackson was witness to Jared's being killed. I lived with Jared's secret, then endured the guilt that I didn't talk to Dad about it, which might have given him an opportunity to let go of the grief that caused his heart to quit on him. And you've got Eli's death."

And the fact that he'd promised Eli's pregnant wife he'd get her husband home alive.

Jesse sat up, swung his long legs off the lounge,

leaned toward Jake, and pointed. "Nothing you could have done that day would have made any difference."

Jake leaned back and sighed with doubt.

"I promise you, it wouldn't have. It's fucked up, but it wouldn't have mattered if you'd tackled him, padded him with a double layer of armor from head to toe, or had him call in sick for the mission. If it was his time, it was his time."

"I call bullshit on that."

"The only way you could count yourself responsible . . ." Jesse clamped a hand over Jake's shoulder. "Is if you'd pulled that trigger yourself."

More than anything, Jake wanted to nod and agree. After a lifetime of advice on everything from how to properly rope a calf, to how to stretch the truth to save your sorry ass, right down to the secrets of all-night sex, his brothers' lectures were like the unwanted voices in his head. But for what it was worth, usually they were right.

"That's not going to matter to Eli's wife or his baby when it's born," Jake said.

"Is that what this is all about? You really think his wife will blame *you*?" Jesse gave him the big-brother glare, folded his hands together, and dropped them between his knees. "Or tell their child *you* were the reason his daddy died?"

Jake shrugged, even while his subconscious screamed *yes*.

"Got news for you. There's an enemy out there. And it isn't you. You, Eli, and your entire company were betrayed. You were ambushed. Call it what you want, that day the enemy played a better hand. Doesn't mean you did anything wrong. Just means they did something right. Just like the day they pulled the trigger on the bullet that killed our brother. Are you going to blame Jackson for Jared's death just because he was there that day? Because he was a witness to what happened?"

"Hell no."

"So what makes you any different?" Jesse punched his shoulder. "War is fucked up, brother. Fucked. Up. The best thing you can do now is to face your demons head-on and find a way to move forward with your life. Freedom. It's what we all fight for whether on the battlefield or here at home. We fight for the freedom to live our lives to the best of our abilities and ultimately find a little happiness along the way."

Jake's gut, though twisted in knots, told him his older brother might be right. But the heaviness in his heart wasn't buying it.

Always one of the more observant brothers, Jesse sensed it was time for a change of subject. He leaned back again and propped his arm behind his head.

"So . . . you go home alone from the party last night?"

"Jess. I'm staying with Mom. Of course I went home alone."

Jesse's wide shoulders came up. "Question's not out of line for you. It's not like you haven't made use of the hayloft before. Or taken a date for a drive out by the creek. Or gone home with someone."

"Just trying to reacclimate first."

"Bullshit. You know what you need?"

"No. But I'm sure you're about to tell me."

"Damn straight I am. You need a woman. A good woman. One who'll be with you through the good times and the bad."

"Jesus." Jake ran a hand over his now-grown-out buzz cut. "I kind of hoped the bad times were behind me."

"With any luck." Jesse squinted. "But just in case, it's nice to have someone who looks up at you every day with love and hope in her eyes. Kind of beats the alternative to shit."

"Pretty sure that's not really on my agenda right now."

Or any time in the near future.

First, he had to figure out what the hell to do with the rest of his life. Deciding where he planned to live would be a good start. With his mother's getting married, Jake figured she'd move her new husband into the house on Wilder Ranch. But even as massive as the ranch-style home was, it would never be big enough for him to give the newly-weds their space. And then there was always the fact that he was an adult and really should have a home of his own.

"You should listen to what I'm telling you. I'm a doctor."

"Jess, you're a freaking vet. And I'm not a dog."

"That's not what Jessica Holt said the last time you were home on leave, then you didn't . . ." He lifted his hands, made air quotes, and raised his voice an octave. "Keep in touch like you promised."

"I don't remember promising anything like that."

"Maybe that's why Jessica thinks you're a dog." Laughter rolled up through his brother's broad chest. "No surprise. The heat of the moment makes you say all kinds of crazy shit."

"Sorry to disappoint you, brother, but even in the heat of the moment, I choose my words carefully. No promises. No four-letter words that start with L unless it's *lick*. Jessica and I are on the same page. We have a mutual understanding. And a casual hookup is all we'll ever be."

"So maybe you should go ahead and give your *casual hookup* a call. I'm sure she'd be happy to help you forget your troubles for a few hours."

"Maybe." Trouble was, he didn't want Jessica Holt. No matter how fancy her private underwear collection might be. He didn't know why, he just didn't.

"But . . ." A grin spread across Jesse's face. "Then you'll be right back where you started. Alone and still ugly as sin."

"You do realize we're brothers, and we look alike, right?"

Jesse laughed. "You keep thinking that."

The empty bottle rolled between Jake's fingers. He looked at his surroundings and the life his brother had created for himself. The perfect house. The perfect yard. The perfect wife. The perfect life.

Jesse had it all.

But Jake knew that with the emptiness in his soul, he'd never find that nirvana. That perfect life. That happily-ever-after. Not when another man's wife and child had been left out in the cold because *he'd* failed them in a major way.

"So what are your plans for the rest of the day?" Jesse asked. "I've got spare shorts if you want to go for a swim."

"Nope." Jake stood, dropped the empty bottle in the trash, and headed toward the gate. "Looks like I might have some making up to do with Jessica Holt and her never-ending array of circus tricks."

𝒟rips of sweet dark chocolate were everywhere. Annie had tried to be careful, so there'd be less cleanup, but she'd missed the mark. Like usual. She might as well have kept Max home. He couldn't have made a bigger mess than she had on her own.

Her plan had been to make enough batches to fulfill her regular orders, then add a few more for the extra cash. Christmas was coming up fast. Soon the stores would put the Halloween decorations on sale, and the aisles would be overloaded with holly and jolly.

Max was old enough now to notice the lights and the festiveness. He'd spot the pretty packages and want to tear into them on sight. She wanted to make this a wonderful holiday for him, here in their own home. Even if he'd never remember it when he grew up.

The two-story they lived in had belonged to her parents before they moved to Florida, aka party central. Abby had come back from Houston after her divorce to renovate it and to put it up for sale. When Annie became pregnant, her sister had sent her an airline ticket to come home. By the time Annie arrived, Abby had everything done, and she'd purchased the house from their parents with some of the money she'd received in her divorce settlement. Since Abby had been married to the owner of the Houston Stallions NFL team, she had the means to make it happen. Still, Annie didn't take that for granted. She paid a fair amount of rent each month even though her sister didn't want to take it. Annie had always paid her own way, and she'd worked hard to make it happen. She might never be a millionaire, she might live from paycheck to paycheck, but that was perfectly okay with her.

Even though it was just her and Max there, the place was more of a home now than it had ever been while she'd been growing up. And she was very grateful for the love of a sister like Abby.

So far today, she'd completed three batches with at least five more to go. A quick glance at the clock told her she'd better bust her can and get moving. Jana's generosity wasn't one she wanted to abuse. If she couldn't get at least two more batches done in the next hour or so, she'd have to wrap it up and continue later tonight after she put Max to bed.

Just as she'd slipped on a new pair of gloves and started pouring the chocolate over the caramel, the doorbell rang.

Startled in the process of moving the pot of chocolate, a huge glob poured out. Instinctively, she reached out to catch it and ended up burning her fingers through the thin plastic glove.

"Ouch!" *Dammit.* "Come in," she shouted, caring not that whoever was at the door could possibly be a stranger but only that she free her hand from the glove and get it under some cold water. In pain and in a hurry, she did a little *ow-ow* dance while she tried to remove the chocolate-laden glove without also removing the burned skin.

"What the hell are you doing yelling 'come in'? I could have been a serial killer."

Annie's gaze shot up from her burned hand to Jake's dark expression where his brows had collided over his blue eyes.

"I'm a little too busy at the moment to care. So unless you're a doctor, I really could do without the lecture."

"What did you do?" he asked, hands on hips like he really was preparing a lecture.

Duh came to mind, but she wasn't so far gone she'd be that rude. She held up her hand as Exhibit A. "The doorbell startled me, and I poured hot chocolate over my hand. So either get helping or get gone. This hurts, and I'm losing my cheerful attitude quickly."

"Like you ever had one," he muttered so low she almost didn't hear him. "Let me see."

When he came toward her, she noticed he was without his cane. She could ask why later; right now she just needed a little assistance. Maybe some sympathy. Definitely a strong drink.

The glove was halfway off her hand but still covered the burned area. He gently took her hand in his, and she was sure she'd feel a rush of tingles—if she didn't feel like howling.

"Let's stick this under the cold water while we remove the glove the rest of the way."

"Good idea," she said.

A smile kicked up one corner of his mouth. "I'm full of them if you'd just pay attention."

While he worked, she looked up, fully entranced by the humor that danced in his eyes for what he thought was such a clever comeback.

"You mean like the night of your high-school graduation, when you and your buddies drove into San Antonio, and you got drunk off your ass and thrown in jail?"

His head came up, eyes narrowed again. "How'd you know about that?"

"Jake. This is Sweet. *Everybody* knew about that."

"Pretty sad a man can't make a fool of himself without everybody and their brother knowing."

"I do believe your brothers were the ones who told."

"Mom never knew."

"Really?" She snorted. "Something that big is going to happen, and she's not going to know?"

"Glove's off."

"What?"

"While you were tripping down memory lane on my behalf, I got the glove off."

"Oh." She looked down and, sure enough, the chocolate-covered plastic was crumpled in the sink, and Jake was holding her burned hand under the cold water. Fortunately, the burn appeared to be minor but still stung like crazy. "Thanks."

"You got some ointment and a bandage?"

"In the bathroom."

He let go of her hand and disappeared through the living room. When he came back, he was loaded down with hydrogen peroxide, triple antibiotic ointment, and a box of multisized bandages that sported the goofy face of SpongeBob SquarePants.

"You seriously should invest in Spider-Man bandages," he said. "They make the healing go much quicker."

"I'm shocked." Once again, he took her hand in his. This time, she *did* feel the tingle.

"Why's that?"

"You seem more like a Superman or Batman kind of guy."

"Nope. It's Spidey all the way for me." He paused and looked up. "What's with the grin?"

"I'm trying to picture you in a pair of Spider-Man Underroos."

"They don't make them in my size."

"Too bad." Laughter bubbled up from her chest. "I'd pay money to see that."

He chuckled as he grabbed the clean towel off the counter, blotted the water from her hand, and went to work applying the ointment and bandage.

"Looks like this isn't your first rodeo bandaging up someone," she said, watching the deft way he worked, his eyes intently focused on what he was doing.

"They give everyone basic medical training in the Marines. You never know when it might come in handy."

Annie bit her lip to keep from saying, *Like the day you had to use a tourniquet and rescue yourself so you could make it back home?*

"You ever think of going into the medical field?" she asked instead.

"Never entered my mind. I always thought I'd retire a soldier."

"You should give it some thought, Jake. You have a nice touch."

His head came up, and those dark blue eyes bored right into hers. "What kind of thought?"

"I don't know." She shrugged. "Maybe you could be a paramedic."

For a moment, he searched her face, then he frowned. "Thought you were going to say I should become a doctor."

"You could if you wanted to."

A chuckle rumbled deep in his chest. "Like you don't have enough doctors sniffing around you already?"

She knew he was referring to Bo Jennings. But this conversation wasn't about Bo. She didn't give a rat's patooty about Bo. But Jake? He was everything.

"Is that what you're doing here, Jake? *Sniffing* around?"

Refocusing on her hand, he lightly tapped the ends of the bandage in place. "I don't sniff unless there's a really good barbecue on the grill."

"Then what *are* you doing here?"

His long pause gave her heart a ridiculously hopeful nudge.

"If you'll remember, my mom said I should come help you."

"I also remember your saying you didn't wear aprons." She couldn't help the taunt that brushed her lips.

"I don't. Yours looks good on you, though."

"Aw, gee. Thanks. You do say the sweetest things to a woman."

"Can I be honest with you?" he asked.

"Aren't you always? And usually brutally so?"

"I never realized you were a woman."

She choked on a laugh of surprise. "Excuse me?"

"Inside my head . . ." He pointed, just in case she didn't know what a head looked like. "Inside my memories? You were always a little girl, like Izzy. Just a little girl, skipping around, getting into trouble, and mouthing off. I never noticed you'd turned into a woman."

Though the comprehension of the way he viewed her stung like the burn on her hand, she gave his broad chest beneath that worn-out gray Marines T-shirt an understanding pat with her un-burned hand. "I know. But it happens to the best of us female types."

His big hand came up and captured hers against his chest.

"Annie?"

"Yeah?"

His gaze slowly traveled over her face, down to her lips, then back up to her eyes. "I'm noticing now."

$\mathcal{B}$eneath their clasped hands, Jake's heart pounded.

What the hell was he doing?

Thinking?

This was Annie.

She'd been like a little sister to him most of his life. She was a great big pain in the ass. Okay, maybe she leaned more toward petite and curvy with a backside that completely rocked a tight pair of jeans. And she was definitely delectable with the sweet scent of chocolate and warm woman that rolled off her like some kind of double-dipped aphrodisiac.

But this was Annie.

Annie, for Christ's sake!

Thank God her eyes were looking up at him and not down to the zipper on his jeans. Or she'd figure out pretty damned fast just how much he really did notice.

She sighed, and he pressed his lips together to keep from kissing her.

"I guess when someone is toting a one-year-old around on her hip all the time, it's hard not to notice the change."

Yeah. Not even close to what he'd been talking about, but he grabbed her misunderstanding like a life preserver.

Gently, he squeezed her hand then let go. "No doubt Max is a pretty big boy."

"And getting bigger every day. Imagine carrying all of that big baby around inside you." She turned away to grab the glove from the sink and dump it in the trash. "I guess I was surprised when Max came out so solid and stocky. His sperm donor was tall and lanky."

"*Sperm donor?*" Jake noted when she came back around that her expression was anything but apologetic. "Is that what you're going to call him when you tell Max about him?"

"I have a long time before I need to worry about what I'm going to tell him." She shrugged those slim shoulders. "By then, I should have figured something out. Because telling him the truth, while it might be the right thing to do, would just be heartbreaking for him. It's my hope that when the time comes, I'll be married to someone wonderful, and Max will be such a happy, well-adjusted kid, he'll never need to ask."

The idea of Annie's being married was like another shot to the gut. Of course she'd want to get married someday. Find a man who'd be a good father to Max. Why should that surprise him?

And why the hell should it bother him?

"Maybe you should try to get Max's father involved in his life early on. It's always better to work things out or get the truth out before they ask. Look at Reno. He was five when Mom and Dad got custody of him. They could have kept a lot of the sordid facts to themselves about his mother's drug addiction and the way she abandoned him. Instead, they gave him the information they thought he could comprehend, then they kept that door open in case he wanted to ask further questions. He never did because—"

"He was a happy, well-adjusted kid after he came to live with your family."

"Yeah." Jake did a mental shake of his head. Annie knew so much about him, about his family. It was like she could effortlessly slide in and out of the collective members. Or like she was a special ingredient that mixed right into the big pot of crazy soup they all created.

"Thanks for your concern," she said. "But involving my ex in Max's life isn't going to happen."

"You don't think he'll eventually come around?"

. "I have higher hopes that flying cars will be invented." She shook her head. "Sorry. My doubt really has nothing to do with Max. Because he's an adorable little boy if I must say so myself."

"He is. So I'm not following your reason. Why wouldn't a man want to claim his son?"

"I guess you'd have to be a man who cared to answer that." She waved her nonburned hand. "Never mind. It's a long story. And I'm sure you're not really interested."

"Would you be surprised if I said I was?"

"Yes." She laughed. "Very."

He captured her hand midair and held it against his chest. "Well, bring out the party favors because I'm interested."

Her hand slipped from his grasp, and she took a step back. Jake was unsure if the retreat was because of their close proximity or the subject matter. "Not something you normally like to discuss?" he asked.

"More like I don't care to admit what a complete loser I was by being in that relationship in the first place." She grabbed some paper towels and began wiping drips of chocolate from the counter with the hand that was burned.

The task looked painful and awkward, so he took the paper towel and did the job for her. "I don't think you're a loser."

"Seriously? Because in my mind, I get to wear the crown and be their queen." She shook her head. "At the time, I thought I was so smart, being all mature and everything by packing up and running away from here. I never imagined I'd be making the biggest mistake of my life."

"We all make mistakes."

"Yeah, but not usually ones that drive you almost two thousand miles away from everyone and everything you've ever known just to prove a point."

He tossed the paper towel in the trash, leaned his backside against the counter, and folded his arms. "And what point was that?"

"That I didn't need anyone. That I could make it on my own. That I didn't care if . . . my parents had repeatedly abandoned me my entire life."

Most of the thoughtful conversations he and Annie shared over the years involved her parents' style of child rearing. Which wasn't much. Mostly, her parents were absentee. Abby, as her big sister, had carried a lot of the parenting load. Annie's way to deal with her parents' blatant disregard had been quiet consternation. When she finally rebelled, she'd done it in a big way.

"But you did care," he said. "Even I knew that."

Her eyes snapped up like he'd surprised her. Again.

"Of course I cared. I still do," she admitted. "I was just a full-blown idiot at the time. Little did I know that moving so far away wouldn't eliminate the hurt but only add to it."

"Don't get flustered. I'm only asking because I care. And I'm interested. So how about you tell me the whole story so I understand."

Her slim shoulders lifted and dropped like the weight of the world had been parked there for a while. "Once I got to Seattle, I had all these big ideas. Big plans. I must have had a crack in my head that let all the good brain cells seep out because being a candy maker in Austin did not prepare me for the outside world."

"I guess dipping chocolates isn't the same as pushing papers or working on a computer?"

"No. And after almost a year of not being able to land a job other than waitressing, and sharing my cheap and cheaply furnished apartment with nothing but a begonia named Bernice, I realized the true meaning of pie in the sky. There was no reward coming for me because I'd taken a stand and moved away. Plus, I was so lonely, I couldn't see straight. I mean . . . really? I was talking to a plant that didn't even have the heart to bloom. About a year and a half after I moved to Seattle, I met . . . Doug."

"*Doug?* Like that sweater-vest-wearing little cartoon dude?"

"You sure know a lot about cartoons."

"I watch them with Izzy."

"Uh-huh."

"I swear . . ." He raised his hand. "I never watch them alone because I'm bored and there's nothing else on TV."

"No need to explain. You're talking to a girl who knows you worshipped the Teenage Mutant Ninja Turtles until you were thirteen, when someone mercifully yanked them off the airwaves." The corners of her pretty mouth kicked upward.

"They're popular again, you know."

"And you would know this how?" Her head tilted, and her ponytail swayed.

"From the commercials I see when I watch Nickelodeon with Izzy."

"Uh-huh."

"So . . ." He grinned, even though his secret cartoon-watching fascination had been outed. "Back to *Doug*."

"Must we?"

"Not if it makes you feel bad."

"Actually, I'm numb to it."

"Liar."

"Fine." She wrinkled her cute nose. "Where was I?"

"Meeting Doug."

"Right. Well, he and his band came into the restaurant where I worked after they'd played a gig at Neumos. They were a fun and animated bunch, and before they left, Doug asked for my number. A couple weeks later, he moved in, and Bernice the Begonia got pushed aside for guitar cases and amps." She looked up at the ceiling and sighed loudly. "I was so happy for someone to talk to that it took me a while—two years to be exact—to realize I was still paying all the rent, as well as stocking the cupboards and refrigerator, and paying the utility bills. Basically, I supported his musical dream while I balanced plates of greasy burgers."

"He never supported you on anything? Not even getting a better job or going back to school?"

"Emotional equality is not in his blood."

"What a dick."

"Yeah. But really, I had no one to blame but myself. People can't use you as a doormat unless you allow them to, right?"

"Just because a person is lonely doesn't give someone the right to take advantage."

"Maybe." She shrugged. "But even in my blinded

state of reality, I should have realized I needed to focus on myself just a little. Maybe take some community-college classes or something. But I didn't. I was too busy supporting him. And to be honest, at the time, I was afraid if I didn't support him, he would leave."

"Not much of a man if he put all that pressure on you."

"Tell me about it. And just so you know, I never tried to cut Doug out of Max's life. He made that decision himself the minute I told him I was pregnant. And he did it while I had my head hanging over the toilet because the morning sickness was so bad. When I came out of that bathroom with a cold, wet washcloth pressed to my forehead because I felt like I would pass out, he was gone. How he packed up his shit and got out of there so fast I'll never know. But he did. After that, he never sent me a forwarding address or took my calls. It would have been easy enough to find him, but after being tossed aside like a bag of trash, I honestly didn't want to."

"You're a good person, Annie. Unfortunately, you just got tangled up with a complete asshole."

"I appreciate the sentiment. And I agree. But that really doesn't erase the situation. Or the lingering questions."

"Questions?"

She looked down at the floor, then pressed her finger to a nonexistent piece of something on the counter and flicked it in the sink. She looked everywhere but at him. Finally, he tucked his fingers beneath her chin and forced her to look up.

There was sadness in her eyes. Doubt. And self-reproach.

"Annie, tell me. Please?"

Each tick of the clock on her hesitation felt like a hot poker to his heart.

"It doesn't stop me from asking why everyone leaves me? What did I do that was so bad it makes them not want to stay?"

Her words crushed him.

Completely.

No one deserved to feel that way. Especially not when they tried so hard.

He'd never been good at finding the right words to say, which was just only one of the reasons he'd yet to contact Eli's wife. If Doug were around, Jake wouldn't hesitate to take him to task. But for all he knew, he'd never come face-to-face with the man. So in that moment all Jake could do was reach out and draw Annie into his arms.

For a long moment, they stood together—heart to heart. His arms around her, offering silent comfort. Her arms around him, accepting solace. She never allowed any tears to fall, but they still dampened a little place on his shirt, right next to where his heart pumped with admiration and something else he couldn't quite name.

Eventually, she backed away, trying to look calm and cool. "Now you know . . . why I'll never try to involve Doug in Max's life. If he truly wanted to be included, I wouldn't refuse. For Max's sake. But Doug only sees what's in it for him. And Max isn't even on his radar. The only thing he can see is the next gig, the sparkle of a big record deal, and whatever stupid girl he can charm into taking care of him so he can follow his dream."

"I'm really sorry he treated you so badly."

"It's okay. Really," she said. "Imagine if he'd stuck around? He'd have been miserable. Both Max and I would have been miserable. Life would have sucked. At least this way, Max and I have a chance at happiness."

The word *happiness* rang like an endless echo through Jake's heart. Not everyone would find it in their lifetime. Some of that was his fault. But tonight, he'd try to push aside his demons and accomplish what he'd originally come here for.

"So . . . thanks. For this." She held up her bandaged hand and gave him a sweet smile. "And the compassion. Although I imagine that's way more than what you bargained for. I wouldn't blame you if you hit the door running."

"Not all men leave, Annie. And I'm staying put." Once the words were out of his mouth, even he wasn't sure what they meant as far as he was involved. So before she tilted her head in that cute way that made him want to cup her face between his hands and kiss her senseless, he glanced around the kitchen at all the pans, molds, and the now-congealed chocolate. "So how about I give you a hand here?"

"You're kidding." Eyes wide, her head went back. "You really want to help?"

"Unless you can think of another damsel in distress who could use my talents . . ." He held up his hands. "I'm all yours."

One sleek brow lifted as she smiled. "And you'll wear an apron?"

"Only if you insist and promise not to sneak photos or tell those jackasses I'm related to."

She promised.

For the rest of the day and into the night he battled dipping the perfect chocolate truffle, eating too many, and trying to keep his hands on the candy and not on Annie.

When Annie closed the door after watching Jake walk out to his truck, she was still shaking off the surprise of his visit. Not really being a kitcheny kind of guy, his offer to help make chocolates had floored her. Running as far behind as she had been, she'd been happy for his help and the company.

At first it felt strange telling him about her life in Seattle and her relationship with Doug. When he came home last year for Jackson and Abby's wedding, he didn't seem all that interested in her wretched life. Then he'd been all about a wink, a grin, and having a good time. Even though she didn't like to bring up her past, somehow Jake had managed to get her to talk, then he relieved the embarrassment she usually carted around.

He didn't make her feel like she'd been irrational when she'd gone in search of a new life. He didn't laugh, point fingers because she'd gotten involved with such a loser, or offer unwanted advice on how to raise her son. Instead, he'd held her in his arms and offered comfort. A safe place. He'd listened.

And he'd agreed that Max was an amazing little boy—which was something her son's own father had failed to do.

Remarkably, it had felt good telling him about what had happened. Much like the old times when they'd sit in the hayloft and talk for hours. The man who'd shown up not only to lend her a hand in the kitchen, and who'd also rescued her burned hand, seemed very much like the Jake she used to know. And while she didn't want to be some kind of charity case who only used his gorgeous broad shoulders to cry on, she did appreciate his genuine compassion.

To top it off, the man had put on an apron.

An apron.

Like she really needed anything else to make her fall more in love?

There were hardly enough words to express how she felt about seeing his six-foot-four muscular frame wrapped in the cute little scrap of printed bluebonnets and smiling suns. What didn't surprise her was that while he helped her make the German chocolate cake and triple-toffee truffles, several of them went missing. The smear of chocolate at the corners of his smooth, masculine mouth was a telltale sign of where the candy had disappeared. For her, it had taken startling control not to lift to her toes and lick the chocolate from those lips.

After he'd called his mother and explained that she was running behind because she'd burned her hand, they'd worked late into the night, boxing up the confections. Jana had been concerned about the burn but was infinitely more intrigued that Jake was lending her a hand in the kitchen. She'd told Annie not to hurry and to keep Jake for as long as she wanted. According to Jana, Max was as happy as a kitten under a leaky cow, and for her not to worry. She could pick him up in the morning.

Jana was a godsend.

Jake—a curiosity.

Annie couldn't figure out what had possessed him to walk through her door other than maybe boredom. But for a woman with a wishful heart, there was that one hurrah moment when he'd told her he'd noticed she was a woman and no longer a girl. Something had been different in his tone and the way he'd swept those deep blue eyes down and back up her body. But again, wishful thinking on her part did not equal reality.

There was nothing really different about her now other than she was a little smarter and a bit more rounded than she'd been prebaby. Nothing remotely interesting about a woman who served up burgers and fries to the community, then spent hours alone in her kitchen sticking her hands in chocolate to tempt the sweet tooth in the residents of Sweet, Texas, or wiping baby barf off her newest blouse.

In essence, she was still just regular old Annie Morgan.

And he was still smoking-hot, sexy, mouthwatering Jake Wilder.

Jake didn't see her *that* way.

He never would.

He viewed her as a friend.

That's all.

Still, a girl with a wishful heart had a right to capitalize on keeping the fantasy alive. And when Annie slipped into bed that night, there was only one man who stepped into her dreams.

Chapter 5

After an exhausting week of work and dealing with Max's teething-induced crankiness, Annie knocked on the door of her sister's house with her irritable son perched on her hip. She smiled when she heard Izzy's little feet run to the door with the slap-slap of Abby's sandals close behind. A delicious dinner provided by your sister who could put Rachael Ray to shame was always a welcome invite. After pushing burgers and fries all day, Annie hoped Abby had made one of her delicious roasts or even a roasted chicken. Anything that was roasted, baked, or grilled, as opposed to breaded and deep-fried sounded heavenly.

When the door opened, Max flashed a gummy grin to his cousin, then held out his chubby arms. Izzy might be just a kid herself, but she loved Max. He was someone to play with until her new cousin Adeline grew up and her new baby sister cooked in her stepmama's oven a little longer. If Annie was honest, she was giddy with the relief that for a few hours, Max would have someone to entertain him and, hopefully, divert his attention away from his aching gums.

"Come 'ere, you cute little booger."

"Izzy." Abby's tone was admonishing. But the grin on her face told a whole different story. She adored her stepdaughter, and while Annie thought divorce was an awful end to a promising life, she also recognized that Izzy was a lucky little girl to have two sets of parents who thought she walked on water.

Watching Izzy struggle with hauling Max into the living room made Annie laugh.

"She's going to be a handful when she grows up," Abby said, still grinning.

"Just like her father." Annie leaned in and gave her sister a hug over her baby belly, then handed over the loaf of zucchini bread she'd made from the vegetables she'd been given from Reno and Charli's garden.

"Very true." Abby gave her rounded stomach a rub. "And with the level of activity in this little one, I'm pretty sure she'll follow in the Wilder footsteps too."

"Better take out good insurance for all those bumps and bruises. I seem to remember Jackson always being bandaged up or having something in a sling."

As they entered the kitchen, Jackson, caught sneaking a handful of black olives, looked up. "What?"

"Nothing." Abby gave him a kiss on the cheek, and he pulled her into his arms for a liplock.

"Oh, you guys." Annie rolled her eyes and laughed. "Stop."

"You're just jealous." Jackson gave his wife another quick peck on the lips.

"So true."

The conspiring look her sister and brother-in-law gave each other piqued her interest. They were up to something.

"Oh my God. You guys didn't invite Bo to dinner, did you?"

They said nothing. Just gave each other that look again.

"Aww, come on. Y'all don't need to be trying to fix me up with someone. I told you I'm not interested in him."

"Little sister." Jackson clamped his big hand over her shoulder. "How can you not be interested in someone who is clearly fascinated by you?"

"Seriously?" Annie folded her arms across her chest and tried to ignore the aroma of the pot roast that floated through the air when Abby opened the oven door. "I suggest you don't go down that road. None of you Wilder boys has ever gone about things the easy way. Even when the right thing was right in your face. For years!"

Surprisingly, he didn't flinch at the reference she'd just dropped like the gauntlet of all gauntlets. Abby had been in love with him for most of her life. But Jackson, stubborn man that he was, refused to acknowledge that he'd been in love with her too. Which had resulted in Abby's leaving Sweet and Jackson behind. With a divorce for each of them later, Jackson finally owned up that he couldn't live without Abby.

Talk about taking the long way around something.

"So some of us are slow learners," he said.

"Some?" Abby jacked up an eyebrow.

"Point taken." Now he flinched. But then that big Wilder smile was back on his handsome face as he winked at Annie. "But your sister and the trouble she caused me was well worth the wait."

"Hey." Abby laughed as she lifted the delicious-smelling roasting pan from the oven. "You want to reexamine who caused who more trouble?"

"We just want the best for you, Annie." Jackson gave his wife an apologetic look, then snagged an arm around Annie's shoulder. "That's all."

From the living room, Izzy's and Max's laughter rang out.

"Right now," she said, "I've got my hands full just trying to provide for my son."

Jackson pulled her in closer for a buddy hug. "We just want you to keep your eyes—"

"*And* your heart open," Abby added.

"I'll get right on that," Annie said. "Between wiping down tables at the diner and wiping Max's messy butt."

The doorbell rang, and Izzy shouted, "Got it."

For a moment, there was a low murmur, then a round of girly giggles and the gleeful shout of a male child who'd yet to learn his volume control. Annie braced herself for an evening of being gracious to Bo while feeling a bit uneasy about the whole *setup* thing Abby and Jackson had tossed them into.

An uneven sound of boots thudded across the stone entry floor until those size thirteen and a half scuffed-up shitkickers appeared in the kitchen.

They did not, however, belong to Bo Jennings.

"Jake." Annie took a breath to calm her racing heart. "What are you doing here?"

"What are *you* doing here?"

"Sugar?" Jackson shot Abby a look of panic. "Was that Izzy calling us?"

"We'd better check." Abby tossed the potholders onto the counter. Like two mice who'd spied the trap, they scurried out of the kitchen.

"Weird." Jake watched the two until they disappeared, then he turned his attention back to her. "How's the hand?"

"Good as new." She held it up and wiggled her fingers. "Thanks again."

"Glad I could help."

Annie did her best not to sigh at the smile he gave her as she leaned back against the kitchen island for support. Jake Wilder all messed up and looking like a rugged cowboy was one thing. Jake Wilder all cleaned up and looking like a cover boy had the ability to noodle a girl's knees. "What are you doing here?"

"Paying a visit to my brother and sister-in-law."

"Bad timing." Annie shook her head. "Your brother and my sister invited me to dinner. And they invited Bo Jennings too. I know you're not fond of him so . . . you might want to make this a quick visit."

"Wait a minute, Miss Bossypants." His blue gaze took a slow ride down her body. When it came back up to her face, he was smiling. Sort of. It could have been a grimace. Or maybe gas pains. "Why are you always assuming the worst of me? I never said I wasn't fond of Bo."

"You called him *that guy*."

"Well, he is a guy." His hands dropped to his hips. "So what would you prefer I call him?"

"I prefer you call him nothing. And you won't have to if you leave before he gets here."

"I don't think my brother intended his kitchen to be a drive-thru."

"What are you talking about?"

"Jackson invited *me* for dinner. And when that dinner smells as delicious as whatever is in that pot, I'm not going anywhere."

Crap. How could this have happened? Dinner was really going to be awkward now. Apparently, Abby and Jackson hadn't conferred with each other on the guest list.

Or had they?

"Great. Just try to be nice when he arrives."

"I'm always nice."

She snorted.

"What?" His brows lifted. "You don't think I'm nice?"

Oh, she thought he was nice all right.

She ran her gaze up and down his body as he'd done hers earlier.

He was *very* nice.

"It depends on the situation," she said. "Like the other night, when you came by and helped me with the chocolates and bandaged my hand? That was very nice. Or the time when you found me and my busted-up Nissan broken down on Highway 46 and you not only offered me a ride home but you got my car towed to the auto repair? That was really nice. But—"

"Now, Annabelle . . ." He turned that charming Wilder grin up to high voltage. "Don't go ruining all those pretty words with a *but*."

"*But* . . . that summer we were all camped out by the creek, and you put a tarantula in my sleeping bag?" She shook her head. "Not nice. And the time I finally wore a dress to school, and you and your football buddies followed me around all day calling me *legs*? Not nice."

"Darlin', we were kids then. I'm a man now."

Yes, he was. In every way and more.

"And by the way . . ." He leaned forward, bringing with him the subtle scent of citrusy, woodsy, warm male. "We weren't making fun of your legs. That was simple male appreciation."

"Bull." She'd been made fun of too many times to buy into that. Still, that he'd noticed her at all sent a sweet little shiver down her spine.

"I swear." His hand came up in the three-finger Boy Scout pledge.

Annie couldn't help but laugh. "You might be many things, Jake. But an innocent Boy Scout isn't one of them."

"Should I be offended?" The playful grin on his face said he was anything but offended.

"Probably."

He chuckled, then that smile slipped, and his

expression grew grim. "Bo Jennings isn't the one for you, Annie."

That he didn't seem to care for Bo wasn't a shocker, but his honest declaration took her back. "How do you know who is or isn't the one for me?"

Before he could respond, Abby and Jackson reappeared in the kitchen, chatting away like they'd never left the room. Annie and Jake looked at each other, knowing the discussion was tabled but far from over.

"I made tiramisu ice cream and peach cobbler for dessert so you'll have a choice," Abby said, moving them all toward the long, dining-room table Jackson and his fireman buddy Mike Halsey—now Izzy's new stepdaddy—had built from an old oak tree that had once grown on Wilder Ranch.

Jake's eyebrows lifted. "I have to make a choice?"

"That's what I asked," Jackson agreed.

"You can have both," Abby said. "I just wonder about the taste factor putting them together."

"It's ice cream and pie, sugar." Jackson grabbed a large platter from the kitchen cupboard and poured the contents of the roasting pan onto the sleek white surface. "What's to wonder?"

As Abby called out to Izzy to wash her hands, Annie headed to the living room to grab Max. "Shouldn't we wait for Bo?"

Abby poked a fork in the moist whole red potatoes to check for doneness. "Bo?"

"Yes." Annie's brows pulled together. There was more than pot roast cooking around here. "You know, Bo Jennings. ER doctor. Guy you're trying to fix me up with and invited for dinner?"

Her sister finally looked up. "I never said we invited Bo to dinner. You just assumed."

"Yeah, Annie." Jackson lifted the platter and carried it to the table.

Annie shot Jake a look, but he was too busy sitting down at the table and taking a large gulp from his glass of sweet tea to look up. Or maybe that was intentional. She swung her gaze back to her sister, and whispered, "Abby? What are you up to?"

"Putting dinner on the table." She scrunched her nose and flashed a smile. "Time to eat."

While Annie headed to the living room to get Max, she glanced at the well-meaning couple and Lieutenant Clueless.

Yes, Annie had always had a thing for Jake Wilder, and she appreciated her sister and brother-in-law's sneaky efforts. But there wasn't a snowball's chance on the Sweet Pickens Bar-B-Q grill that he'd ever return that interest in her direction. So she might as well just enjoy the dinner and conversation. Afterward, she could go home to the superhot and sexy romance novel she'd picked up during her last trip to the grocery store. The hero on the cover was a dead ringer for Jake Wilder, and Annie figured that was about as close as she'd get to getting naked with the real thing.

$\mathcal{D}$essert had been served, and Jake's stomach was deliriously full and happy as he settled into the bright red Adirondack on his brother's back patio with a cold bottle of Shiner in his hand. Across from him sat Annie, looking extra tasty in a tight pair of jeans, red halter, and red boots. Beside her were his brother and sister-in-law, looking like contented cats on a warm day. On the lawn, little Max was doing his toddling best to chase down Izzy, but his unsteady little baby steps could hardly keep up with his long-legged and quick-footed cousin.

While the nearby creek meandered by, spilling over rocks and the roots of oak and cypress trees, and the buzz of cicadas hummed from those same trees, Jake briefly closed his eyes.

For months at war, then months stuck in a hospital bed, he'd dreamed of this. Being home with his family. Enjoying their company. Feeling the warmth of the Texas sun as it rode off into the west for the night. Hearing the sound of children at play, dogs barking, and the general peace he'd only ever felt at home.

Home was where the heart was.

But Jake's heart was still shattered.

And his future remained in limbo.

He took a long sip of ale and glanced across the flickering fire-pit flames at Annie, who laughed every time little Max squealed with delight. Liberty—Jackson and Abby's mutt-of-questionable-breed—slurped the little boy up the side of his face, and a hearty chortle bubbled through his tiny lips. The sound of a child's laughter had always filled Jake with joy. Now, Jake couldn't laugh. Couldn't find the joy. Because now, that delightful sound served only as a reminder of his poor decisions. His inability to lead. His failures.

"Jesse says I need a dog," he said, breaking the silence and, hopefully, the tension in his chest.

"Are you looking for a puppy?" Abby asked. "Or one that's already outgrown the chewing-everything-to-shreds stage?"

The animal rescue center Abby had created along with the secondhand store to support it was often crowded with abandoned or lost pets. Abby worked hard to find them all homes. She never gave up until she was able to place each animal with the right family.

During his last visit home, Jake had visited her center and found it to be more like a day care than a shelter. No animal went into an enclosure unless it had a behavioral issue. If it did, Abby brought in experts to help the animal work it out. A pretty amazing and admirable feat, Jake thought, as pride filled an empty spot in his soul. His brother had married a remarkable woman.

"I'm not looking for either," he said.

"You'd make a perfect parent," Annie argued.

Jake knew she meant a parent of the four-legged kind of kid, but a suggestion of the two-legged type still dangled between them. Jake appreciated her vote of confidence, but uncertainty ruled.

Having grown up in a big family, Jake had always wanted children of his own. He loved the noise, the chaos, the love, and the sense of togetherness. But the troubling conversation he'd once had with his best friend—of hearing Eli's regret of being abandoned by his own father and the deep abiding fear that he'd leave his own child fatherless because of the career he'd chosen—would stay with Jake forever. That he hadn't even been able to face Eli's widow since the ambush said a lot about his character. Right now, it was shakier than hell. And right now, he felt that since he'd stripped the opportunity to be a father away from Eli, he didn't deserve that privilege. An eye for an eye might not make sense to anyone else, but it did to Jake.

"Why don't you come by the center tomorrow and take a look anyway?" Abby shrugged. "You never know."

"No offense, but I can barely get my own shit together, let alone care for some poor defenseless animal."

"Baloney."

Annie's tone was so sharp, it snapped Jake's head around.

"A dog really asks nothing of you aside from food, water, a place to sleep, and a little love. In return, the love and loyalty of a dog is limitless." Annie's delicately arched brows pulled together over a fierce look in her eye. "You can trust them with all your anguish. All your sorrow. And they will never betray you or your trust *or* withhold comfort when you need it. You're a Marine, Jake. Surely you've heard of service dogs? Have you never heard of a wounded warrior who's been given a dog to help them heal in both heart and mind?"

Jake swallowed.

How did this woman continue to nail him on everything? How did she know him so damned well when he knew so little about her?

"I'm familiar," he finally mumbled.

"Then why not go to Abby's shelter tomorrow?" Annie brushed away a fleck of ash from the fire pit that had floated down and landed on the leg of her jeans. When she looked up at him, ferocity still darkened her eyes. "Why not take a chance on finding that kind of friend?"

Jake took a deep breath as the truth grabbed hold of his heart and squeezed. And he realized that, once again, Annie proved she knew him a hell of a lot better than he knew her, or himself.

$\mathcal{A}$ walk after a heavy dinner and dessert was always a good idea. Annie tried to either speed walk or run on a regular basis, but finding the time often became the impossible dream. After putting Max down with a bottle in Izzy's room and waiting till he fell asleep, Annie took up her sister's offer to watch him while she took a stroll around the property.

These days, she rarely got to her own backyard even after several of the Wilder brothers had been kind enough to relandscape for her in a manner that would require less maintenance. While she loved working in the yard, Max tended to eat everything in sight, which often included bugs, plant leaves, and those oh-so-interesting dandelion fluffs. The phrase "Don't put that in your mouth" seldom left her lips fast enough before Max would look up with a horrified expression because, yes, he'd eaten a bug.

However, taking a walk now wasn't generated by the need for exercise. All night, she'd been battling something far more disturbing. One, the fact that she couldn't keep her big mouth shut, and two, Jake Wilder. Or more accurately, her crushing desire for him.

In the flash of a breath, her longings ran the gamut from wanting to wrap her arms around him and draw him in close for a comforting hug, to wanting to wrap her arms around him for a sensual body rub, to wanting to wrap her hands around his neck and squeeze until his eyes bugged out.

The man drove her crazy in too many ways to count. Escape from his extreme hotness and her burning desire had not only been a want, it had become a need. Five more minutes sitting across from him could force her to spontaneously combust. Or worse. She could actually drool.

Yeah, that was a pretty thought.

Maybe in the length of time she toured the property, he'd pack up his badass grumpy self and go home. And maybe in that length of time she'd also learn to keep her yap shut. Doubtful, but as long as she breathed there was always hope. Or hysterical laughter at the thought that she could miraculously acquire the unattainable cone of silence.

For several minutes, she wandered aimlessly. Then, like a woman with PMS drawn to a king-sized Hershey bar, she was pulled toward the old tree house the Wilder brothers had built back when they'd been young and full of mischief.

Other than a few years, not much had changed with those men.

Annie remembered they'd always been building something—go karts, tack boxes for their livestock supplies, jewelry boxes for their mom, even an Army-tank-sized grill for their huge family feasts. When they weren't kept busy, they often found intriguing ways to get into trouble. A fact Jana still lamented. Especially when it required frequent visits to the emergency room.

When Annie reached the tree house nestled beneath a thick canopy of oaks, she noticed the rustic structure had been given new life with a corrugated tin roof, diamond-paned windows, and a deck bordered with a railing made of branches. Someone had obviously put some time into it. And since there was a little floral wreath on the front door, she guessed it had been Jackson, who'd polished up the once "boys only" hideout for Izzy.

The ladder had been rebuilt too, made easier and safer to ascend to the deck. Annie didn't hesitate to climb her way up the short seven steps and open the door into a little girl's paradise.

Walls once covered in Jared's old landscape and wildlife photos had been updated for the softer side with photos of flowers and cute, fluffy animals. A braided rug in vibrant lollipop colors covered a portion of the floor. On top of the rug sat a purple table and chair set with a Minnie Mouse tea set on top of a darling lace doily. From a wall plaque with mermaid hooks and *Isabella* painted in pink and green, several boas and fancy hats waited to be donned by the mistress of the tree house. The entire vignette made Annie wish she could be a little girl again. But maybe with more compassionate parents this time.

From outside the tree house came the shuffle

of leaves and uneven footsteps. Annie stepped out onto the deck and found Jake near the ladder, looking up.

"Do I have to call 'Rapunzel, Rapunzel, let down your hair?'" he asked, squinting against the setting sun.

"Hate to disappoint you." She leaned her elbows on the top of the railing to peer down at the handsome prince. "But these days, damsels in distress often get themselves out of trouble."

A grin spread across his face. "Which begs the question . . . are you a damsel in distress, fair Annabelle?"

"I could be. Let me check to see if the ogre still has a lock on the door." She made a great show of dashing back into the tree house, then back out onto the deck again. "Why, yes, the door is still locked, and there are guards at the gate. How's the leg?"

"My leg?"

"Yes. The guards' legs all seem to have fared the battle well. And yours?"

"Much better. In fact, the castle Blood Letter insists on more exercise."

Enjoying the playfulness in his grin, she batted her eyelashes, then held out her hand. "Then perhaps you could climb up and show me those dashing princely rescue skills."

"I thought damsels could rescue themselves."

"Sometimes . . ." She winked. "A damsel just likes to see a prince in action."

He clasped a hand across his heart. "Alas, fair maiden, unless a dragon lights a fire under my arse, climbing the tower seems an unmanageable feat. For I am not a prince. Just a mere peasant wandering these woods in search of . . ."

"In search of what?"

Truly puzzled, his broad shoulders lifted in a shrug. "What does one usually wander the woods for? Food? Respite? Buried treasure?"

"Doesn't everyone search for love?"

The expression that darkened his eyes caused a logjam of emotion in Annie's throat, and she backtracked. "Buried treasure is all good and well, kind sir. But how does one defeat an ogre? The door is locked tight. How will I survive alone in this tower?"

With his bottom lip snagged between his teeth and his hands on his hips, he continued to look up at her. She knew he thought the task of climbing that ladder might be difficult with the injury to his leg. But the doctor apparently wanted him to exercise it more, and the tree house was only seven easy steps off the ground. A tough Marine like Jake who'd regularly gone through strenuous training could scale the short distance using the power of his massive arms alone. His ogre—his doubts—were self-imposed, and the defeat in his eyes broke her heart.

In her mind, Jake Wilder had always been able to accomplish anything he set his heart to. Right now, it seemed he just needed a little reminding.

She knelt on the deck, held her hand out between the rails, and implored, "Come on. You can do this. I know you can."

His broad shoulders lifted and dropped on a frustrated sigh. "Annie . . ."

"Come rescue me." She wiggled her fingers. "Please don't let the ogre be victorious."

For a moment, she thought he would walk away because the horrific incident in Afghanistan and its dreadful outcome had swallowed him whole. Then she caught a subtle twitch in his jaw. His hands dropped from his hips, and he muttered under his breath. Finally, he crossed the path to the ladder. With one hand on the rung level to his shoulder, he looked up.

Her heart leaped.

"I don't know if this will work." He dropped his gaze. Shook his head.

It will, she encouraged silently. *It will.* She would never put him at risk. Challenge him? Indeed. Hurt him in any way? Never.

He looked up again, and caught her gaze. "But I'll give it a shot."

She smiled down at him. "That's all any damsel in distress could ask."

Once again, he muttered something incoherent while she kept her hand stretched out to him from between the rails.

He placed the foot of his good leg on the first rung, slowly bent his knee and eased up the other foot.

"That's good, Jake."

Frowning, he looked up. "Annie? I'm only a foot off the ground. There's a ways to go."

"But that's a foot higher than a second ago. Come on, Jake. Seven steps total. That's it." She brushed the hair from her eyes, then popped her hand back out. "Easy for a tough Marine like you."

"I'm not so tough."

Annie heard the unspoken "anymore" beneath that grumbled statement. But she rejected it.

"Are you kidding? You're the best dragon slayer in the Texas Hill Country. Everyone knows that."

Brows slammed together, he looked up at her. "Anyone ever tell you you're a pain-in-the-ass kind of princess?"

"Yes. You. Frequently." She wiggled her hand. "Six more steps. That's all. Come on. I believe in you."

Using the strength in his arms, he pulled himself up and managed to skip a rung, quickly making it to the third. Watching him slowly bend and lift his injured leg nearly brought her to tears, but she'd never let them fall. Jake hated pity. And so, instead, she offered him strength.

"That was great." She grinned. "I'll bet those boot-camp obstacle courses were child's play for you."

"Shut up, Annie." The muscles in his forearms and biceps bulged while he pulled himself up another two rungs. He sucked in a breath, then bent his knee and got his bad leg steadily beneath him.

"Almost there," she encouraged.

He looked up again. Squinted his eye. And gave her a crooked grin. "What kind of reward do I get when I get to the top?"

"Make it to the top, and you'll find out." She grinned too.

"Yeah?"

"Yeah. Better get that body moving, soldier."

"I thought I was a prince."

"We'll see about that once you get up here."

"Doesn't the princess always grant the prince a kiss after a good deed?"

"It's been known to happen a time or two."

The next two rungs went much quicker, and Annie had to wonder if he'd mastered those steps to reap the reward or if he'd just gotten tired of hanging on that ladder.

Once he pulled himself up onto the deck, he leaned his head back against the wood siding and let go a long sigh.

"I knew you could do it." A ridiculous amount of pride rippled through her heart.

Head down, he picked up a twig from the deck and twirled it between his forefinger and thumb. "A few months ago, I wouldn't have had to think about it. I would have grabbed hold and made it to the top in a split second."

"Speed is overrated." Annie sat down beside him and covered his twig-twirling fingers with hers. "Life isn't about having it rush by so fast you can't see it. Sometimes, you have to sit back, take a breath, and let it happen. We aren't always dealt a fair hand, Jake. But that's when paying attention matters the most."

"How's that?"

"If you're observant, then you can find a way out of the muck. You can figure out a way to assess the situation and move forward. Sort of like what they probably trained you for in the Marines."

His head came up then, eyes focused on her. "Is that what you did when Doug walked out?"

She nodded. "After I used every foul word I could think of."

"I've already gone that route. It doesn't change anything."

"Ah, Prince Charming, that's where you're wrong. Verbally giving it life changes a lot. Admitting the truth. Lashing out at the unfairness gives you the power to fight back. To breathe. To live. To find happiness you might never have imagined."

The last drop of sunlight sparkled in his eyes. "When did you get so smart?"

"Just because I didn't get straight A's in school and because I wasn't a big butt-kisser like you doesn't mean I'm a dim bulb."

Laughter barked deep from within his chest. "You're a pistol, Annie."

"Takes one to know one." She squeezed his fingers. "Give yourself some time to heal, Jake. And when you're ready, I promise the light at the end of the tunnel will be so bright, you'll need shades. I'm proof that it can happen."

His responding smile was weak by Jake Wilder's normal, gleaming standards. But it was still a smile. And Annie would take what she could get.

"I thought you said the princess rewards the prince with a kiss for rescuing her from the ogre."

"Sometimes it happens the other way around."

"Yeah." His gaze turned serious as he slipped his fingers around the back of her neck and drew her in. "Maybe sometimes it does."

Their lips gently met, and Annie's heart sighed. His mouth was warm and delicious just before he broke the very brief kiss. His head went back and he looked at her with utter surprise and curiosity. Then he leaned forward and kissed her hungrily, and as if he was no longer startled that after all these years, they were in each other's arms. Either that, or he was just accepting something he might not completely understand.

Lucky for him, she did.

When he leaned away again, he gave her the full-on impact of his smile.

"You weave one hell of a fairy tale, Annabelle." He pressed one more kiss to her tingling lips. "I'm looking forward to the next chapter."

For years, Annie had dreamed and fantasized about kissing Jake Wilder. This kiss didn't come anywhere close to her imagination.

It was so much better.

Chapter 6

$\mathcal{L}$eave it to a mother to bang her pots and pans loud enough to wake the dead. Or in this case, him. Not that it was her first rodeo of starting up the "get your sorry ass out of bed" symphony. Back in the day, she reserved that special tune for when she knew Jake or one of his brothers had been out late the night before, tying one on, and had slept with a pillow over his head and his hand on the bottle of Tylenol.

Today, he had no such hangover. Yet with what sounded like an entire cascade of aluminum cookware hitting the floor, Jake bolted up in bed and looked at the clock. Eight o'clock had come way too quick for someone who'd been up half the night trying to solve the mysteries of life.

Or more specifically, wondering what in the hell had possessed him to kiss Annie Morgan.

He was truly perplexed.

Because not only had he kissed her, he'd wanted

to do it again and again. Hell, he'd wanted to lay her back on that deck beneath the stars and ease those jeans down her shapely hips. He'd wanted to untie that pretty red halter top and use his hands and mouth to explore everything that suddenly made her so intriguing.

When the hell had Annie become so intriguing?

It had been a struggle for him to get up that ladder—a feat at one time he could have accomplished without even thinking. But thinking was what he was doing now. And wondering why he'd even bothered to make the climb. What did he think he had to prove?

He ran a hand through his hair, then scrubbed it over his face.

Maybe nothing other than to himself that he could do it.

Or maybe it had been the way she'd looked at him—not like he was damaged, but instead like he could save the world or at least rescue the princess from the evil ogre. Even if the villain was really only his own fears.

He flopped back down to the mattress.

Yeah, that had been it. He'd just needed to prove he could make the climb.

So then, what had been his excuse for even thinking about the reward? For standing down on the ground, looking up at the promise and encouragement she offered, and wondering what those plump pink lips would taste like?

Whatever had been the catalyst for the ascent, he'd found out.

Her kiss had been like honey—a nectar he'd

needed to sweeten something inside him that had bittered since that bullet had shredded everything he'd believed, worked for, wanted.

Promised.

Once he'd climbed to the deck of the tree house, he'd had no choice but to kiss her. Not because of all the teasing that had gone on between them but because he'd been moved to.

I believe in you.

Her four words were straightforward, easily spoken. And for that reason alone, he simply couldn't not kiss her.

She believed in him when he didn't have the nerve to believe in himself.

Was there any doubt why every time he looked across a room and found her there, he smiled.

She believed in him.

If he told any one of his brothers how he felt, they'd laugh their asses off. Then they'd tell him he was a goner. He wasn't gone. But he also wasn't whole enough to think he could put any kind of meaning behind the curiosity he felt. Not even if the way he felt when he was around Annie was damned good.

Once they quit their sparring.

He liked kissing her. Just the thought planted a warm tingle right in the center of his chest.

He liked kissing her.

But there couldn't be more.

As much as every cell in his body wanted her, he had to keep her in the friend zone. It wouldn't be fair for him to start something he couldn't finish, or to make a promise he couldn't keep. Annie wasn't a see-you-once-in-a-while kind of girl like Jessica Holt. Annie was a forever kind of girl. Unfortunately, at this point in his life, he was a barely there kind of guy.

Another cacophony of metal pots hitting against each other crashed loudly from the kitchen.

Unable to delay the inevitable any longer, he threw off the covers, dressed, and stumbled into the mess in the kitchen. Pots and pans, cooking utensils, plates, bowls, and other various kitchen necessities were piled high on the countertops. The kitchen table had disappeared beneath stacks of linens and cookbooks.

"Good Lord, woman, what are you doing?"

Amid the disaster and dressed in her customary jeans, button-down shirt, and big blond Texas-sized hairdo, his mother chuckled. Then she wandered over to the table and plopped a *Sweet on Texas* dessert cookbook down with the other piles. "You sound just like your daddy when he'd wander in during the midst of my spring cleaning."

"Mom?" He scratched his head. "In case you haven't noticed, it's early fall."

"I have noticed, son. Which means if I plan to hold to the November wedding date Martin has requested, I'd best get the backside of my jeans in gear."

"I didn't know you two had set a date." He pulled out a chair and sat down, not because his leg was aching but because he was truly surprised.

"Happened last night," she said in a much-too-nonchalant manner. "You want some coffee?"

"If you've got some handy."

"Got a fresh pot right here behind this red cook-ware." She retrieved the carafe, then filled a mug that was already sitting on the table in front of him. Automatically, she set the bowl of sugar down and went to the refrigerator for the pitcher of cream.

"Good for you finally setting a date," he said. When she didn't respond, he looked up from the curl of steam from his mug. "You nervous?"

She shook her head. "Not nervous about marry-ing Martin. But . . . I wanted to wait."

"For?" He lifted the mug and sipped, careful not to burn his tongue just in case he had the op-portunity to kiss Annie again soon.

"Well . . ." A long sigh blew through his moth-er's lips. "I wanted all my babies to have found their happily-ever-afters and be married before I took that step myself."

"I'd say you've done a pretty good job making that happen. You've even got a new granddaugh-ter, with another one on the way."

She sat in the chair next to him and gave a moth-erly shake of her head. "Perhaps you missed the part where I said *all* my babies."

"Don't look at me."

"You're my son, aren't you? My baby boy?"

"I'm not much of a baby anymore. And mar-riage is the last thing on my mind."

"Why? You're not getting any younger."

"Geez." He choked on the sip of coffee he'd just taken. "Seriously? I'm only thirty-one."

"Like I said, not getting any younger. Your twenties are behind you. Partying days are over."

"Says who?" He folded his arms across his

chest just to protect himself from all those crazy thoughts she was aiming at his heart. "Jesse built himself a bachelor's paradise and got to enjoy the hell out of it before he hooked up with Allie. And he's sneaking up on thirty-five. I think three out of four brothers is pretty good odds. You should just let it go at that."

"I should have had a five out of five. But that option was taken away from me."

The reminder of the loss of his oldest brother slammed home like the blade of a sharp knife.

"So . . ." His mother laid her hand on the table, leaned in close, and gave him the stink-eye. "Are you really going to deny me four out of four?"

"Mom." He leaned away from the all-knowing, all-seeing power in her eyes. Sometimes, his mom just scared the shit out of him. "I just came home. I haven't even had time to go out on a date yet."

"Don't be silly. Since when have you ever *dated*?" She slapped her hand down on the small space of tabletop that was actually visible. "Which reminds me . . . you'd do well to stay away from that Jessica Holt."

How the hell did she know about Jessica?

"She's no good for you."

Last time she'd been on top of him playing bronc rider, she'd been pretty good.

"She's nothing but trouble with a big bra size," his mother continued. "What you need is a nice girl. Not one you'd worry about her messin' around with someone else every time your back was turned."

"Rest assured, I'm not planning on hooking up with Jessica Holt." How could he when there was only a cute, fiery little blonde on his mind?

"I'm not resting at all until *all* my babies are settled and happy." She poked her finger into the front of his T-shirt. "You hear me, son? I said *all*. That includes *you*."

Jake brushed her hand away and tried to keep from laughing. His mother had the same MO every time she tried to make a point, which was to make herself seem big and tough and like she could kick any one of him or his brother's sorry asses anytime she wanted. He didn't doubt she could do just that. At the same time, the twinkle in her blue eyes was tinged with laughter as if she knew it was ridiculous for her to be trying to *tough guy* someone who was a foot taller and a mile broader.

"I've got a long way to go before I'm ready to find settled and happy, Mom. So you'd best just keep making those wedding plans of yours and forget about the rest."

She leaned back in the chair and sighed. "I really do have to get better at my *I'll kick your ass* voice, don't I?"

"Believe me." Jake laughed. "You do just fine." He set down his mug and took her hand. "And I appreciate your concern. But life isn't about having it rush by so fast you can't see it. Sometimes, you have to sit back, take a breath, and let it happen."

Her head went back. "Where'd you hear that?"

Annie. "Just popped into my head."

"Uh-huh."

Uh-oh. He could tell by that head tilt that she'd switched on her Mom radar. Seemed like a good time for a diversion. Or a quick exit.

"Besides, now that the Marines have said *adios*, I need to figure out what the hell to do with my life. What woman in her right mind would want to hook up with a guy who didn't have things figured out?"

"Sugarplum, I know it hurt you down deep when you received the honorable discharge. I know you feel you could have given more. And I know you see it as some kind of punishment for what happened. But I wish you wouldn't do that. As much as you want to beat yourself up about it, what happened that day comes down to circumstance and tragedy. Neither of which you had any control over. Personally, I couldn't be happier you aren't going back. I've grown fond of sleeping through the night knowing my boys are home. Living their lives and finding happiness. You've got your whole life ahead of you, with plenty of time to figure things out. So what is it you think you might like to do?"

The weight on his shoulders barely budged when he shrugged. "I guess I could go back to college and finish getting my degree."

"That's a good idea."

"I'd probably like to stick with horticulture and landscaping."

"An excellent idea. And one you're very good at. What else?"

An uncontrollable sigh pushed from his lungs. "Finding a way to face the past so I can move forward?" He grinned, knowing that's exactly what she'd wanted him to say.

She grinned in response. "That sounds like the best idea yet."

"Funny how I knew you'd say that."

"The possibilities are endless." She cupped his cheek in her hand. "And I'm more than happy to do my share with helping you get to your happily-ever-after. So you might want to ask why I'm cleaning out everything."

From Chutes and Ladders to Monopoly, his mother loved to play games. "Fine. I'll bite." He leaned forward and put on an eager face. "So what's up with the spring cleaning in the fall?"

"Well, I've got to go through things before I move out. See what you and your brothers or the girls might want."

"Move out?"

"Sugarplum, I'm marrying Martin in a few months. Just in case you missed that part."

"I didn't miss it I just thought you'd—"

"Live here?"

He nodded.

"Your daddy and I built this place together. It wouldn't feel right to bring another man in to live here. I have such special memories of me and your daddy putting this place together with all of you boys underfoot. I don't want to wash those memories away. I'd rather keep them in my heart and see them in my mind whenever I walked through the front door."

The fear of her intent sliced through Jake. His father had willed portions of the hundreds of acres to him and his brothers, but the will never specifically mentioned the main ranch house. He'd always assumed his mother would live there until one day she passed. Did she intend to sell?

"But this is your home, Mom."

"And it's been a wonderful home for all these years. But I'm starting a new chapter. You should too." She gave his hand a little pat. "And now you can, because this place will be yours."

"What?"

"Your brothers all have their own homes, their own parcels of land. You have a piece of land too. But I plan to move out sometime in the next couple of weeks. And then Wilder Ranch is all yours."

His heart pounded out of control. Like someone had put a lock on his brain and his mouth, words escaped him, and he just stared at her.

On the several hundreds of acres attached to the main portion of this land, they'd explored, dreamed, grown, and discovered who they were as boys and men. Until each brother had worked his own way out into the world and joined the Marines, they'd all lived together under one roof, trying not to step on anyone, learning how to get along and be a family. They'd fought, laughed, prayed, and held each other's hands through the tough times.

All within these walls.

Though as his mother had said, his brothers all had their own places. But by moving out of the ranch house, she—the glue who held them all together—would change the dynamics of their family forever.

"Unless you don't want it," she said.

"It's not that I don't want it, Mom. It's—"

"Nothing ever stays the same, son." She patted his hand. "Most of the time, change is good. Sometimes it's painful and hard to let go. But that's why God gave us memories. We get to hold on to those for the rest of our lives. In the meantime, we build—or rebuild—from the ground up. Our family will continue to grow. And that's a very good thing. It would have made your father and your brother very happy."

"I don't know." He leaned back and tried to catch his breath. There were too many things coming his way. Too many issues he didn't know how to deal with. In his mind, he'd always been a rough-and-tough son of a bitch. But everything that had taken place in recent months had left him feeling weak and vulnerable. He didn't like it, but there wasn't a damn thing he could do to save his own ass at this point.

His mother leaned forward and tucked her fingers beneath his chin the same way she'd done when he'd been a little boy. He had no choice but to look smack-dab into the goodness sparkling in her eyes.

"You've grown into a fine man, son. And you're going to be all right. I promise. Even if right now *all right* seems a million miles away. Cherish the good memories. Banish the bad. Build new ones. And stay away from women like Jessica Holt. Don't be the kind of man a woman just wants to go to bed with. Be the kind of man she wants to spend the rest of her life with."

He couldn't help laugh. "How many speeches like that have you given at this very table?"

"Dozens." Her grin lit up the room. "And I'm not done yet. Although I'll be giving those speeches from a different kitchen and a different table from now on."

She slurped down the rest of her coffee, then shoved a pile of recipe books in front of him. "In the meantime, you might want to get reading some of those because you'll be cooking for yourself. And figuring out which room you're going to give a new coat of paint first."

"Why would I want to change anything?" His mom had gone on a redecorating tangent about the time Charli and her makeover show rolled into town, but she had pretty good taste. Even if she did have a pink rhinestone-studded cow skull over her bed.

"Because this is how *I* wanted the house to look. You've got your own style."

"Camo and empty Shiner bottles?"

"I certainly hope not." Her laughter tickled his heart. "But don't think you're going to be able to steal the John Wayne painting from Jesse either. I think he's got it under twenty-four-hour surveillance." With a little shrug, she turned to continue her cleaning.

Over the years, his parents had been supportive, understanding, and loving. Jake knew he was lucky. Especially when there were others like Annie, Abby, and Reno—before he'd come to live on Wilder Ranch—who hadn't been dealt such a good hand.

"Hey, Mom?"

She turned.

"Thanks."

"Why, son, you don't have to thank me for giving you a house that's always been yours."

"Not the house, though that's appreciated. I'm thanking you for being my mom."

"Oh, sugarplum." A sigh lifted her chest. "It's my pleasure."

The call from Jake came from nowhere and surprised Annie so much, she'd stuttered for her first few responses. When he showed up at her door a bit later, she'd had to compose herself and not let the fact that after last night's kiss at the tree house, she'd done nothing but think of him until dawn peeked through the crack in her curtains and shed a harsh light on a longtime fantasy.

One kiss did not equal a relationship.

One kiss did not equal the opportunity for another.

One kiss did not equal the possibility that he thought of her in the same way as she did him.

Now they were headed to a secret location, which didn't matter much to Max, who sat in his car seat in the backseat of Jake's big truck, babbling at everything that passed by the window. Though Jake had strapped the actual seat in place, he'd not offered to carry Max to the truck and settle him in the seat. Now that Annie thought about it, she'd not seen Jake engage much with his two nieces either. He'd watch, but he'd definitely kept his distance.

Before, he'd have been down on the floor playing like a big kid. His lack of proximity and participation unsettled her. Not for the first time did she wonder what she could do to help him come out from the cave of reservations he'd backed into.

"And where exactly are you rushing us off to?" she asked him while he sat behind the wheel concentrating so hard the corners of his eyes crinkled.

"Abby's."

"Abby's house? Abby's secondhand store? Or Abby's rescue center?"

"*You* said I needed a dog."

"I say a lot of things, and you've never heard any of it before." She folded her arms. "So why now?"

He shrugged and flipped on the turn signal. "Maybe this time you made sense."

"I always make sense."

"Annabelle. Those purple-and-orange-striped socks you wore with your cargo pants in high school made no sense whatsoever."

"While I appreciate that you even bothered to notice—or remember, you keep referring to things I did in high school. In case all that partying you've done in the past has affected your brain, I graduated from high school ten years ago."

His dark blue gaze slipped across the seat, and he gave her as intimate a perusal as driving a half-ton truck would allow. "Well, I'll at least admit that your selections in clothing have gotten better."

"Thank you, Ralph Lauren. I'm so glad you approve." She sighed and dove into the unavoidable elephant in the truck. "So what makes you think Bo isn't the guy for me?"

"You're too different."

"Haven't you heard? Opposites attract."

"Yeah, but you're talking about fire and gasoline. With him and you, it's more like pablum and sass."

"Which do I get to be?"

"Darlin', you are all sass, all the time."

It was hard to take that as a slam when he had such a cute grin on his face. "Funny. When I look at Bo, I don't see bland."

"Then what do you see?"

"A good-looking nice guy with a fantastic career and a lot to offer a woman."

He scoffed. "Haven't you ever heard not to judge a book by its cover?"

"Yes. And it's a good thing I don't because you would not fare well, my friend."

Brows slammed together, he turned his head and speared her with a glare. "What's that supposed to mean?"

Uh-oh. She hadn't meant to rattle the tiger's cage. Time to change tactics. "Why do you think we argue all the time?" she asked, truly unsure why it always seemed like he was a walking firebomb, and she was a match.

"I wouldn't exactly call it arguing." He pulled the truck into the lot of the Sweet Reprieve Animal Rescue Center and parked near the door.

"Seriously?" She unbuckled her seat belt while he did the same. "Because from where I'm sitting, it seems we can never agree on anything."

She let go a surprised squeak as his big hand reached out, clasped her by the waist, and dragged her across the bench seat until their thighs were pressed together.

"Then how's the view look from over here?" A hard-to-resist smile lit up his blue eyes.

"I'm not sure." She tried to keep a giggle from escaping, but was unsuccessful.

"Ah. Now I see the real problem."

"Which is?"

"It's not the view," he said, as his eyes fell to her lips, then climbed slowly back up to her eyes. "It's that mouth. It has far too much time to wreak havoc."

"Jake, I—"

Annie wasn't a woman who liked to have what she was about to say interrupted. But when he leaned in, curled his long fingers at the nape of her neck, and pressed his lips against hers? Well, she wouldn't mind being sidetracked like that every day of the week.

He kept the kiss sweet—for about a split second. Then he traced the seam of her lips with his tongue, and she opened to let him in. His tongue slicked against hers, enticing her to join in and play. Jake had been a bit of a hell-raiser most of his life, and when he kissed, it came with a Molotov-cocktail blast of heat and passion.

Had they not been in a truck in a public parking lot in broad daylight with her one-year-old in the backseat, she might very well have torn off Jake's faded gray Marine Corps T-shirt and let her hands have a field day over all that tight skin and hard muscle.

"Geeeeee!" Max let out a gleeful shout that reminded them they weren't alone.

Jake didn't jump. Didn't back away quickly as though he'd been caught with his hand in the cookie jar. Nope. That wouldn't be his style. What he did do was barely lean his head back and look her in the eye as he swept his thumb across her moist bottom lip.

"Don't count that as being saved by the bell," he said. "Or in this case, a squealing baby."

"Then what do I count it as?"

His gaze searched her face. "A promise."

"Of?"

He gave her a sly look, opened the truck door, and held out his hand. When she slid across the seat he was right there, with his big body blocking the way from her actually getting out.

"Let's go find that dog you're so hell-bent on me getting," he said.

"Me?" She pointed to herself and received a nod for her efforts.

The only thing she was currently *hell-bent* on was bringing his lips back down to hers to finish where they'd left off. What she got instead was a gentle push toward the backseat of the truck to retrieve her squirming little boy.

"Maybe I'm not interested in what you're promising," she said.

"You're interested." His chuckle of male confidence sent a skitter of lusty anticipation through her chest.

Yeah. She was totally interested.

"You should probably have had your head checked while you were in that hospital." She reached for the door, but his big hand covered hers, and he used it to reel her in.

"My head—in that direction—is just fine." He moved in close. His broad, muscular chest pressed against her breasts, and her heart reacted with a hearty kick. "And you've got too much fire stored up for me to just walk away and let it go."

Annie took a breath. A long, stuttering breath. He smelled so damn good, like a woodsy forest, clean cotton, and warm, virile male.

He dipped his nose to the side of her throat, and his warm breath tickled her skin, her senses. All those long-ignored womanly parts deep down low were perking up. Raising their attention toward the first sign of possible activity in almost two years.

"So . . ." He lifted his head and tucked his fingers beneath her chin. "What do you say we just light the fuse and blow all this sexual tension to hell?"

There were moments in her life she wasn't proud of. Moments where she'd like a "do-over" to erase her bad decisions or embarrassing displays of jumping off a cliff without looking where she'd land. But the moment she realized Jake was engaged in whatever this was between them made her want to jump up and do the "Tequila" dance.

"Hmmm." She slipped out from his arms, opened the truck door, and hurriedly took wiggling Max from his car seat. Then she gave Jake's chest a little pat. "I've blown many things in my life, Jake. This won't be one of them."

The grin dropped from Jake's face.

Damn.

He'd done it again. Kissed her like there was no tomorrow and still wanted more. He had to get a handle on this *Annie* thing. Find something about her that turned him off so he wouldn't be so tempted to press his lips against hers over and over.

He watched her walk toward the entrance of the rescue center in her short light blue dress and boots. Nope. That wasn't going to turn him off anytime soon. And she smelled so damned good, he wasn't going to get any help in that department either. Plus, she tasted as sweet as a ripe strawberry. And everyone knew strawberries were his favorite.

Damn.

He was officially screwed.

And what the hell had she meant anyway?

He knew she was interested. That hadn't been his first kiss. Wouldn't be his last. He had enough experience to know when a woman liked what he was giving her.

Annie liked.

Despite what she said.

She fucking liked.

As she neared the door, Jake kicked it in gear and somehow, even with a bum leg and no cane for support, still made it there in time to open it for her. When she flashed him a polite thank-you, he was tempted to draw her back into his arms again. Just to make sure he hadn't been hallucinating as he had when he'd been on the heavy doses of pain medication. Instead, he safely backed off.

Max held out his chubby little arms, and while Jake wanted to pick up the little guy and accommodate the request, he just couldn't. Instead, he smiled, hoping a one-year-old wouldn't understand the depth of his fuckedupness. Max was a cute baby, with chubby cheeks and Annie's big blue eyes. And he had an unending wealth of energy Jake was sure helped Annie sleep well at night.

He could think of better ways to help her sleep.

As he followed her inside the building, he realized that he either had to stop thinking about stuff like that or invest in a nice white jacket with heavy-duty buckles.

A bell over the door chimed, and Abby waddled in from the back wearing one of Jackson's old SAFD T-shirts. Even as pregnant as she was, the shirt fit like a flour sack over her protruding belly.

"What a surprise." Abby clapped her hands together. "I never thought you'd actually get him to consider it."

Jake hadn't called Abby ahead of time to let her know he was coming in. Or that he'd be bringing Annie and Max. Or that he'd most likely be taking a dog home even if he wasn't sure he agreed a dog would help him through his troubles. But at this point he was open to just about anything. Even if he believed a long night of great sex with a warm woman might be the only cure he needed.

"I can't take the credit." Annie shrugged. "He actually called *me*."

"He did?" Abby's eyes widened. "Well, something must have changed his mind. What do you think that was?"

"Hard to tell with all those frowns going on. Could have been anything." A smirk touched Annie's luscious lips. "Maybe he's just tired of sleeping alone."

"Hel-lo?" Jake waved his hand to break them from talking about him like he wasn't there. "I'm standing right here."

"And so you are." Abby gave his arm a pat. "Good for you."

He turned his gaze toward Annie to make a point. "And who says I'm sleeping alone."

"Oh. That's right." Annie gave him the full smirk this time. "You have Jessica Holt on speed-booty dial."

"So." Abby clapped her hands again, and Max jumped. Then he burst out in a full giggle when Abby held out her arms. "How about I take this little guy, and you both go on back to the playroom to see if there's anyone there you might be interested in."

Jake was interested in why Annie had brought up Jessica. Again. Jealousy? He doubted it. Still, there was always a chance. And to be honest, he wasn't sure how he felt about that.

"Sounds great." Annie tweaked Max's plump little cheeks, engaged in some baby talk, then led the way through the door.

"Jessica Holt?" he asked, following her down a

hallway with plumbing drains set in the concrete floor about every twenty feet. "Why does everyone keep bringing her up?"

"Maybe because you keep calling her up." She stopped to look at the directional sign on the wall. "I know you've been to some of the biggest parts of the world, but don't forget that you still live in Sweet, where gossip flies faster than Angus Pepper's homing pigeons."

"It's not like I've been announcing to the world when I see her."

"Ha!" She squinted up at the top of the sign, then pointed down the hall. "Little dudes are this way."

"Who says I want a little dude? The word *little* doesn't fit me. At all."

"Gosh, Jake. I wish I had half your ego. I'm sure I could really go places."

"Tsk tsk, Annabelle. It's not ego. Just the confidence the Marines instilled in me."

"More than likely it's the same bullshit you and your brothers have fed each other all these years."

She was right, but he figured he'd refrain from giving her a leg up on him. Unless it was in a more interesting fashion. Like, without clothes.

"Big dudes are this way." He pointed in the opposite direction.

Her sleek brows pulled together. "You'd think at some point, we could at least go in the same direction."

"Opposition opens more doors, don't you think?"

"I think it leads to more arguments."

Mischief brushed his lips. "Which always makes makeup sex more fun."

"Maybe," she said, heading down the hall toward the big dog door. "But we're not having sex."

"Yet."

She stopped abruptly, and he had to shift his gaze up from where it had been watching the way she made the back side of that dress swing and sway.

"What did you say?"

He kept walking until he invaded her personal space. "I said . . . yet."

"I'm not Jessica Holt, Jake. I've had my spin with the love 'em and leave 'em kind. I didn't think it was a very fun ride."

"Who says I'm that way?"

Her pretty blond head shook side to side. "How about close to every girl in town our age?"

"That's a lot of women."

"From what I hear, you got around pretty good. And I also hear you never send flowers."

Okay. That stung. He'd sent flowers before. Maybe once. But he couldn't remember to whom. Shit. It had probably been his mom for her birthday or something. Man, he hated when Annie pinned him to the wall like a dried-out bug.

"Did Doug ever send you flowers?"

"Nope. All I got was the bill for the sixty-inch TV and the surround-sound system he charged in my name."

"Jackass."

"Pretty much." She slid one hand to her hip. "So . . . are we going to look at dogs or stand here nipping at each other all day?"

"Dogs." But as she walked ahead of him again, he saw plenty of places on Annie's sweet body where he wouldn't mind taking a bite.

As soon as they opened the door and walked inside the big-dog playroom, they were surrounded by wagging tails. All except one black Lab who remained on a piece of carpet across the room and studied the newcomers with watchful eyes. There was a bit of silver on the old boy's face, and Jake wondered how a dog who'd obviously lived a while could end up here. Not that Abby's place wasn't great. She'd done an amazing job of providing an environment where the animals wouldn't feel like they were imprisoned, or being punished simply for being alive. There were dog toys everywhere and a door they could also use to run outside and play.

"This is heartbreaking," Annie said, dropping to her knees and stroking the necks and heads of the pooches that surrounded her, trying to steal a slurp up the side of her face. "These are all adult dogs. How can people just let them go?"

"Believe me . . ." As much as his leg would allow, he crouched down beside her and petted several dogs that came his way. "There are assholes of every kind in this world. I've seen my share."

"I'm sure you have."

Again, Jake looked across the room to where the older black dog remained. Watching. And if Jake wasn't mistaken, waiting.

"I don't know how you're going to choose just one."

"I know this sounds crazy, but I think I've made up my mind."

"What?" She looked up and got a sneaky slurp attack from a border collie. "Already?"

"Yep." He eased up to his feet, took a breath to still the pain that shot up his thigh, and slowly crossed the room. The big black dog watched him carefully. Never took those dark brown eyes off Jake for one second. When he came to where the dog's front paws were extended, he eased himself down to sit in front of him. The dog watched every painfully slow movement.

"Hey, boy. How you doin'?" He extended his hand slowly so the dog could smell him. The dog didn't. And that made Jake wonder. He turned his hand palm up to see if that would interest the dog any further. The dog still didn't react, and his eyes remained on Jake's face.

Intuition told him this dog didn't have a sensory problem; he had a trust issue. He'd had a life that had somehow gone horribly awry, and he'd ended up here.

"Life can sure take a shitty turn, can't it?" Jake said to the dog. Not that he expected an answer, but the dog's ears perked up at the sound of his voice. "I think you might be a little bit like me, old boy. You did your best and have seen some hard times. Now you're just wondering where this path will take you."

Jake extended his hand again.

This time, the dog's long pink tongue slipped out and took a taste of Jake's fingers. Jake gently stroked the top of the dog's head. The show of affection was rewarded when the dog belly crawled the few remaining inches to Jake's lap.

Something inside Jake broke, like a dam that had been holding back a river of emotion. For the first time since he'd carried his friend's lifeless body to the medevac, Jake had no fear of letting go. Instead, he felt like he might have just found the first piece of solace in his screwed-up life.

He wrapped his arms around the dog and, ignoring the pain in his thigh, coerced the animal onto his lap. For a moment, Jake looked up at Annie, who stood across the room with her fingertips pressed to her mouth and tears in her eyes.

How did she always seem to know what he needed?

Especially when he had no clue?

When he looked back down to the dog's face, he could swear the dog was smiling. The poor guy had probably been passed over so many times in favor of a younger dog that he'd grown doubtful of ever finding a home. Or maybe he'd just been waiting for Jake to come along.

Jake looked back up at Annie and gave her a nod. He had a feeling they were a match made in somebody's crazy idea of heaven.

Sure, he'd probably cry a river a few years down the road when the dog passed on. In the meantime, they were going to have one hell of a good time.

Chapter 7

"Well, this should be interesting."

Jake closed the door to the truck after the dog jumped down from the backseat. During the ride home, Max had gleefully pulled his ears, poked his face, and stuck his hands in the dog's mouth. The dog hadn't so much as blinked. In fact, every time Max stopped, the dog licked his fingers or cheek and sent the baby into a fit of giggles.

Before they'd gotten in the truck to go home, they'd spent some time in the get-to-know-each-other room in Abby's facility. After just a few minutes, there had been no doubt the dog wasn't just used to babies, he adored them. He'd put his stamp of approval all over Max's face in the form of slobbery kisses.

Now that the dog had all four feet on Wilder Ranch, he was being greeted by Miss Giddy, who seemed as though she had even more girth than when Jake had left this morning. Her blue satin ribbon drooped—a clear sign his mother was busy inside the house going through more of her stuff in preparation for the move.

"Yep. He's proven he's baby-proof." Annie grinned as she took Max from his car seat. "Let's see if he's goat-proof."

Dog and goat ended up making a large circle as they sniffed each other.

"Is that goat getting fat, or is it just my imagination?" Jake asked.

"Your mom says it's because Miss Giddy's getting older and doesn't have to watch her waistline anymore."

"Please tell me that's not true."

"Sorry. It is. I asked your mom that same question last week. I don't know who was more insulted, your mom or the goat."

"She sure loves that animal. I wonder if she'll take her with her when she goes."

Annie looked up. "Where's she going?"

"She says she's moving in with Martin. I guess they plan to get married in November."

"What about the house?"

Jake shoved his hands in the pockets of his jeans. "It's mine now."

"What?" Annie twisted her head around to look at him. Surprise widened her already big blue eyes.

"She doesn't want to start her new marriage in the home she and my dad built together. So they'll be living in Martin's house. She said since the brothers already have their own homes, she wanted to give me Wilder Ranch."

"Oh my God!" She grabbed his arm. "Jake, that's such a wonderful gift. You love this place."

"I know. I almost feel bad for accepting it."

"Why? Your mom wants you to have it. And your dad would be thrilled."

"It's a lot of property. The cattle are a big responsibility. And I'm not even sure I can ride a horse anymore."

"Well, you can't ride one any less."

"What?"

The sound of her laughter sent a funny tickle through his heart.

"Have you even tried to ride one since you've come home?"

"No."

"Well, you big baby. Stop assuming you can't do something before you even give it a go. Call your doctor first. Ask his opinion. If he clears you, grab a saddle, and get back on."

He watched the dog playfully drop to his front legs and wiggle his entire back end in an invitation for Miss Giddy to play. She gave a little kick and complied.

"I'm not a big baby."

"Scaredy cat?"

"No."

"Chicken liver?"

"Hell no."

When Annie grinned, it was near blinding.

"Then as soon as you show your nameless dog around the ranch, get on the phone and make the call."

Stunned that once again, Annie seemed to know what he really needed, he remained silent. She, of course, did not, and started making chicken sounds.

"Okay. Okay. I'll call."

"Yay." She jumped up and down a couple of times, which sent Max into another fit of giggles.

Then she kissed Jake's cheek.

A small little gesture that didn't feel so small when the tingling sensation traveled from his cheek down his neck and straight into his heart.

"Can I go too?" she asked. "I haven't ridden in so long."

Jake tilted his head, picturing exactly how she'd look up on a horse wearing that dress. "Do you even remember how?"

"Care to put me to the test?"

While there were a lot of things he wanted to do to Annie, testing her was the last thing on his mind. Getting her alone, however, sounded like a damn fine idea.

$\mathcal{T}$here was something about a man who wore jeans like they'd been made just for him—to lovingly caress all those spectacular body parts. A man in a well-worn straw hat with the tip lowered over his forehead and a pair of Ray-Bans covering his eyes was infinitely even more special to observe. A man who wore boots with miles and miles of walking on the heels, and who currently had them tucked into a pair of stirrups with hand-sewn leather made such a pretty picture, Annie could hardly maintain her breathing. A man who wore nothing but a simple white T-shirt that lay like a second skin over a ladder of stomach muscles, wide shoulders, and thick biceps then controlled a frisky horse like nobody's business was truly something to behold.

Jake, in his current position atop Rocky, was manly perfection.

She should be thoughtful and take out her cell phone. Snap a shot to share with the ladies on Facebook who appreciated the male physique.

She should. But she wouldn't.

Sharing Jake was the last thing she wanted to do.

Once he'd been cleared by the doctor for the ride with orders to not overdo, he'd spurred into action. Jana had offered to watch the new dog and Max, but before they rode away, Annie had taken Max for a little ride. Her baby loved it, and she hoped he'd have plenty of opportunities to grow up with the Western way of life. Living in a house in town probably wouldn't cut it, but maybe someday she could sell enough chocolates and serve up enough burgers to save some money and find a little ranch to buy for the two of them.

Now, as she and Jake rode beneath the canopy of oak and cypress that trailed the creek, she could see the sheer happiness on his face.

This was what he'd been born to do.

How could he have forgotten?

And why would he have tortured himself by preventing himself such a small pleasure?

"So what are you going to name your new dog?"

He looked up, and though she couldn't see his

eyes from behind those Ray-Bans, she could feel the heat of them all over her body. Or maybe it was just the fact that she still wore the sundress she put on earlier that day and riding astride a horse in a dress—a short one at that—made for interesting circumstances.

"I'm not sure," he said. "Most likely he had a name before."

"Abby said he didn't have a collar on when she found him by the side of the road. Maybe you could name him after your friend." She hesitated to bring up the memory, but at some point Jake was going to have to learn to deal with the loss. Not that she wanted to be harsh; she just lived in the real world. And to her experience, tiptoeing around subjects just didn't work.

"I'm not naming him after Eli. If I were to have children I'd probably name my first son after him. But that's never going to happen."

"Never?" This newsflash shocked her. "Why?"

His shoulders came up in a tight shrug, and his expression darkened. "Life got too complicated."

From personal knowledge, she knew the Wilder brothers could beat themselves up for things that were completely out of their control. Reno, Jackson, and Jesse had already proven that point where their oldest brother had been concerned. So to know that Jake blamed himself for his friend's death followed suit and didn't surprise her at all. Still, she couldn't help but sigh her frustration.

She'd like nothing more than to probe the topic further. Make him realize that denying himself anything that might bring him joy was a bad idea.

Instead, she took the pressure off an obviously difficult subject.

"Maybe you could name him after your favorite country singer," she said.

"Interesting idea. But I just don't see him as a Blake, Brad, or Keith."

"No, he's definitely not a Keith." She laughed. "Who was Jared's favorite?"

"Waylon Jennings." His mouth broke wide. "Jared loved the good old boys—Johnny, Waylon, Willy, and Hank. I don't know how many times he played those guys on the stereo at full throttle."

"Any one of those would be a great name, don't you think?"

"Maybe. He kind of looks like a Hank."

"I agree."

"Let's just hope he isn't as much of a hell-raiser."

"If he is . . ." She slid him a deadpan look. "At least he's in the hands of an expert."

A bark of laughter left his lips and sent a twirl of happiness through her heart. It was good to hear Jake laugh. Darned good.

"You're a pistol, Annie."

"I do my best. So Hank it is?"

He nodded. "Hank it is."

"You guys are going to have some great conversations."

"Darlin', I hate to burst your pretty little bubble, but dogs don't talk."

"Then please explain how out of all those other dogs, he got you to come over, fall in love, and take him home."

"I don't fall in love."

"Liar."

"Don't get your hopes up, girl," he said, without giving her a glance.

She tried not to let his remark sting. She did know better than to fall in love with him. But it had happened so long ago, she couldn't take it back now. A blatant lie seemed the best solution, considering the circumstances.

"How long have I known you, Jake?"

"Seems like forever."

"Exactly. So what makes you think I'd put any kind of thought in that direction?"

"I don't know. There's something in the way you kiss."

She grinned to throw him off the truth. "Maybe I'm just a good kisser."

"Maybe you're good at a lot of things." The corners of his mouth lifted suggestively.

"Oh. I am." She settled in the saddle a little more, which rearranged the short dress around her legs and lifted the fabric a little higher up her legs. Though hidden behind those sunglasses, she felt Jake's gaze follow the fabric up. "Too bad you'll never find out."

"We'll see."

We'll see?

On any other terms and with any other man, that might have sounded like a threat. Annie hoped it was more of a promise. Just like he'd said in his truck earlier.

They rode a little farther before he spoke again. "How about we take a break?"

"Does your leg hurt?"

He frowned, and she knew that even if his thigh screamed in agony, he'd never admit it.

"Nope. Just want a break." He nudged his heels into Rocky's flanks and headed toward a shady area near a wild tumble of rocks in the creek. Though it couldn't really be classified as a waterfall, it was very scenic, and the water tumbling over the rocks was soothing.

Watching him swing his good leg over the horse's back and putting all his weight on his bad leg made her cringe. But again, Wilder men had a tendency to take tough to the limit, and Jake didn't flinch. In fact, he even helped her down from her horse, then snagged both sets of reins on a tree branch beneath the shade. He tucked the arm of his sunglasses into his white T-shirt so they hung down the front as they walked together to the creek. Instead of sitting down, Jake continued to stroll along the bank.

"Been sitting too long," he said in way of an explanation. "Need to get some circulation going." Then he let go a cynical laugh.

"What?"

"I sound like an old man."

"I don't see it that way at all."

In front of a large oak, he stopped abruptly and turned. She bounced off his chest, and his hands captured her waist to steady her. "Then how *do* you see me?"

Me, he'd said. Not *it*.

She searched his face beneath the brim of that battered straw hat and watched as he briefly pressed his lips together. "I don't think it's wise of me to say."

"Annabelle Morgan, when have you ever been shy about having your say?"

"Because sometimes it gets me into trouble. Even I realize that."

"Sounds interesting." He arched a brow over blue eyes that snapped with curiosity. "What kind of trouble?"

"Plenty. That's what kind."

"That's not a kind. That's an amount."

"Same thing when you're talking in terms of trouble." She stepped back to break his hold on her waist and the tingles his touch sent down to her lower region. The ladies in the lingerie department were getting restless, and Annie didn't have the courage to tell them that today they would not be able to ring up a big sale.

He didn't release her. Instead, he dug his fingers in and pulled her closer. "How do you see me, Annie?"

A rush of air pushed from her lungs, and her mouth took the challenge before her brain engaged.

"Besides naked? I see you as smarter than you let on and ornerier than you need to be. I see you as someone who can have anything he wants because you've got the talent and the willpower to make it happen. I see you as a good brother, an amazing son, and a loving uncle. And I see you as a hero, Jake. Yes. I know things went bad in Afghanistan. Really bad. But any way you want to review it, in my eyes, you come out a hero."

She folded her arms over her chest. "You happy now?"

He grinned. "You picture me naked?"

"Is that all you got out of what I just said?"

"Pretty much."

She let go a combination growl and sigh. "Then yes. I picture you naked."

"Then I'm happy."

"Should I call CNN?"

He shook his head. "You should unfold those arms."

"Why?"

"Because if I let go of you to do it myself, you'll run like a rabbit. Hell, I can feel your heart pounding out of your chest all the way over here."

"You are so full of it."

"Maybe. But I'm not wrong." He tugged her closer. "Unfold your arms, Annie. So I can kiss you."

"Okay." She did as he asked. Simply because she wasn't a stupid woman. If Jake wanted to kiss her, she had no choice but to make it very easy for him to do.

"Now wrap those pretty arms around my neck."

She did.

"Now . . ." He lowered his head. "Don't say stop."

Stop?

The word wasn't even in her vocabulary. Not when it came to him.

Foolish?

Yes.

Crazy?

Absolutely.

But when he pressed his mouth to hers, she really didn't care about foolish or crazy.

*J*ake lost all thought the moment she parted those pretty lips and their tongues met. The only thing he knew now was the heat of passion, her sweet scent, and the need to lose himself inside her warm, luscious body.

Whatever she thought of him was wrong.

He wasn't anybody's hero.

If he had even a spark of such, he wouldn't be having the single-minded thought of slipping her panties down her legs and losing himself altogether. For an hour, two hours, however long it took to forget what had happened and to try and remember who he'd been.

Filling his hands with the delectable curve of her rear end, he pressed his erection into the soft center of her thighs. Her moan filled his mouth and, if it was possible, he got even harder.

Switching their positions, he backed her up to the tree, leaned in, and pressed against her harder. Thought halted and sensation took over as he lifted his hands to her face, kissed her thoroughly, then filled his hands with her luscious breasts.

Beneath the pretty blue sundress, Annie wore no bra.

Hallelujah.

She was both firm and soft. Heavy and light. She felt like heaven in his arms.

Desire pulsed through his veins and arrowed

down into his cock, which throbbed and ached with lust. Not just for the first time in a long time.

He lusted for *her*.

He lowered his mouth to the sweet arch of her throat, ran his tongue slowly down the length, and nearly exploded when she quivered in his arms. Her head dropped back to give him better access, and he took full advantage, kissing his way down, lifting her breasts in his hands, then sliding his tongue along the plump flesh that rose above the fabric of her dress.

"More." Her breathless plea turned him on. Raised the bar. Made him eager to please.

"Tell me you're interested," he said, throwing her denial back at her just so he knew they were on the same page.

"Interested." She moaned when he opened his mouth over the skin just above where her nipple hid beneath the dress. "Very. Very. Interested."

"That makes me happy, Annie. Really fucking happy." Using his thumbs, he tugged the blue cotton down until her breasts came free of the material. Then he swirled his thumbs over her tight, hard nipples just before he lowered his head and gently sucked one into his mouth.

"Oh my God." Her pleasure was expressed in a lusty sigh. "Do that again."

He loved that she appeared to be as verbal when it came to passion as she was the rest of the time. So he complied. This time he took hold of the other tightened nipple and rolled it between his lips before he sucked it into his mouth. She rewarded him with a long, breathy moan.

She'd been grabbing onto his T-shirt with both hands. Now, she reached up, took off his hat, and tossed it aside. Then her hands explored his chest. She yanked the bottom of the shirt from his pants and her hands were all over him—touching, tweaking, lightly scratching.

God, he couldn't wait to be inside her. Might even be driven to madness if it didn't happen soon.

"Touch me, Annie."

She took his meaning and lowered her hand below his belt to his zipper. Just her touch nearly sent him over the edge. But when she curled that palm around his cock and squeezed, his eyes nearly crossed.

Resting his forehead against her, he closed his eyes. "Fuck that feels good."

She gave him an extra squeeze. Then her fingers slipped down behind his belt and her warm, soft hand was on his bare, rock-hard flesh.

"Is that better?"

He couldn't speak, so he just nodded as she stroked him inside the constrictive quarters of his jeans. Her fingertips brushed the head of his cock, then wrapped around him again with a long, slow stroke.

He could come.

Right now.

Right there in her hand without any further encouragement.

But he didn't play that way.

No matter how hard he might be, no matter how much he ached, no matter how long it had been or how bad he wanted it, a man always took care of his woman first.

"Baby, take your hand out of my pants."

She complied quickly. Almost too quickly, as the final squeeze and slide of her palm nearly undid him. He groaned. Loudly.

"Oh!" Concern puckered her forehead. "Does your leg hurt?"

"Yeah." He chuckled. "But not the one you're thinking of."

Annie's knees went weak as Jake kissed her again. She lost herself in the heat of his mouth. The warmth of his skin. And the fact that after all these years, she was finally in Jake Wilder's arms. Against a tree. In a forest. Then he made his descent, kissing, licking, and sucking his way down her neck and across her breasts.

In all the fantasies she'd had of him over the years, he'd been good. Jake Wilder in the flesh blew her expectations out of the water.

And they'd only just begun.

When he eased down to his knees, started to lift the bottom of her dress, then stopped and looked up at her with a flash of sunlight in his blue eyes, her knees literally wobbled.

"What color panties are you wearing, Annie?"

"What's your favorite?"

"Whatever you have on."

"Then it looks like you're in . . ." She gasped as those light blue panties that matched the lace in her dress were torn off and his tongue slipped between her legs. "Luck."

He moaned, or said something that was completely muffled, because his lips were too busy sucking her sensitive skin into the warmth of his mouth. Maybe she was the lucky one because his tongue knew all the secret places to stroke and swirl.

It had been a long, long time since Annie had been touched. And she'd *never* been touched like this. So it didn't take much before she exploded and melted like a marshmallow held over the campfire too long. Her legs threatened to buckle beneath her, and she reached back and grabbed the bark on the tree for stability. A long, broken moan left her lips with Jake's favorite four-letter word. Not a word she normally used, but completely appropriate for the shocks and tingles that fired through her body.

As she began her tumble back to earth, he wiped the moisture from between her legs with her torn panties, then he tucked the ripped nylon into his back jeans pocket.

Still throbbing from the most delicious orgasm she'd ever had—and she meant *ever*—he came to his full height and pressed into her.

"I want you, Annie." He kissed her and she tasted herself on his lips. "I want you really bad."

"I want you, too." She reached down and cupped the huge erection straining against his jeans. Then reality popped up its nasty little head. "Please tell me you have a condom."

His mouth stilled on the curve of her shoulder. Then his head came up. Disappointment darkened his eyes. "I don't."

"Then we can't do this." *Dammit.* "The last time

I took that chance, I got pregnant. I don't think you need that kind of added problem right now."

"Fuck." He dropped his forehead to hers.

"Yeah. I know."

Several long, thoughtful breaths later he said, "Annie? I'd never see you as a problem."

She chuckled. "Are you saying that just because you want to get laid?"

"No."

The sincerity in his tone gave her no choice but to believe him.

"Then consider turnabout fair play."

His gorgeous head came up. Comprehension put a strain in that normally smooth forehead. But that didn't stop his hands from wandering down her backside. "Annie. You don't need to—"

"Do you remember the night of my sixteenth birthday when you wandered naked through your house in search of the refrigerator?"

"Not really."

"I do. And it's not nice to keep a lady waiting to see that again."

A grin broke wide across his face. "So you're saying you want to see me naked?"

"Completely. And on your back." She dragged a finger down the center of his chest. "How opposed are you to getting that nice white T-shirt a little dirty?"

"Darlin', *dirty* is my favorite word."

"No, it's not." She laughed as she reached for the bottom of his fresh-smelling cotton shirt and pulled it over his head. "That word starts with an F."

Laughter screeched to a halt when his broad

chest—lightly covered with short, soft, silky hair—and washboard stomach were revealed. He might have been in the hospital and rehab for months, but he certainly hadn't let any fat grow under his skin. Jake was lean, and muscular, and as mouth-watering as she remembered.

The tribal tattoo of an eagle on his forearm was familiar. He'd had it inked over the scar he'd received the time he and his brothers had constructed their huge barbecue grill. The tribal-cross tattoo with firebird wings and a shield that said "Protect thy Family" was new. If you'd asked her any other time what she thought of tattoos, she'd have said, "Meh, they're okay." On Jake Wilder's warm, tan skin, they took sexy to another level.

Eager to touch and taste, she wasted no more time. Leaning forward, she pressed her mouth to his skin. Tasted the peaks of his taut nipples. And slid her tongue down that lean, tight, rippled belly.

He reached for his belt.

She got there first.

Good or bad, unbuckling a belt quickly was something she'd become quite an expert at, and she wasted no time relieving the hand-tooled leather from its job of holding up his pants. Likewise, she was more than happy to liberate the zipper from its job of guarding his valuables from her eager touch.

When she pushed the dark blue boxer briefs and jeans from his hips and down his thighs, she tried not to gasp at the series of red, angry-looking scars marking an otherwise perfect section of mascu-line flesh.

"Not such a pretty sight," he muttered.

The combination of wariness and anger in his tone forced her to look up, away from the wound that had forced so many changes to his life, and into the blue eyes she'd loved from the moment they'd met.

"They say beauty is in the eye of the beholder." She pressed her lips gently to each and every scar. Then she curled her fingers around the erection that momentarily seemed to be affected by what Jake saw when he looked down at that mangled fragment of skin. She wanted to give him something better to look at. "In my eyes, you're perfect."

And then, with her mouth and her hands, her sighs and her moans, she proceeded to live out all of those fantasies she'd been dreaming of for years and years.

Well, almost all of them.

Chapter 8

The grit of sand and blood filled his mouth, dug into the crevices between his teeth. The dive he'd taken to the ground had been involuntary. Marine Lieutenant Jake Wilder never backed down from the enemy.

Never.

Unless they drilled a bullet from an assault rifle through the center of his thigh.

The sharp, burning pain stole his breath. Momentarily rocked his brain while he lay there on the sand, looking up at a sky brown with dirt and debris from the firefight engaged around him. At first, the shouts that came from his troops were warnings. Curses. Then quickly the sounds turned to chaos, pleas for help, and bursts of anger that were nearly drowned out by the ear-shattering blasts.

While the bullets flew and zinged all around him, Jake adjusted his helmet, rolled to his stomach, and tried to get up on his hands and knees.

Pain shocked his system, and nausea roiled in his stomach. He knew he'd been hit, but he was still surprised at the inability to control the actions of his own body. Only sheer Texan tenacity had enabled him to make it to his feet.

He found cover behind an outcropping of boulders and through eyes coated with grit, made a quick scan of the dire situation. His heart raced, pounded the blood through his veins. And then he spotted Eli, unmoving, on the ground about twenty feet away. A little farther in the distance, several more soldiers dragged themselves toward a safer location.

Sweat rolled down Jake's face and back—not just from the desert heat, or the white-hot pain in his leg. Dread strangled him like nothing he'd known since the day he'd discovered his big brother had been shot and killed on the same damn dusty patch of hell.

He awoke with a start. Opened his eyes to get his bearings. Took in a shuddering breath. Then he squeezed his eyes closed again to ward off the anguish stabbing at him. A moment later, a long, wet tongue licked his face. Rolling to his side, he looked into a pair of soulful brown eyes and felt the thump of a wagging tail against the mattress. "Hey, Hank."

The thumping increased as Hank inched closer and nudged Jake's hand with his warm, moist nose. Jake stroked his palm between the dog's ears. Hank inched closer, laid his head on Jake's chest, and gave a long, canine sigh.

Jake lost track of time as he lay there next to

his new companion, who unknowingly gave Jake comfort from his recurring nightmare.

Annie had been right.

Again.

He should probably be pissed that someone could have his number, have figured him out so completely they knew every move he'd make or needed to make before it even entered his mind. But he'd bet she hadn't seen yesterday coming. And that made him smile.

The horrific vision of the tragedy in the sands of Afghanistan was replaced by the vision of Annie up against that tree, with his hands on her curvy body and passion on her lovely face. He'd touched her, tasted her, and made her moan. But the one thing he'd wanted more than anything hadn't happened. He'd wanted to bury himself inside her. To feel her legs wrapped around him. To feel her heart beating against his chest as he looked into her eyes while she exploded around him.

Yet even without that, he'd felt more connected to her than he had anyone in months.

How had that happened?

For years, they'd sniped at each other every chance they got. They'd started out that way yesterday too. And then everything changed. For days he'd looked at her differently. If you'd asked him just weeks ago what he thought of Annabelle Morgan, he'd have told anyone that she was nothing but a pain in the ass.

Now he knew she was the complete opposite.

Now he knew she might very well be the only thing that could save his wretched soul.

He just didn't know what to do with all that. He'd let down his best friend. Let down his best friend's wife and unborn child.

He couldn't let Annie down too.

How the hell could he reach out and find happiness when Rebecca Harris was husbandless, her child fatherless, and Eli's parents without the son they'd loved? How could he accept something that gave him joy when he couldn't find the nerve to face his best friend's wife and tell her he was sorry?

He couldn't.

Not with a clear conscience.

And so, even with Hank lying there patiently as Jake pondered the future, he knew he had to back off. He had to leave Annie alone, so he didn't screw up her life. So she could find happiness with someone who was whole, not so broken he'd never find peace. Even if she drove him total-bat-shit crazy at times, he couldn't do that to her.

Not even if he still had her sweet blue panties in the back pocket of his jeans and she, very likely, had a firm grasp on his unsalvageable heart.

$\mathcal{B}$ud's Diner was hopping with the lunch crowd. Annie ran an arm across her forehead to dislodge the loose strands of hair that stuck there like they'd been glued. It was only noon, yet her feet already ached from the numerous trips she'd made from the dining room to the kitchen.

Paige had gone into labor that morning, so Annie had volunteered to take over her shift. Short notice had left Annie without a babysitter. But as always,

Jana came through like a gift from the heavens. She'd even come to the house and picked up Max, so Annie could get to work faster. So while they all awaited the news from Paige and Aiden on their new little bundle of joy, Annie put her heart and soul into delivering Bud's newest lunchtime concoction of Hot Stuffed Smokin' Mama Burgers to the Sweet City Council, the Digging Divas Garden Club, and Chester Banks with his crony entourage.

Chester, who never failed to put the flirt on from the moment he entered the place, looked up with rheumy hazel eyes that seemed a bit bloodshot today.

"You got any aspirin in the back, little darlin'?"

Annie propped her fist on the waistband of her apron. "You hit the George Dickel a little too hard last night, Chester?"

"That I did." He gave her a crooked grin that jostled his false teeth. "Took Virginia Luckenbill out for a spin. Took the hills a little too hard trying to please the infernal woman's urges to go faster, harder."

Annie hated to remind Chester that Virginia was near ninety as was he, and that reality might not live up to their expectations. Then again, she just hoped Chester was talking about the actual hills on the ground and not any of Virginia's saggy body parts. "I take it that didn't go so well?"

"Nope." He sipped his coffee. "Might even make me have to reconsider going back to the younger set. These older women are too hard on my creaky old bones."

"Chester? When did you ever stop going after the younger women?"

Roy Babcock, one of Chester's oldest and dearest partners in crime, gave a hoot of a laugh. "Since they started takin' off runnin' when they'd see the old coot coming down the road."

Chester frowned, and for a flash of an instant, Annie felt sorry for him. Until he slipped his hand around the back of her uniform skirt and gave her a pat on her derriere.

"Hands off, buster." She removed the offending groper. "I'm not your type."

"You're young and pretty, aren't you?"

"I'll take that as a compliment." She refilled his cup with fresh coffee. "But since you went where you weren't invited, I'm not going to bother looking for that aspirin."

As she spun on the heel of her tennis shoe, she heard Chester's *compadres* giving him a bad time. When she got back behind the counter and checked the orders up on the window, Sarah Randall laughed.

"Chester getting fresh again?"

"I think the older he gets, the bolder he gets." Annie sighed. "I know he's old as dirt, but sometimes I'd just like to pop him in that gigantic nose."

"I imagine all those ex-wives of his did a little damage over the years."

"Doesn't seem to have helped."

Annie grabbed two plates piled high with sweet-potato fries still sizzling from the fryer and Diablo burgers dripping with cheese. She carried the orders to a young couple in the back booth, then looked up when the bell over the door jingled. To her surprise, the Wilder brothers strolled in in full force. Not for the first time did Annie have to admit they were quite an awesome sight. Joe and Jana Wilder had produced some fine-looking sons. Everyone in town knew it, even if the brothers paid no attention. Unless it was to their advantage, of course.

In her eyes, Jake was undoubtedly the best-looking in the group. And though she'd put a smile on his face just yesterday, he walked in the diner wearing a frown and seemed unable to meet her gaze.

Her imagination?

Not when she tried again, and he snapped his gaze away so fast, it drowned all those oogly-googly warm feelings she'd been having.

So that was the way he wanted to play it?

Fine.

She snatched up some menus and met them at the booth near the window. Setting out the menus and silverware, she gave them her courtesy smile. "You boys want water?"

"Coffee," Reno told her. "All around please."

Please?

Since when did they feel the need to be so polite with her when all they'd done most of her life was treat her like a pesky little sister? And no, she wasn't imagining things. Jake refused to look up. Refused to acknowledge that not even twenty-four hours ago, they'd been touching each other in places polite people didn't discuss. Moaning each other's names. And wishing to hell one of them had brought a condom to the party. Instead, he planted his nose in the menu even though she knew he'd order the same thing he did every time he walked through the door.

The moment she walked away, all those gorgeous Wilder male heads came together over the table like they were up to something. Even Gladys Lewis and Arlene Potter, who were seated in the next booth, strained to hear what those boys were saying.

While Annie gathered up the coffee carafe and cups, she tossed another glance in Jake's direction. Their gazes collided, and he looked away as though he'd been stung.

That stung.

Saddled with parents who could barely be considered as such, Annie learned that life didn't always play fair. No one always got what they wanted or what they'd wished for all their life. What was that song Garth Brooks used to sing? Oh yeah, "Unanswered Prayers." Maybe Jake's sudden cold shoulder was one of those. Personally, she'd rather have him crawling up her backside giving her a load of bullshit than ignoring her. But apparently he had other plans.

It wasn't like after yesterday she expected him to drop to one knee and propose, but a little, "Good afternoon, Annie. I hope you slept well after I rocked your freaking world yesterday" would have been nice.

Annie was ashamed to say that once she got in a snit, she followed it through. Right or wrong, she planned to let *Mr. Avoidance* know that wasn't okay with her. She'd been down that road once before with Doug. And though Jake owed her nothing, she wasn't about to let him treat her like a stranger.

After all, the man had taken her underwear home in his pocket.

It didn't get more personal than that.

$\mathcal{N}$othing in the diner could keep Jake from copiously trying to watch Annie's every move. Not the conversation his brothers tried to drag him into. Not the delicious scent of burgers and fries. Not even the fact that one of Sweet's oldest cougars, Arlene Potter, kept reaching across the back of the booth and tickling the back of his neck with her wrinkly old fingers.

Annie's blue-eyed glares had made it clear that she didn't appreciate his avoiding her. Even if it was for her own good. He was too broken. Too fucked up in the head and heart to be good for anyone. Except a dog. Annie had been right once again. She'd been on target when she'd said the loyalty and love of a dog was limitless. When he'd woken up that morning in a cold sweat, battling the recurring nightmare, Hank had been there with a warm nose, a nuzzle, and soulful eyes that somehow said he understood.

Judging by the fire snapping in Annie's eyes, she wasn't on the same wavelength.

By the time she came back to their booth, she was all sweetness and sunshine. Carefully, she set the coffee cups in front of his brothers. His, she slammed down on the table. As though she were pouring pure gold, she cautiously poured the steaming liquid into their cups. His, she sloshed over the sides, and he had to jump back to keep from getting burned.

"Oops." Her mouth spouted an apology while her narrowed gaze told him, "Yeah, I did that on purpose, buster. What are you going to do about it?"

His brothers looked up in unison and grinned. Great. Now he'd never hear the end of their guessing game about what was going on and why Annie had singled him out in a seek-and-destroy mission.

"Are y'all ready to order?" She pulled the order pad and pencil from the pocket of her apron.

"You okay there, Annie?" Reno asked.

"Yeah." Jesse piped in. "You seem a little tense."

"Anyone's ass need kicking that I need to know about?" Jackson added.

"Everything's great. I don't know why you'd even ask."

"Max okay?" Reno asked, completely aware that whatever had ticked her off had nothing to do with baby problems.

"He's as perfect as always. Your mom is watching him for me today. It wasn't my usual workday, but Paige went into labor, so I'm covering for her."

Reno chuckled. "Aiden must be a wreck."

"I think he's surrounded by lots of friends and family."

"The hell with that." Jackson set his cup down. "He'd better be in there holding his wife's hand."

"I'm sure he is." Annie laughed. "Or he'd never hear the end of it. So, are you ready to order now or would you like a few more minutes?"

It was unusual for Jake to remain so tight-lipped during a conversation, but with Annie flashing him a dirty look between responses, he figured silence was golden.

All his brothers ordered the usual heart attack on a plate. When it came his turn, she walked away.

"Hey," he protested. "You didn't get my order."

She stopped and came back to the table. "I'm sorry. Did you want something other than a double Diablo burger with extra peppers, a side of sweet-potato fries—extra crispy, and a chocolate-banana shake?"

That's exactly what he wanted, but he absolutely wasn't going to let her win this time.

"Yeah." He opened the menu again because for the life of him he couldn't remember what else was on it. "Give me a . . . meat-loaf sandwich on wheat, curly fries, and a Diet Coke."

Her pencil remained perched over the order pad. "Seriously?"

"Seriously." He pushed the menu across the table in her direction. "Can't afford to have someone thinking they know me so well."

"Oh, believe me, Jake Wilder, I would never assume to know how that brain of yours works. It's too dark, and there are too many cobwebs in there to figure it out." She snatched up the menu and spun in her little white sneakers off to the window, where she jammed the slip of paper up on the order wheel and barked out the list to Bud in the kitchen.

"Something we need to know about, little brother?" Jesse asked, one eyebrow quirked halfway up his forehead.

"No."

"You sure?" Reno asked.

"Damn sure."

"Hell, you could have fooled me," Jackson threw in for good measure. "I figured I was going to have to hide my knife with you two going at it like that."

As soon as Annie disappeared into the kitchen, Jake stretched and watched through the order window as she then slipped out the back door. He got up and followed without a word to his brothers. Unfortunately, he didn't miss their snickers and chuckles as he left the table.

Outside, he found her leaning against the building, popping a watermelon-flavored Jolly Rancher into her mouth.

"What the hell was that all about?" He slammed his hands down on his hips. "And do not respond with 'what was what?' You know what I'm talking about."

She looked up. "Hi, Jake, how's it going?"

"You been drinking?"

"Not hardly." A fake laugh bubbled through her pretty lips. "I just don't like dropping my panties for someone, then have the person act like he'd never laid eyes on me before."

"Technically, you didn't drop them, I tore them off."

"And that's suppose to make it better?"

"So you're pissed," he said.

"Curious."

"About what?"

"About how you can be so wonderful one day and such a total jackass the next."

He let go of the breath he'd been holding. He'd never meant to hurt her. Never meant to take advantage. Unfortunately, where Annie was concerned, he was learning fast that his control was miniscule. "I think you're mistaking the wonderful part. But . . ." He shrugged. "It's for your own good that you see me as I really am."

"Oh really." She folded her arms across the breasts he'd paid careful attention to just yesterday afternoon. He liked her much better half-naked and happy than fully clothed and ticked off. "How the heck do you know what's good for me or not?"

"Look, Annie. I never meant for yesterday to happen."

"Doesn't take a brainiac to figure that out."

"I like you but—"

"Stop." Her hand went up like she was controlling an unruly bunch of pedestrians. "Dear God, do not give me the 'I like you but' speech. I've known you far too long for you to puss out like that."

"That's not my intention, Annie. But you have to understand that I'm not the guy you used to know. I'm not the guy you think I've been all these years. That guy perished in the desert. You deserve better than what I've become."

The truth hurt just to think it, let alone verbalize it. But Annie did deserve better than he could ever give her.

He'd made a mistake yesterday, letting things go so far. But he couldn't take it back.

He wouldn't even want to.

Yesterday, she'd given him a moment where he

didn't have to think. All he had to do was feel. Lucky for him, she'd been within reach with all her soft, sweet-smelling skin, and her long, silky hair.

For the first time in months, he'd had a glimpse of the man he used to be. But he didn't try to fool himself. Moments like that were fleeting. At least for him. Annie? She'd been through enough. She had a great life ahead of her. She deserved that. If she was happy, she'd raise a happy son. And that meant a lot to Jake. Especially with recent circumstances. He might never have a son or a daughter of his own, but he wanted the very best for Annie's little boy. For his sweet nieces. And for Eli's child.

"So you're saying, when we look at you, we're seeing two different people," Annie said.

He shrugged. "I guess so."

She shifted her weight from one hip to the other. His gaze followed. One thing was for sure, Annie looked dynamite in that short skirt and tight little T-shirt. "Huh."

"Huh?" His gaze snapped up. "That's it?"

The Jolly Rancher rolled on her tongue, and the scent of the watermelon candy tickled his nose. He looked at her glossy lips and thought of the way they tasted. The way they felt against his skin.

Damn, but he wanted to kiss her again.

Her hands came up. "I'm not sure what you want me to say here, Jake. I've only got a few minutes before I have to go back in there and serve up everyone's lunch with a heap of happy. But right now?" She pulled a great amount of air into her lungs, which expanded her chest, which drew his gaze right down to the front of that snug little shirt. "Right now you just make me want to cry."

"I'm sorry."

"I know. And I guess I should thank you for being honest." She looked down to the ground and scraped the toe of her tennis shoe in a small arc on the gravel. "Well, at least now I can feel free to accept Bo's invitation to go out Friday night."

What?

"You're going out with Jennings?" He didn't like that idea at all. Hadn't she heard what he'd said about Bo's being not the right guy for her?

"Why shouldn't I?" She gave a little shrug. "You and I? We had a great time yesterday, but as you said yourself, it can't be anything more than that. Just friends. Right?"

"Right." No. It wasn't right. But . . . shit. He jammed his fingers through the top of his hair. He'd never be able to sleep again if every time he closed his eyes, he pictured Annie in Bo's arms.

"All righty then." Annie's face lit up, and she bounced to the toes of her tennis shoes to plant a quick kiss to his cheek. A friendship kiss. Nothing more. "So I guess I'll see you around."

"Yeah." Fuck.

He watched her go back inside the diner. Listened to the screen door slam behind her. And felt his heart hit the gravel at his feet. He kicked a rock into the nearby bushes, then followed her inside. Bud gave him a questioning look as he stalked like an angry bear through the kitchen. By the time he got back to his table, Annie had already delivered their orders. He slid into the booth next to Jesse and grabbed his fork.

Meat loaf.

What the fuck had he been thinking? He hated meat loaf. And curly fries. He wanted his damned chocolate-banana milk shake.

"Everything okay, little bro?" Reno asked just before he sank his teeth into the double Diablo burger dripping with melted cheese. Jesse and Jackson grinned, like they knew something was up. Hell, all his brothers probably did. They'd gone through some challenges with the women in their lives. Not that Annie was in his life.

"No. Everything is *not* okay. Why the hell did you guys let me order meat loaf?"

Chapter 9

A single mom constantly battled the balance of trying to be a good parent while still maintaining a life that made her feel like a desirable woman. Annie knew that struggle only too well as a surge of guilt spread through her chest while she drove to meet Bo at the new restaurant that had opened up just a few weeks ago.

Word on the street had it that *Dolce Italiano Grill* offered an intimate and unforgettable dining experience with a bubbling fountain, soft lights, and a menu bursting with handmade pastas and creative dishes. All in all, Annie wasn't sure she was ready for a romantic evening with Bo Jennings.

Admittedly, she was more of a barbecued brisket kind of girl, and she wondered now about the choice of leaving her baby in the care of her sister just to go out with a man she didn't know very well. Then again, maybe she should just cut the BS and admit that she wasn't really all that hyped up to go to a romantic anything with anyone other than Jake.

How pathetic was that?

He'd flat out told her that even though they'd shared a really intimate naked moment, and even though he couldn't seem to keep his lips off hers, he planned to keep her in the friend zone. So here she was pining away. Again.

After she parked in the lot behind the restaurant, she got out of her little car and smoothed her hands down the dress she'd chosen to wear. She always felt more comfortable in jeans, and for the most part, jeans would be acceptable in any dining establishment in Sweet. But she wanted to make a good impression. Just in case Bo might be more than she expected. Just in case he was truly sincere about his interest in her—a never-married, single mom who slung hash for a living—while he had the ultimately important job of saving lives. And just in case she could find more than a small spark of attraction to him. Although at this moment, it was a six-foot-four package of nothing but trouble who held the top position with her fascination.

Taking a "you can do this" breath, she opened the door of the restaurant, and Bo was right there, waiting with a bouquet of pink roses.

"You look lovely," he said, handing her the bouquet and giving her a chaste kiss on the cheek.

"Thank you." She'd curled her hair, shaved her legs, and spritzed on her best body mist. She'd also taken the extra time to apply her makeup just the way the girl at the department store had shown her. And she'd put on the strappy black stilettos and pretty little black dress Abby had loaned her while promising it was a sure thing.

Annie wasn't so sure she wanted to be a sure thing. Heck, she didn't even know if she wanted to be a maybe thing.

Bo cupped her elbow in his hand as they followed the hostess to a table for four near the fountain. With any luck, Annie would refrain from saying anything embarrassing and have to throw herself face-first in the fountain to drown her humiliation.

Once they were seated, Bo ordered a bottle of wine and reached across the table for her hand.

"You know . . ." He gave her a charming smile. "My mother was a little surprised that I'd asked you out."

"Oh?" Ding, ding, ding. Warning bells clanged in her head, and she wondered why the subject of his mother would be his opening conversation. Shouldn't it be something about the two of them? And what was wrong with his asking her out? It wasn't like she had cooties or anything. She was just a simple, hardworking waitress in a low-paying job. An unwed mother who'd refused to put her ex's name on her son's birth certificate because she believed a man who'd walk away from his child gave up his rights. A woman who was over the moon about a man who'd made it painfully clear that he didn't return her affections even though he had a keen interest in her body.

Okay, so maybe Bo's mother had a reason for concern about who her physician son dated.

Bo nodded, and the candlelight gleamed against

his brown hair. "She thinks I should only see professional women. But I told her that I preferred to see you."

"Oh." She tried to decide whether he'd just given her a backhanded insult or whether he was just being naively honest. Whichever way the bat swung, she refused to apologize for having her beautiful son or how she earned a living. The only part that might be an issue was her loving a man who didn't love her back.

"My mother believes that if you've worked hard to succeed in your profession, you have the skills to make anything happen."

Again with the mother. Annie had a feeling if the matron of the Jennings household continued to be the topic of discussion, the night would crawl by at a snail's pace.

She thought about throwing in a "Hey, how about those Houston Stallions beating Green Bay last week?" or "Did you know that I not only make delicious chocolates but I know the best places to smear it on a body?"

Like an angel of perfect timing to save her from herself, the waiter showed up with their wine. He poured a small amount into their glasses. Annie watched as Bo swirled the burgundy liquid, then stuck his nose in the glass before he took a small sip.

"Excellent," he told the waiter, who then filled their glasses half-full.

Annie lifted her glass, took a drink, and somehow refrained from sticking her tongue out and wiping off the bitter taste with her napkin.

"Good?" Bo asked.

"Mmmmm." She nodded. She'd never been a fan of wine. She was a simple country girl who, depending on the cause of the celebration, preferred Shiner Bock Ale and Hard Lemonade. The rest of the time, she was strictly a coffee, lemonade, and sweet teetotaler. The wine Bo had ordered tasted dry and sour, and it left a residue in her mouth that grossed her out.

"Anyway, back to what my mother said . . ."

Again?

Annie leaned back in her chair and did her best to appear interested in what was clearly a three-way date. She tried not to flinch when he bragged that his mother still did his laundry and changed the sheets on his bed. Whew. Had she ever had a totally different image of him before she'd arrived at the restaurant.

"I had no idea you and your mother were so close."

"Best buddies." His grin said it all. Mama's boy.

While the Wilder boys loved their mother, they lived their own lives and ran the show their own way. And Annie was pretty sure none of them had asked the woman to do their laundry or change their sheets for at least a decade.

"I don't do anything in life until I get my mother's approval," he said.

"Nothing?"

"Nope." His grin widened, like having to get his mother's okey–dokey should gain him extra points.

Annie cringed to think that might include mommy dearest giving him the go-ahead to have sex. Surreptitiously, she glanced at her watch and discovered they'd been there all of ten minutes. While Bo continued to spout the rewards of having such a close relationship with the woman who'd given him life, Annie lifted her glass and took a long drink of wine that now didn't taste so bad. Because all the signs said it was going to be a really, really, *really* long night.

$\mathcal{P}$arked on Main Street several doors down from the *Dolce Italiano Grill*, Jake called himself ten kinds of stupid.

Why, on this perfect, warm evening was he sitting inside the cab of his truck like some kind of stalker? Why had he gone to great lengths and used his supersecret investigative skills to find out where Bo Jennings had invited Annie on a date? And for shit's sake, why the hell was he actually considering going inside the restaurant to break up that date?

Insanity had surely seeped into his brain. Or maybe some kind of sandworm from the desert had taken over and was now punching the buttons on the computer inside his head.

Why did he care if Annie was on a date with Bo? She deserved to go out and have a little fun. She deserved to find a man who'd treat her and little Max well. She deserved to find love, security, and happiness.

But Jake knew she'd never find that with Bo Jennings.

He was way too much of a mama's boy to ever

put Annie and her son first in his life. Jake had seen
firsthand what a tight grip the mother had on Bo.
In high school, she'd hovered over him and never
allowed him to compete in any sports in which
he might be injured. She'd never allowed him to
go out to school functions with the other kids because apparently, in her mind, every single kid in
the town of Sweet was a bad influence. Yeah, okay,
maybe that would hold true for a few of them, but
every single kid?

The only activities Bo had been allowed to
attend or join were ones like the school debate
team or the chess club, where Mrs. Jennings could
sit and watch her boy like a mother bird.

There had been rumors back then about what
kind of hold Mother Jennings *really* had on her son,
but no one had any evidence of anything beyond
an overprotective mother and a seriously pansy-
ass kid. It had been weird as hell though.

Jake glanced back up at the restaurant down the
street.

Reality struck home. It really wasn't any of his
business what Annie did or who she went out
with.

He turned the key in the ignition, and the engine
rumbled to life.

Nope.

Not any of his damned business at all.

Annie slugged down another drink of wine,
then held her glass out for a refill, which Bo per-
formed with a raised brow.

Screw it. Let him think she was a lush. No way in hell was she going to sit there and listen to another story about how his mother carefully arranged his clean white T-shirts in his drawer. The creep factor went beyond the idea that a man who saved lives for a living voluntarily chose to live at home. Jake currently lived at home too. But he'd just come back injured from the war, and it was just a matter of time before he'd be doing his own thing.

The waiter returned to take their orders, and Annie nearly applauded the interruption of Bo's nauseating tale of his mother's laundry prowess. No sooner had Bo handed the waiter back the menu—from which he'd taken the liberty and ordered for her—than she felt a quiver of awareness tickle the back of her neck.

"Well, fancy finding you two here."

Annie didn't need to look up to realize the overblown *shit howdy* Southern drawl came from none other than Jake Wilder. Just to make sure she knew he was there—like he was the one person she'd ever miss?—he pulled out a chair next to Bo and sat down.

"What are you doing here, Jake?" she asked, refraining from giving him an eye roll.

He grinned, literally from ear to ear, like he was in on some funny secret. "The brothers sent me in to talk to the owner about catering for Mom's wedding."

"At seven o'clock at night?" Bo asked, clearly displeased their date—aka praises of his saintly mother—had been interrupted.

"Is it that late?" Jake made a great show of looking at his watch. "Yep. I guess it is."

"I thought your mom wanted to keep things simple," Annie said, not buying the reason for his sudden appearance. Although really, what else would bring him to the restaurant. He was a meat-and-potatoes kind of guy, not pasta. So maybe he was telling the truth. Then again, the evil little twinkle in his eyes said otherwise.

"She did," Jake said with a laugh. "But then she made the mistake of turning over some of the duties to the brothers. And, well, you know how that goes."

Not for one minute did Annie believe Jana would turn over the planning of her wedding to her sons. The same sons who'd been pretty tough on poor Martin Lane since he started dating their mother. Their wives, yes? Her sons? Absofricking-lutely not.

"I hope I'm not interrupting anything important here," Jake said, gesturing his hand between Annie and Bo.

"As a matter of fact, you are." Bo leaned back in his chair and puffed out his chest like he was claiming his territory. "Annie and I are here on a date."

"A *date*?" Jake's brows spiked up his forehead. "Well, I'll be. I suppose that's what the roses are for." He turned his blue eyes on Annie, and the intensity was enough to make her squirm. "Although, Annabelle darlin'? I thought you weren't fond of roses because they made you think of the flowers they put on coffins."

It took everything she had not to snort. She didn't know what this good-old-boy act was all about, and, humorous as it was, it was rude.

"I like roses just fine. Don't you have an appointment you need to get to?"

His head cocked. "Appointment?"

Bo sat in silence, obviously unsure what was going on. Unsure whether he should ask Jake to go. Unsure whether he wanted to punch Jake in the mouth. On second thought, he was probably pretty sure about that one.

"Your appointment?" Annie reminded him. "With the owner?"

"Oh." Jake waved a hand. "I can talk to him anytime. The wedding isn't for a couple of months."

"And yet . . . here you are," Bo said. "Tonight. Butting your nose into our date."

"I do apologize. I just saw Annabelle sitting here when I walked through the door and thought I'd come over and say hello."

"Well, you've said hello," Bo's tone got tighter with each word. "So maybe you could leave now."

As wrong as it was, Annie didn't want Jake to leave. To be honest, she never should have accepted the date in the first place. She wasn't interested in Bo no matter how much she'd primped or hoped. Jake Wilder was all she'd ever wanted.

Even if he didn't want her.

"You bet. I could sure do that. Sorry to have overstepped." Jake stood, reached out his hand, and shook Bo's. As soon as he let go of Bo's hand he turned to Annie. "If I could just talk to you outside for a minute? I forgot that I have a message."

Something deep in his eyes beckoned her to go along with the ruse. Annie had never refused him anything. She wouldn't dream of starting now.

"Is there a problem?" Bo asked.

Jake nodded. "It's highly possible."

"Oh, dear." Annie pushed away from the table and apologized to Bo before she followed Jake out the door. Once they were outside on the boardwalk, she folded her arms across her little black dress. "Okay, so what's up?"

"What are you doing here with him, Annie?"

"Having dinner and conversation. By the way, that's not a message, it's a question. So why do you care where I am or who I'm with?"

Those broad shoulders shrugged. "I just do."

"Well, sorry, buddy, you had your chance." She turned to go. Her stilettos caught in a crack in the boardwalk, and she wobbled.

Jake reached out to steady her. His hands went to her waist and he pulled her close. Looked down into her eyes like they were somewhere private and not standing on Main Street, where anyone who drove by could see them.

"Ah hell, Annie. Do you really want to be on a date with that guy?"

Her hesitation gave her away.

"I'll take that as a no."

"Don't assume anything," she said. "You don't know me that well."

He tightened his grip around her waist. "I know you well enough to know you deserve better."

"Better than what? Sitting at home alone every night?"

Next thing she knew he had her over his shoulder and she was fighting like crazy to keep the short dress down and her derriere from being exposed to the entire town.

"Jake! What are you doing?" She tried not to be concerned that his limp became more prominent as he carted her down to where his truck was parked on the street. Still, she couldn't ignore the intense thrill that shot up her middle at his ridiculous caveman action.

"Friends don't let friends go out on bad dates." He opened the passenger door, set her inside, and pulled the seat belt over her lap. Then he leaned in and grinned. "I'm removing you from a bad situation."

"I didn't ask to be removed."

"Too bad. I'm doing it anyway."

"So . . . what. You're kidnapping me?"

"Guess so."

*J*ake had done some truly asinine things in his life. He'd done a lot without thinking of the consequences. This one rated right up there at the top. Funny. He didn't give a shit. He was doing it anyway.

Annie looked too wild and hot in that little black dress and those sexy high heels to have to suffer through a boring date with Bo Jennings. If she wanted to have a little fun, he'd be happy to give it to her.

As a friend.

That's all.

As he climbed up into the driver's seat, he could feel the heat of her glare. He turned his head and almost laughed. The whole pissed-off thing she had going on was completely ruined by the mirth playing at the corners of her luscious mouth.

"You can't just kidnap me. I'm on a date. That's not very nice to Bo. He made a real effort to do something romantic. He even bought me flowers. Which, by the way, are still sitting on the table."

"Annie? I don't really give a shit about Bo. And if you want flowers, I'll buy you flowers. But when I walked into that restaurant and saw the misery on your face, not to mention that you were slugging down a good amount of wine—which you never drink—well, I knew I couldn't just stand by and let you suffer. I've only got your best interest at heart."

"My best interest? Ha. That's what you said the other day when you told me there could never be anything between us."

"It's the truth, Annie. And you know it."

"Yet here you are butting your nose into my business. Thinking you know what I want or what I need. Maybe I was having a good time. Maybe what you describe as *misery* was really keen interest in what Bo was saying. Maybe I discovered I *like* wine."

"You can lie to me, Annie, but you can't lie to yourself."

"You're a jackass, Jake." She huffed. "A bona fide one hundred percent jackass who makes no sense at all. Especially when your lips are moving."

He couldn't help but smile. He loved the way

she got all fired up and feisty. "So what you're saying is, I don't explain myself very well."

"Amongst other things."

"Huh." He laughed when she narrowed her eyes. "Maybe we should discuss this over a cold Shiner."

"Maybe I should just *give* you a shiner."

Another laugh rumbled in his chest. "You're a pistol, Annie." He turned the key in the ignition.

"Wait!" She turned to look back at the restaurant. "What about Bo?"

"I figure in about five more minutes, he'll get the clue that you aren't coming back."

"You can't just leave him in there waiting for me."

"Sure I can."

"That is so rude."

"Annabelle. You can hardly call it kidnapping if you tell someone who you took and where you're going."

She folded her arms across that hot little black dress and refused to look at him.

"Fine." He groaned.

She still didn't give him as much as a glance as he got out of the truck and went back into the restaurant. Ditto for when he came back and slid into the seat next to her.

"Happy now?"

Finally, she looked his way. "What did you tell him?"

"To pay for his wine and go home. You weren't coming back because he bored the snot out of you."

"Oh my God." She gasped. "Is that really what you said?"

"Maybe." He put the truck in DRIVE and pulled away from the curb.

"You are such a shit, Jake."

"Not the worst thing I've ever been called."

"I can come up with quite a list." She grinned. "Want to hear it?"

"Nope."

$\mathcal{T}$he Blue Armadillo beer garden was the last place Annie imagined Jake would have in mind. Seven Devils' loud and rowdy honky-tonk saloon was more his style. Then again, he was just full of surprises lately. And that sparked all kinds of ideas in her head. Call her crazy, but she knew by the look he'd had in his eye the other day by the creek, he liked being with her. And judging by the sounds he'd made and the things he'd said, he really liked what they'd been together. With that in mind, she wasn't ready to give up.

Not yet.

It seemed the Armadillo was having a busy night, as there were no available spots on Main Street to park. Jake finally found a place down a darkened side street. When he got out of the truck, he came around, opened her door, and held out his hand.

"So *now* you want to be the gentleman?"

"Just don't want you breaking your pretty neck in those shoes. It's pretty dark, and there could be cracks in the sidewalk."

"You're afraid I'll tell your mother, right?"

"Damn straight. I'm way more afraid of her than I am you."

She took his arm, and they walked down the sidewalk that did indeed have cracks. "You should probably rethink that strategy."

He looked down at her, and even through the shadows, she could see the white gleam of his smile. "Is that a threat?"

"Do I look like the type who'd threaten someone?"

"Hell, you look like the type who could take an opponent to the mat and pin their shoulders before they even blinked."

"I've had to learn to be tough. So I'll take that as a compliment."

They rounded the corner onto Main Street and walked down a couple of blocks. Then they cut in between the Rusty Junk antique shop and The Tipsy Tulip, a floral shop that also sold local wines. The Blue Armadillo sat back about fifty feet off Main Street, which was originally an old homestead with a huge lot. When they got to the garden-arbor entrance, Jake stopped and looked down into her face.

"Once we cross this threshold," he said, "no more sniping, arguing, or thinking bad thoughts, okay?"

"Then how will we ever have a conversation?" She was joking but his expression turned serious.

"I think we can do just fine without all that."

So did she. Because in the end, it was all just teasing. She'd never hurt him in any way. She hoped the feeling was mutual.

"Would you mind waiting here for just a minute?" he asked.

"First you kidnap me, now you want to dump me?"

"Not a chance." He chuckled. "I just forgot something."

"Fine. Do you want me to go ahead and try to find a table?"

"Nope. I want you to wait right here." With that he disappeared back from where they came. A few minutes later he came around the corner of the building holding the biggest bouquet of luscious lilies and cheerful daisies she'd ever seen. He held them out with a smile.

"For you."

"Jake." She reached out to take them, but he didn't let go. "You didn't have to."

"You should know by now I don't do anything I don't want to. And by the way . . ." He pointed at the bouquet. "*Not* funeral flowers."

"I appreciate that. And thank you. They're beautiful." She tried to take them again, but he still held the bouquet tightly in his hand.

"Before I let go, you have to admit one thing."

"What's that?" She couldn't help but smile at the mischievous curve to his mouth.

"Admit you were miserable sitting there listening to Bo talk about his mother."

She sighed. "Sooooo miserable."

"See." His grin doubled as he let go of the flowers. "Friends don't let friends go on bad dates."

She lifted the bouquet and inhaled the sweet fragrance. "How did you know?"

"I went to school with the guy. A leopard can't change its spots, so I figured it was a good guess he's still a mama's boy."

"You have no idea." A chuckle tickled her chest.

"By the way, in case I forgot to mention it, you look amazing."

"Are you saying that just so I'll be nice?"

"Annabelle? Have you ever known me not to tell the truth?"

"Back at the restaurant comes to mind."

"No bullshit." His big hands came up and gently cupped her face. "You. Look. Amazing."

"Way to win me over, big guy." The National Guard couldn't have stopped the flurry of hot tingles that danced through her stomach. "Okay. You've got a deal. No sniping, arguing, or thinking bad thoughts."

"That's my girl." He kissed her forehead, and she had to do everything she could to keep from melting. Because aside from the fact that they were just friends, *this* felt like a real date.

With his warm hand settled on the small of her back, they walked beneath the arbor lit up with white fairy lights and into the patio area of the Blue Armadillo. Set back beneath a small grapevine-covered gazebo, the band's female vocalist sang Allison Krause's "Let Me Touch You For A While." Ivy-covered latticework surrounded the patio, and a three-tiered fountain provided a comfortable atmosphere.

Jake, a head taller than she, looked over the crowd and spotted an empty table back in the corner. No sooner had they sat down than an attractive redhead showed up to take their order. Annie didn't have to wonder if Jake's sexy smile and good-old-boy shtick charmed the woman as he placed their order. The poor thing was just about evaporating in her Daisy Dukes.

"You and your brothers should find a way to market that," Annie said.

"Market what?"

"The charm that oozes out of you like warm honey."

"Ah. So now you think I'm charming."

"Yes. I think you're charming."

She watched the redheaded server approach with their Shiners with an eager smile on her face.

Setting two bottles of ale down on the table should take a matter of seconds. The redhead managed to turn it into a process that included flirting, fawning, and if she'd had her way, fornicating with Jake. Annie figured she should be insulted that the woman didn't see her as a threat. Apparently the way Jake looked at her said *friends only*. And no matter what spin she tried to put on it, that was just disappointing.

When the woman finally left to tend to other customers, Jake stretched out his leg and leaned back in his chair. He lifted his bottle and tilted it toward hers. Their amber bottles clinked together, then he took a long drink as if he'd been dying of thirst.

Annie took a sip of ale and set the bottle down on the little cocktail napkin that read "Why limit happy to an hour?" "So how's Hank working out?"

"Great. Well, except when he gives me the sad puppy face so he can have table scraps, then proceeds to have no discretion later on letting it all go. If you know what I mean."

She laughed. "I imagine it's about like Max. Who, unfortunately, is all boy and thinks body noises are hysterical."

"You'd better be glad he's all boy. You wouldn't want him to end up like Bo Jennings."

The thought of what went on behind the scenes in the Jennings household made her giggle. "Lucky for Max I'd never be that kind of mother."

"You're a great mom. I always thought that women became great mothers because they had great role models. But you're just a natural. Max is a lucky little boy."

"Awww. There you go being all sweet again."

"Please don't tell my brothers. They'd kick my ass if I started getting all wimpy."

"Don't worry." She reached across the table and patted the top of his hand. "I'll protect you."

"I believe you." With a gaze directly to her eyes, he turned his hand over and his fingers intertwined through her own. The heat of his palm traveled all the way to her heart.

"Life isn't always fair, Jake." She squeezed his big hand. "And I don't always have the answers. But I want to be that soft landing place for you. I want to be that heart that understands. Because . . . we're friends, right?"

He searched her face several times before he simply nodded.

"My phone is always on, and my ears and heart are always open. Just in case you ever need someone to talk to. Okay?"

A sigh expanded his chest. "Okay."

From the small stage at the front of the enclosed

garden, the band rolled into Dierks Bentley's "Come a Little Closer."

Jake stood and tugged her hand. "Dance with me."

"Are you sure? I noticed you were limping a little after tossing me over your shoulder."

"Crazy as it sounds . . ." His smile warmed her from the inside out. "When I'm with you, it doesn't seem so bad."

The huge lump in her throat made it difficult to speak.

"Now what's a girl supposed to say to that?"

"How about, 'yes, Jake, I'd love to dance with you.'"

"Funny. That's exactly what I was about to say." She stood and took his hand. He didn't lead her to the dance floor. Instead, he took her in his arms right there, and they danced in the narrow space between their table and the lattice wall. Above them, the fairy lights twinkled, and the night air was scented with something sweet and promising.

The night had started out bad, but right now, Annie felt like she'd floated up and gone to heaven.

When Jake got lost in the moment and enjoyed himself, he felt good. Like he could breathe without the constriction of the guilt that hung around his neck like an ever-tightening noose.

He drew Annie in close just like the song said. Breathed in her sweet perfume. Stroked her soft skin beneath his fingers. Felt the quickened thump of her heart against his chest. As they moved slowly together, he wondered again how she'd evaded his radar all these years. Ridiculous. Especially when they'd practically been raised together.

He didn't think of her as a kid or a sister now.

Now she was definitely all woman. So new and fascinating to him that he felt like he was waiting for Christmas morning. Waiting to unwrap that one highly anticipated gift that would make his eyes pop and his jaw drop.

He smoothed his hand across the silky fabric of her dress and pictured easing that zipper down her back and slipping it off her shoulders. He imagined tossing it aside, continuing to caress all that soft skin, and finding even more ways to make her moan and sigh. Laugh and smile.

She'd offered him friendship, a warm heart, and a soft place to land.

As he gazed down into her pretty blue eyes, he realized that she was more than just a soft place to land.

Right now, with her, was the only place he wanted to be.

Chapter 10

$\mathcal{S}$ome things in life were worth waiting for.

At almost twenty-nine years old, Annie realized Jake was the first guy to walk her to her front door after a date. True, he hadn't actually started out as her date. But she'd always been a firm believer that how you began the dance didn't matter half as much as how you ended it.

She still felt a little bad about abandoning Bo at the restaurant, and she hoped he wouldn't hold it against her if she ever needed his skills in the emergency room. But she was really glad that it was Jake holding her hand up the walkway to her front door. That it was Jake taking her keys and opening that door. That it was Jake who walked inside the house, turned on a light, and checked to see that all was well inside before he said good night.

After the Blue Armadillo, he'd taken her back to the restaurant to pick up her car. Then he'd followed her home to make sure she got there safe.

"Are you sure you don't want me to take you to pick up Max?" he asked on his way back to the door.

"It's late. Abby said it was no problem letting him stay the night. I'm sure everyone over there is already asleep. Morning will be fine. Plus, they have Izzy this weekend and Max is crazy about his cousin. He won't even miss me."

"I'm sure you're wrong about that."

"I'd like to be, but he's a pretty independent little boy already. He barely tolerates me smooching on him anymore."

His hand—curled around the doorknob—paused. Flirtation pushed up the corners of his sexy mouth. "Need a substitute?"

"For?"

"Smooching."

She laughed.

He didn't.

Instead, he let go of the knob, slipped an arm around her waist, and pulled her in close. "I should say I'm sorry I ruined your date tonight. Even if it wasn't exactly what you expected." He slid his fingers into the hair at her temple, cupped the back of her head, and stared into her face. The hunger that burned hot in his eyes sizzled all the way down between her thighs. "But I'd be lying."

Before she could protest—not that she would—he'd pinned her between his hard body and the wall. Her breasts crushed against his chest. His thigh thrust between her legs and rubbed against her. Her heart pounded. And then he kissed her with all the hunger that had been burning in his eyes. Kissed her with a desire that stole her breath. Kissed her like he needed her, like she was everything to him.

She'd been starved for this. Needed to hold on so she could maintain reason. But how could she when he was everything she'd ever wanted? She wrapped her arms around his broad shoulders, his hard biceps. She clutched and grasped at everything she could reach while he filled his hands with the curve of her butt, the swell of her breasts.

Beneath the clingy dress and the black silk of her barely existent panties, she grew damp and needy. When they both needed air, he lowered his mouth to that sensitive place beneath her ear. He licked, nibbled, and sucked his way down her throat, sending a wild shot of desire skittering across her skin, into her breasts, and down through her stomach. Between her legs, she ached for him, for the erection that pulsed beneath her palm as she pressed it against the zipper of his pants. He rocked into her, and then his mouth was back on hers as his strong fingers gathered up the bottom of her dress and inched it upward.

"I want you, Annie." His words came broken between harsh breaths. "Want you so bad I'm about to explode."

The thought that he wanted her that much nearly pushed her over the edge. He rubbed that muscled thigh between her legs again, cupped his hands over her breasts, and gently squeezed. She was so damned excited, she could barely breathe. He pushed the top of her dress down, exposed her nipples, and greedily sucked one into his warm mouth.

"Please tell me you have a condom."

He smiled against her skin. "More than one."

"Thank God." Her head dropped back with a thunk to the wall as he drew the other nipple into his mouth and gently rolled it between his teeth.

"And . . ." His mouth moved back up her neck. "We've got all night."

"I like the sound of that." She panted because that was the only way she could breathe when he slid his thumb beneath the strings holding up her black lace panties.

"I'll give you everything you want tonight, Annie."

Hallelujah.

"But tomorrow . . . we have to go back to being just friends again. Okay?" His fingers teased close to the flesh between her legs, and her aching need almost drowned out his words.

"Just friends?" she murmured.

"*Good* friends." He nodded against her shoulder just as his fingers slid into home base.

Ice water rushed over all those warm, moist places his mouth and fingers had traveled. Even as she wanted to strip him down and see how high the rest of these fireworks could fly, she placed her hand on the wall behind her and walked her fingers across the surface until she felt the cold steel of the doorknob. With a quick twist, she yanked it open, shoved him outside, and nearly cried at the utter surprise on his face just before she slammed the door shut and locked it tight.

"Annie, what the hell?" He pounded on the door. "Open up."

Tears and disappointment clogged her throat as she leaned back against the barrier between her and her one desire.

"I'm not your booty call, Jake Wilder." She rested her palms and forehead against the door. "Not yours. Not anybody's."

"I know that." His sigh of frustration was audible. "Open the door."

"I'll always be your friend, Jake. I'll always be here for you . . . as your friend." She wiped the moisture from the corner of her eye. "But if you want my body, it comes as a package deal with my heart. It's not on loan just because I'm your *friend*. Take it or leave it."

"Annie . . ."

"Take it or leave it."

"Will you please just open the door?"

A woman who'd been burned didn't readily stick her heart in the fire a second time. "Open the door" was not the same as "I'll take it." Or "I'll take *you*." Or "I *need you*, Annie." "Open the door" meant get out the heavy-duty bandages because you're going to need them when I crush your heart like a dried rose.

"Please?" he implored.

She inhaled her self-respect, turned the dead bolt, and opened the door just wide enough to see his face through the crack.

"Annie?"

His hands went to his hips, and she caught the slight grimace on his face. Pain or regret? She didn't know.

"Let me come in so we can talk," he said. A

muscle twitched in his jaw—a clear sign of his frustration.

Too bad.

"Talking leads to touching," she said. "Not that I'm opposed to either, but I have a past of listening to pretty words that are empty just so a man can have what he wants. I deserve to be more than a one-night stand. More than just a cheerleader. More than just someone who pays the bills, cooks, and cleans. More than a doormat. I deserve to give myself to someone who's willing to give himself back to me. One hundred percent. If you can't do that, then these panties—no matter how small— are staying in place."

For a long moment, they stood there, looking at each other. Annie's heart chanted "*please, please, please,*" while Jake's jaw twitched and clenched. Eventually, he dropped his head and slowly shook it from side to side. Her hopeful heart seized up so hard and fast it brought tears to her eyes.

"Maybe you'd best give Jessica Holt a call. Good night, Jake."

In the dark of the night, the click of the closing door sounded more like the hard slam of a guillotine blade on all her hopes and dreams.

*J*ake limped back to his truck, slid onto the seat, and slammed the door shut.

"Fuck!" He pounded the steering wheel with both fists. "Fuck. Fuck. Fuck!"

How could one person fuck up so many times without even trying?

"Fuck!" The steering wheel suffered another forceful wallop.

Anger, frustration, and disappointment swirled through him so fast he didn't know which way to turn. Inside, he felt like he might explode.

And it had *nothing* to do with sexual frustration.

Yes, more than anything, he'd wanted to take Annie in his arms and make love to her. All fucking night long. Until neither of them could breathe or think. But he wasn't that immature. At least not in that way. His frustration came from wanting to give but being too damn fearful to cross that line.

Annie was dead-on. She deserved someone who would love her and treat her well. Even if sometimes she drove him bat-shit crazy in the head, he wanted that for her.

But could he ever be the one to give it to her?

For the first time in his life, he was scared.

More scared than when he'd first planted his boots in the enemy's playground. More scared than when the bullet had sliced through his leg and he didn't know if another one would follow to completely take him out.

For the first time in his life, he was confused. Genuinely a jumbled, tangled, fucked-up mess in the heart.

He was scared he might never figure things out.

And for the first time in his life, he wished someone would just step up and tell him what to do.

Minutes later, the tires of his truck kicked up dust as he roared down the gravel road toward Wilder Ranch. Neutral ground, for the time being.

The darkened house and silent property created

the perfect scenario for a man who needed to put in some serious thinking time.

Parking the truck near the barn, he knew going into the house would be a mistake. He'd probably end up waking his mother, which would make her start to worry, which would have her end up going into the kitchen to bake something, which wouldn't help the situation at all. Tonight, he didn't need calories, he needed clarity. Best he kept his troubles to himself.

Looking for a way to expend his energy, he walked the perimeter of the house.

Much of the land between the multiple barns near the house were corrals and grass areas shaded by large oaks. Because the majority of the work to be done at Wilder Ranch was in front, his father had never made use of the portion of the land behind the house. A substantial part of the property had amazing views of the surrounding hills that were overgrown with aged oaks, shrubs, and tall grass. The creek that ran through the property split off in several locations. The main section ran by Jackson's place. Another by Jesse's. Another large segment ran about fifty yards behind the main house. Because the cattle were fenced off, the water in the creek was cool and pristine.

When he and his brothers had been very young, they mostly played in the creek behind the house. When they'd gotten older, they'd moved out to the larger vein close to where Jackson and Abby had built their home. At the time their mother had questioned why they'd want to stray so far from the house. It had been hard to tell her that, as boys, they'd been trying to spread their wings. See what trouble their hell-raising ways could get them into. Often, those ways had required a trip to the emergency room. Other times, it had landed them on restriction. But it had always been fun.

Jake walked along the sandy bank, watched the water tumble over the rocks beneath the bright moonlight. He'd always loved to work with the gifts Mother Nature offered that so many overlooked. He remembered the joy he'd felt when he'd been in college, learning the types of plants and how to care for them. Learning the necessities of design, then expanding on an original idea. Immersing himself in what the earth offered had always given him a sense of peace, of fulfillment. And that's exactly what he needed now.

Carefully, he knelt by the edge where the water lapped up onto the sandy soil. He fished a small quartz out of the water and bounced the weight of the rock in his hand. Then he looked up at his surroundings.

In his mind, he pictured a completely different scenario. Jesse had created a backyard oasis using the natural landscape, native plants, and adding a pool and spa behind his house that offered an enormous outdoor living area worthy of a magazine cover. Why couldn't he do the same? His savings could handle it, and the idea of putting some sweat equity into his new/old home sounded very appealing.

He turned and looked back at the ranch-style house that spread out like giant wings. The front and sides of the house had a wraparound veranda, but the house had no back patio. All the living and partying had been done in the front beneath the shade of the giant oaks. Jackson and Abby had even been married out there. There were plenty more trees in back with a wide-open space to create an entertainment area to rival his brother's. He could picture his family enjoying themselves while his nieces and Annie's little boy played. The project would give him something to do while he figured out what to do with the rest of his life besides feed and drive cattle.

Inspired, he thought of going into the house to grab a pad of paper and pencil and do some sketching, but his mom was a light sleeper. He'd have to find another way to burn off the restlessness scratching at the back of his neck. Returning to Annie's wasn't the answer. Even if it was exactly what he wanted to do.

Plenty of moonlight existed. He could always saddle up Rocky and go for a ride. The horse was sure-footed and could practically cross the grounds blindfolded. So a venture out to unleash a little tension shouldn't be an issue. Forgetting about what had happened at Annie's wouldn't be easy, but if he intended to get any sleep, he had to do something.

With another quick look at the property, he sealed the remodeling idea inside his brain and headed toward the barn. When he got close, he heard an odd noise. As a rule, he didn't carry a weapon, but his father had always kept a shotgun over the front door. Just in case it was needed. Coyotes usually didn't come this close to the house, but one never knew. They might keep a close eye during calving season, but that wasn't till spring. Didn't sound like a coyote anyway.

He eased open the barn door and saw . . . nothing. Still, the strange guttural sound continued. Amplified. He moved inside and grabbed a pitchfork for protection. Yeah. Go figure.

He was a Marine.

With a pitchfork.

Oooh. Scary.

Shaking his head he made his way toward the back stall where the sound seemed to originate. He peeked through the bars and found Miss Giddy pacing and grunting. Her blue satin ribbon was bedraggled as she looked up at him. If a goat could wear a bitch face, Miss Giddy would be sporting one.

Something was wrong.

"You okay, girl?" He stepped inside the large stall.

His mother's favorite farm animal was an affectionate sort, so he was a bit surprised when she didn't trot over for the usual rub between the horns. Instead, she pawed at the straw on the ground, then paced some more. Which made Jake very nervous. He knew squat about goats. That was his mom's area of expertise. Still, he'd lived on a ranch long enough to recognize the signs. If he was correct, Miss Giddy was about to become a mama.

The question was how?

Wilder Ranch spread out for several miles in all directions, and as far as he knew, there wasn't another goat within sneezing distance. Which meant either Miss Giddy had been on the prowl or some Billy had hoofed it past party lines to get a little action.

Whichever it happened to be, he didn't think it wise to leave her alone right now. He cut open a fresh bale of straw and spread it on the ground. Miss Giddy looked at him as if he'd offended her.

"Just want you to have a clean place to deliver if that's what you're going to do." He pulled out his phone and thought about calling Jesse. Couldn't hurt to have a veterinarian on hand in case something went wrong. After all, Miss Giddy was getting up in years. But he knew if he called Jesse, then the whole thing would turn into a big whoop-de-do, and most likely, the entire freaking family would show up. Right now, he really just wanted to be alone. Just him and the goat. And the horses who were standing near the doors of their stalls trying to get a look. And the chickens, who were perched for the night up on the haystacks. Okay, so maybe he really wasn't alone.

For good measure, he checked his phone to see if by any chance Annie had called or left a message to tell him what a total jackass he was. But there was radio silence on that end. No surprise there. He stuffed the cell back in his pocket and pulled a camping chair into the stall to wait.

At first, Miss Giddy didn't seem overly pleased with his presence. Eventually, she gave in and continued her pacing and pawing like he wasn't there. He leaned back and stretched out his legs, folded his hands together across his stomach.

As the time went on, and Miss Giddy seemed to get more uncomfortable, he began to get more worried. At the same time, she seemed like she knew what she was doing, so he tried to keep his concern contained. Sure, he knew when women were giving birth they had a tendency to call their husbands' names, hold their hands tight enough to break bones, and threaten that they'd never let the man touch them again, but in the end there was really only one word for what they went through and how they handled it.

Amazing.

Yeah. He got that from a goat.

About two hours later, Miss Giddy pushed out a cute brown-and-white fuzzy little kid. She hadn't needed any help, and the process had been fascinating. And even though everything appeared to be normal and he could probably close the stall door and Miss Giddy and her baby would be safe, he sat there watching.

Several things came to mind that he wrestled with. He'd been raised on a ranch and had seen countless heifers deliver their calves. Most had a happy ending. But unless there was a problem that required veterinary help, the moms did it all on their own. The dads were nowhere to be found. Not that he was comparing Annie to livestock, but the situation was the same. She'd done it all on her own, without a father around to help her through the tough times. The long, lonely nights. The restless days. He admired the hell out of her. Her strength and willpower made her even more desirable.

Last night, she'd had every right to kick his sorry ass out the door.

She'd offered him a soft place to land. She'd offered friendship. She'd offered her heart. And all he'd wanted to do was bury his troubles between her legs. To momentarily forget the misery that plagued him night and day with the friction of good sex and the release of a powerful orgasm.

Most of his life he'd thought Annie was nothing but a pain.

He'd been wrong.

All along Annie had been something really special.

He thought back to when he'd just started high school, and she'd been in junior high. Some old memories popped up that he'd long forgotten. Memories of Annie with her hair in braids, her complexion imperfect, and her attitude in sore need of adjustment. They'd spent hours sitting on the large stack of hay bales, talking about where they fit in and where they didn't. What they wanted to do and what they refused to do for fear of total humiliation. They talked about their families, his being stable and hers ready to crack at any moment. They talked about dreams and fears and what they would ever do if zombies took over the world. They'd been as close as two people could possibly be without being related.

It took him a few minutes to remember that somewhere along the way after she'd entered high school, he'd taken to ignoring her. In front of his buddies, he treated her like some nerd girl with cooties. A time or two he was sure he'd hurt her feelings and made her cry.

So how the hell did he get lucky enough to have the amazing woman she'd become look at him and not find him a complete toad?

"Sugarplum?" His mother entered the barn in her pajamas, robe, and boots. "What are you doing out here? I got back late from seeing Paige and Aiden's new baby boy, then got up for a glass of water and saw the barn light on."

"Watching."

"What could you possibly be watching at this time of the—Oh! Land sakes, Miss Giddy. What a surprise!" His mother's face lit up as she came into the stall.

Miss Giddy perked up like she was full of pride as she licked the top of the tiny little kid's head. His mother hunkered down and gave Miss Giddy a gentle rub between the horns.

"How did this happen?"

"Mom. You had five sons. You have to ask that question?"

She laughed. "I know how, I just don't know *how*. As far as I know, there aren't any goats around except for the ones Virginia Peabody brought back from her sister's over in Stephenville about six months ago. But they live over a mile away."

"Well, it looks like somehow Miss Giddy has been meeting someone on the sly."

"And all this time I just thought she was putting on some elderly weight. Did everything go okay?"

He nodded. "She handled it like a pro."

"Of course she did. We women know how to take care of things when there's no man around to help. Don't we, girl?"

Point taken. Jake stood and stretched. "Think I'll try to catch a few winks before the sun comes up."

"Did you have a nice time last night?"

He shrugged. "Didn't do anything special."

One all-knowing motherly eyebrow lifted. "You sure about that?"

"Good God." He jammed his fists on his hips. "Who called and ratted me out?"

"Mrs. Jennings. Bo was upset when he stopped by her house after his date mysteriously disappeared."

"She didn't mysteriously disappear."

"Oh?" His mom stood, brushed off her hands, then folded her arms across a striped pair of pajamas. "Then what happened to her?"

"Don't look at me like that."

"I don't know what you mean."

"You're giving me the stink-eye."

"Do you deserve it?"

"Okay, so I might have *persuaded* Annie to leave."

On a good day, his mother's smile was hard to resist. Not that he had to worry about that right now because currently there was a big-ass frown on her face.

"Persuaded?" she asked. "As in you threw her over your shoulder like a sack of potatoes and carted her off to your truck? Son, I thought I raised you to treat a lady better."

"I don't even want to know how you know all that happened."

"Well, that's just fine. Sometimes it's best to keep the confidential informant names . . . confidential."

"Why can't anyone in this town just mind their own business?"

"Now where would the fun be in that?" She closed the distance between them. "Sugarplum, you're my son, and I love you more than life. But I have some real concerns about you."

"Such as?"

"Such as, if you don't have the right intentions in your heart, then please leave Annie alone. She might have had a thing for you for a whole lot of years, but she's been through a rough time, and she deserves to find someone who'll make her happy. If that's Bo Jennings, then so be it. I'd rather have it be you but—"

"There's nothing between me and Annie, Mom. You don't need to worry."

"Ha. Shows you how much you know."

"Now, what's *that* supposed to mean?"

"It means, dear boy, that there's plenty going on. But unless you remove your stubborn head from your rear end, you are never going to find out."

"Didn't you just tell me to leave her alone?"

"I might have misspoke." She flung her hands upward. "It's the middle of the night, and I've got too much on my mind right now to make any sense."

Jake watched his mother stalk off in an obvious snit. "What the hell was that all about?"

Miss Giddy replied, "Meh-eh-eh."

"Yeah, that clears it right up." Jake bid the goats good night, shut the door to the stall, and followed his mother into the house. Trying to sleep now would be a lesson in futility. Because sure as hell, he'd either be thinking of helping Annie out of that hot little black dress and his hands caressing her all over her body, or he'd be thinking of her in Bo Jennings's arms.

Neither was right, but he sure liked the first image a hell of a lot better than the second.

Chapter 11

"I thought you were a shop owner. When did you start running a day care?" Jake asked his mother as he came into the kitchen for a cold glass of water, followed closely on the heels of his dusty boots by Hank. After he'd fed the cattle and checked on Miss Giddy and her baby, he'd spent the greater part of the day out in the back, making plans for the transformation of the yard. Most people would start with changing the colors of the walls in a house once a place was their own. He figured when he got around to that, he'd have to incorporate the help of Charli's design skills. He didn't know moss green from sage green or turquoise from teal.

Hank went to his bowl of water, then lay down on the big dog pillow Jake had bought him and closed his eyes. Guess all that walking around wore the poor guy out.

"I'm not running a day care," his mother insisted while she juggled trying to feed Max his lunch while propping up the bottle for Adeline. "I'm being a grandma."

"Last I checked, Annie's name wasn't on the family tree."

"She's as much a part of our family as anyone else, and you know it."

Yeah. He did. And that didn't make it easy to avoid her.

The problem wasn't because he was embarrassed about what happened just a few nights ago. The problem came because he wasn't sure he could look at Annie without wanting her. Wanting her was wrong. So avoidance became his method of control. He had a shitload of things to focus on and another shitload to deal with, so inevitably both of them were better off with some distance.

"What are you doing out there in the back anyway?" His mother gave Max a piece of banana, which he immediately squished in his chubby hand, then tried to shove in his mouth.

Jake chuckled. The kid was damned cute, with his big eyes and ever-present, toothless grin. Jake just couldn't figure out how the little boy could make him smile and make his heart ache all at the same time.

"I'm making some sketches," he said. "Looking things over."

"Sketches? For what?"

He flipped open the pad of paper and pushed it across the table. Her eyes grew wide.

"Oh, son. That's beautiful. Is that what you plan to do with the backyard?"

"If that's all right with you."

"It's your house now. You can do whatever you want except burn it or knock it down. I might have to come after you if you tried to do that."

"I love this house. You know that. I'm just trying to think of ways we can all enjoy it a little more."

"Your daddy would be so excited to see what you have in mind. He always wanted to do something back there, but he never had the time."

"I know. He worked way too hard." Jake grinned down at the design on the paper. "I think adding a pool like Jesse did would be a great idea. But with all the kids coming along in this family, I think I might go bigger. Add a slide. Maybe a cave. Something to spur on their imaginations. One of those cable shows had extreme backyards. One guy even designed a pirate ship with slides that went into the pool."

"That really sounds like something."

"Geeeeeee," Max shouted.

Jake looked up and answered Max's smile with a grin. "You want a pirate ship, buddy?"

"Ip!" Max threw his hands upward, and the banana went flying. Hank's eyes popped open, and before anyone could blink, he was up off that pillow and snarfing down the squished fruit.

"Oh, dear." His mother grabbed a towel and struggled to hold baby Adeline's bottle in her mouth while reaching to clean up the mess.

"I've got it, Mom." Jake took the towel and cleaned off Max's hands. Then he cleaned the bits of the banana Hank missed off the floor. "You're going to give your mommy a run for her money, aren't you, little man?"

When Jake sat back down at the table, Max clapped his hands together then reached out for Jake with a big grin. Two little bottom and top teeth flashed at him like tiny pearls in a sea of pink.

Jake had no warning of the tidal wave that overtook his emotions and the almost breathtaking need to swoop up the little boy and hug him close. In his mind, Jake pictured Eli and his son sitting at a table just like this one. Eli feeding his son bananas and the son holding his messy little hands up to Eli's gruff face and giggling.

None of that would ever happen.

No hugs.

No kisses.

No laughter.

Jake knew Max wanted him to pick him up. But Jake couldn't do that. He knew if he held that little boy in his arms, he'd completely lose it. Eli would never be able to hold his child. Jake shouldn't have that right either.

"You okay here?" he asked his mother.

"I'm just fine, sugarplum. You okay?"

"Yeah. Just . . . have things to do."

Without a backward glance, he escaped the heat in the kitchen and went in search of something to occupy his mind until the darkness and the reminder that he'd failed to do his duty by Eli's wife drifted away and gave him room to breathe.

Behind him came the click click click of dog toenails on the floor. Just like Annie had said, dogs were loyal. And, apparently, Hank could sense when his buddy Jake was drowning in the deep waters of his own guilt.

$\mathcal{A}$nnie finished placing the last batch of chocolates into their decorative boxes. She tied the ribbons and added the *Dinky Dots Chocolates* cards to the top. Finding a name for her little business venture had been a challenge until she started looking at everything she'd put together for Max. His room had been decorated with dots. His car seat, blankets, and even a lot of his footie sleepers had dots. The name had been staring her in the face.

Finally, she managed to put it all together with coordinating boxes, cards, brochures, and she'd even started to work up a Web site. She'd been trying to take some online classes about conducting an online business, but between the job at Bud's and being a single mom, there was little spare time in her daily bank. As it was, she felt guilty enough for having to ask friends and family to watch Max just so she could get some things done. Or go out on a date that might very well end in disaster.

Jana—bless her heart—had offered to watch him today. And since Annie knew the woman had a to-do list of her own a mile long, she hurried to clean up so she could pick up her son.

Heading down the gravel road that led to Wilder Ranch, Annie banked inside her head a list of chores she needed to do when she got back home. But first she and Max had a date at the grocery store. The cupboards were starting to look a little Old Mother Hubbard, and Annie never liked being caught without the essentials. One thing she'd learned being on her own was that there was nobody to help you out in the middle of the night when you or your child got sick. Or if something prevented you from having the ability to run to the store at a moment's notice. Thinking ahead prevented stress. And though her life was anything but stress-free, she figured why add to the problem by being lazy.

As she eased her car toward the barn and parked, she glanced at the house and noticed Jake sitting in the big blue rocking chair on the veranda. In one arm, he held her sleeping son. In the other arm, he held his equally slumbering niece, Adeline. Eyes closed, Jake's head rested against the back of the chair. Annie wondered if he might be asleep too. Stretched out at Jake's feet, Hank apparently had traveled off to dreamland with the others.

Quietly, Annie got out of her car and closed the door. Her tennis shoes made little sound as she approached the wraparound veranda. It wasn't until she got close that Hank lifted his big black head. When he recognized her, he gave a swinging wag of his tail, then laid his head back down. As Annie reached the steps, she realized that whether Jake was asleep or not, there were wet streaks down both of his chiseled cheeks. His chest heaved as though he was having trouble breathing.

The sight of a man's tears had the ability to destroy her. That this man happened to be Jake, whom she happened to be crazy about no matter what a complete shit he happened to be once in a while, gave her heart an agonizing twist.

She stepped up onto the veranda.

Jake's eyes shot open, filled with utter panic.

"Take them." Arms out, he jolted up from the rocking chair. Neither baby flinched. "Please."

"Sure." While she gathered up the sleeping babies, she noticed that his hands trembled. The moment she had both children in her arms, Jake flew off the veranda and raced toward the barn.

"Are you okay?" she called, fighting back the urge to run after him.

Without giving a response, he kept walking. His dog followed.

She watched until they disappeared into the barn. After she went into the house, she settled both babies in their pack and plays. Neither of them moved a muscle, so Annie went in search of Jana. She came up empty and sat down at the kitchen table to wait. Roughly ten minutes later, Jana came through the kitchen door loaded down with empty cardboard packing boxes.

"Hey, sugarplum. I didn't expect you back so soon."

"I feel bad always having to ask for help, so I thought I'd cut you some slack and get here early."

"Did you get all your chocolates done?" Jana asked, setting the boxes down near the hall door.

"Yes. Thank you." She glanced out the kitchen window and caught sight of Jake just as he rode Rocky out of the barn. Hank followed a short distance, but when Rocky had a pair of heels to his flanks, the horse could run like a rocket. Hank finally gave up and lay down in the middle of the drive to await Jake's return.

"Well. I wonder where *he's* off to in such a hurry." Jana looked out the window too. Then she propped her hands on the hips of her jeans. "I got a call from Eloise Parker, who said she had plenty of boxes I could use but I had to come get them right this minute so they'd quit taking up space in her hobby room. I asked Jake if he could watch the kids for just a few minutes."

"When I drove up, Jake was sitting in the blue rocker on the veranda with both kids sleeping in his arms. I thought he was asleep too, but . . ."

"But what?"

"But when I got close, I noticed streaks of tears down his cheeks."

"Oh dear." Jana dropped into a kitchen chair.

"What do you think happened?"

"You know my son. He doesn't say much unless he's feeding you a line of BS or arguing with his brothers. But I've noticed that since he's been home, he's been keeping a wide berth of the little ones."

"I've noticed too."

"I think he's wrestling with some mighty strong feelings about his friend Eli. Eli's wife is pregnant, you know."

"That doesn't make sense." Annie exhaled her frustration. "I mean, I understand why he feels so horrible about Eli, but the connection with him keeping away from the kids doesn't make sense. He's always been so great with kids. I mean, he adores Izzy, and I can see the way he looks at little Adeline."

"I've tried to get him to talk, and he won't go into details." Jana shrugged. "He just tells me he's fine. Tells me everything will work out just fine. But from this mother's eyes, he's far from fine." She reached across the table and placed her hand over Annie's. "Maybe you can get him to talk."

"I doubt it. All we ever do is argue."

"Could you please at least give it a try?" For the first time since she'd received word that Jake had been wounded, Jana's eyes shone bright with tears. "I'm really worried about my boy."

Annie was worried too.

"I can't promise anything," she said. "But it kills me to see him in so much turmoil. Do you mind watching Max a little longer? He'll probably sleep for a while."

"Sugarplum, the night that baby was born, I told you I'd always be here when you needed me. That offer stands until I take my final breath."

"Thank you." Annie leaned in and kissed Jana's cheek. She could sense her tension, her worry, and it broke Annie's heart to see her so torn up. "I'll go saddle up and see if I can find him."

"Look near the creek. That's always been his favorite place to go work things out."

Annie nodded. She'd look near the creek, over the hilltops, and to the ends of the earth if she had to. Jake drove her crazy for a number of reasons. But she loved him. She always had and always would. And if there was a way to help him through this tough time, she'd do what needed to be done.

Even at the risk of her own heart.

The twig snapped between Jake's fingers as he heard the thunder of hooves beating against the dry earth in the distance. He'd kicked off his boots and was sitting with his feet dangling in the cool water. The bottle of Jack at his hip had several shots missing that now warmed the pit of his stomach. He hated to rely on a bottle to get him through anything. Normally, he wasn't that weak. But holding those babies in his arms had crushed any power he had to overcome the anguish.

Adeline, his newborn niece, had the sweetest little bow lips that moved when she slept like she was sucking a pacifier, and her dark lashes spread like angel wings across her chubby little cheeks. Clean and fresh in her little pink sleeper, he'd wanted to hold her close to inhale that sweet baby scent. To immerse himself in the innocence and try to remember back to a time when life hadn't been so messed up.

Little Max was all boy. When he slept, he let everything go. Mouth open and eyelashes fluttering. His relaxed arms and legs hung limp and flopped like a rag doll. Max played hard, and as Jake held him, he could smell the sweat from his curly blond hair. Jake remembered that smell. It had been hard to get away from when you shared a room with a brother or ended up in a headlock from another.

The last thing he'd intended to do that day was be responsible for two innocent little lives. No one should trust him. He'd proven himself unworthy. But as usual, he'd been pulled in by his mother, and he'd been unable to tell her no.

He'd been out back measuring for a patio when she came outside and asked him to watch the kids for a few minutes while she ran to Mrs. Parker's house to grab some boxes. He'd been hesitant but figured since both little ones seemed content in their playpens, he wouldn't actually have to do anything until his mom came back.

He'd been wrong. So freaking wrong.

No sooner had his mother put her truck in DRIVE than both kids started fussing. The fussing had turned to crying. Adeline produced real tears and even gotten the hiccups. The more Adeline cried, the more Max joined in. Heart torn, Jake fixed up a bottle for each of them, then he faced the real issue. He could load an M27 and keep an eye on the enemy line simultaneously, but he hadn't been able to figure out how to feed and soothe both kids at the same time.

He'd tried several options, but nothing calmed either child until he picked them up. The only solution he'd been able to come up with was to hold a baby in each arm. Max, he learned, could hold his own bottle. Adeline, not so much. When they continued to fuss, he figured rocking them might help calm them down.

What he hadn't realized when he'd gone outside to sit in the big blue rocker was how painful it would be to hold them in his arms. He'd had an idea, but reality was a much harder punch than anything his imagination could conjure up.

While he'd held them, he again thought of Eli and Rebecca, and their unborn child. In his mind, he pictured them all together as a family. And then that picture shattered like jagged shards of glass. It had been Adeline's contented little sigh that completely destroyed him. He'd barely been able to control himself until Annie showed up to rescue him.

Now, as the hoofbeats came closer, Jake wondered who'd been brave enough to follow him after the way he'd stormed off and raced out of the barn. He was in a foul mood, and he felt sorry for whoever had made the choice to seek him out.

Within moments, their sorrel mare, Dandy, and her four white socks appeared through the long Texas grass, with Annie in the saddle.

"Might as well turn that mare right back around," he warned.

"You're not the boss of me, Jake Wilder."

Annie swung down from the saddle and tied Dandy's reins next to Rocky. Then she and her skintight jeans marched right over to where he sat on the creek bank in a big knot of conflict.

"I can go anywhere I want on this ranch."

"Then you should have picked a friendlier spot." He lifted the bottle of Jack to his mouth. Annie's hand snaked out and snatched it away.

"Is this your solution to whatever's got you so tangled up?"

"Doesn't hurt."

"Doesn't help either."

He shrugged. "All a matter of opinion."

"Then how about we both sit here and get completely shit-faced. Afterward, we can try not to complain when the real problems are still waiting for us when we sober up."

He shot her a glare. "I hate it when you make sense."

"And I hate it when you're upset." She put the top on the bottle and tossed it out of reach. Then she sat down by him, close enough that he could feel the warmth from her body. "You don't need Jack when you've got me. I'm your friend. Remember?"

He sighed. Dropped his head and shook it. "You know what a guy hates, Annie?"

"To wear dresses and high heels?"

"No." A sarcastic chuckle rumbled in his chest, but he couldn't look her in the eye. "A guy hates to be weak. He hates to involve other people in his problems. And he hates to have to admit that he doesn't have the answers."

"That's a whole lot of hate going on, Jake."

"Tell me about it."

"Are you still talking to the counselor?"

He nodded. "Isn't doing any good, though."

"How do you know?"

"Because I'm still pissed enough to break a brick wall with my bare hand."

"In my experience, anger comes from confusion, a misunderstanding, or the sense of a lack of control."

"There's no misunderstanding that it's my fault Eli and the others are dead, Annie. There's no confusion that Eli's child will grow up without a father. Or that I have yet to find the balls to go visit his wife after I promised my best friend that I would make sure she was taken care of if he got killed. And as far as control goes? In training, I was given options that, had I not been such a know-it-all smart-ass and paid better attention in class, I probably would have made a better decision that day."

She held her hands up like she was weighing something. "Gee, I don't know. On one hand, you've got four walls, a blackboard, and a pleasant atmosphere. On the other hand, you have rocks, blinding heat, and bullets flying at you all while you're trying to concentrate on a combustible situation."

"I made a mistake, Annie."

"So you're going to compare the ability to make a decision in a safe classroom against a split-second decision made in a real-time war situation?"

"There shouldn't be a difference."

"Of course there is. Because you're perfectly human."

"I'm not a perfect anything."

She settled her hand on his shoulder, and he finally looked up. Though the shade of the sweeping branches of the towering oaks blocked out the direct sun, her eyes were bright with moisture.

"Even machines are fallible, Jake. And you, most certainly, are not a machine. You were taught options. You chose the one for the situation you thought best. You had a fifty-fifty chance of getting it right or wrong. Those aren't exactly great odds."

"The Marines promoted me to second lieutenant because they believed I could do the job. My men trusted me. I failed."

"Did your mission stop the enemy from advancing?"

"That's what the report said."

"And do you think the military is going to lie just to make you feel better?"

"No."

"Then why won't you believe them? You all

may have walked into an ambush, but you accomplished your mission. Lives were lost. And that's horrible. But you didn't fail the mission, Jake."

"I failed my troops."

On an audible exhale, she lifted her hand to his back and slowly stroked him in a comforting manner. "Did you fail them on purpose?"

"You know I'd never do that."

"Then how can you continue to beat yourself up for something that wasn't intentional? If you want to blame anyone, blame the enemy."

"I can't."

"Why?"

"Because they're faceless. When I look in the mirror, I see *me*. I can't see *them*."

"So it's easier to blame what you can visualize?"

"Maybe." He looked away from the confusion in her eyes. It was nearly impossible to explain the way he felt to someone who'd never been in his situation. Which is why he felt it a complete waste of time to talk to a counselor who'd never gone any farther than from behind his desk.

Unable to handle the intensity in the conversation and the insane yearning for this woman who wanted so badly to help, he got up and walked farther down the creek. Barefoot, the rocks and sticks that poked the bottoms of his feet reminded him of the shrapnel that had penetrated his boots that day, and a chill settled in his spine.

A few moments later, Annie caught up to him.

"Haven't you had enough?" He reached down and picked up a floating leaf. At her silence, he came up and found her looking right into his eyes.

She lifted her hand and tenderly weaved her fingers through the hair near his temple. His frustration made him want to flinch, but her touch felt like a life preserver. And he grabbed hold.

"Guess you don't know me as well as you think you do," she said. "Even though you still have possession of my torn panties."

That made him smile.

Hell, everything about Annie made him smile.

She moved closer and brought with her the sweet scent of chocolate and warm woman.

"Everyone has their breaking point, Annie." He trailed his fingers down the soft, silky strands of the hair framing her pretty face. "You should be tired of listening to me whine all the time."

"Stop it. You're not whining. You're feeling. Expressing those feelings. And that's really important to process through everything. I'm here for you, Jake. I don't want to be your booty call—the one you think of when the bar closes, and there's no one else around. But I *want* to be here for you because your heart and soul need me."

"I would never think of you as a booty call." He captured her face between his hands and brushed a kiss to her luscious mouth. Then he pressed his forehead to hers. "And I do need you, Annie. I really do."

When he drew her into his arms, felt her heart beat against his own, nothing felt more right. Nothing took away the ache more than being with her. Nothing gave him an inkling of hope like it did when she wrapped her arms around him and just gave him her heart. He knew that heart was fragile after what she'd been through. And he'd never take that for granted. In her strength he found comfort.

For a long moment, with nothing but the sound of the breeze floating through the leaves and the trickle and splash of water in the creek at their feet, they stood there in each other's arms.

In that moment, he didn't feel so broken.

"I really do need you." He looked down and tilted her face up to meet his gaze. "And I don't mean as just friends."

$\mathcal{A}$nnie's heart leapt with joy. For him to admit that he needed anything was not just a matter of pride for him. It was declaring weakness. Defeat. And anyone within ten counties knew the Wilder brothers didn't readily admit their vulnerabilities.

When Jake had been a boy, he'd tried so hard to keep up with his big brothers, and they'd tortured him. Affectionately, of course. But there were no ends to what he'd do to gain their admiration. He never gave up. Never surrendered to the pressure of the crazy things they'd put him up to.

Annie didn't want to pressure him. She didn't want to ask exactly what he meant or where they'd go from here. She just wanted to be there for him— with him—as a friend, a lover, or whatever he needed right at this moment. Stepping from his arms, she began to unbutton her blouse. Surprise lifted his severely drawn brows.

"What are you doing?" Deep and rich, his voice invisibly touched parts of her that reacted with a warm tingle.

"That should be obvious." She gave him a smile as she tossed her blouse aside where it fluttered down over a large rock. Then she reached for her boots. "As much as you need me, I think I may need you even more."

"Annie—"

"Sssh." She tossed the boots, came forward, and pressed a finger to his lips. "We can talk later."

"What about all the stupid things I've said to you?"

"Oh, they're still stupid. But right now, I'm going to pretend they never happened."

"I don't—"

This time she silenced him with a kiss.

Jake had always been a man of action. And when he pulled her against his hard body, ran his hands down her back, and cupped her rear cheeks in his big palms, she knew—for the moment—he wasn't thinking of anything but her.

They could sort out the messy details later.

He held her close for a long beat, and with his erection pressed against her belly, asked, "Are you sure about this?"

"Jake? I am standing in a forest half-naked. Just how much more sure do you need me to be?"

A grin spread across his face. "Completely naked?"

She reached her hands around to her back to undo the hooks of her bra, but he stopped her.

"God." Briefly he closed his eyes. "Let me do that. You don't know how many times I've pictured it in my head."

She freed her hands and, beneath the soft cotton

of his shirt, slipped them up his chest. Her exploring fingers met taut, warm skin, short soft hairs, and male nipples hardened from arousal. She leaned into him, lifted to her toes, and slowly licked up the side of his throat. "Then don't let me stop you."

An appreciative male groan rumbled from deep within his chest as he unhooked her bra with an expert flick of his fingers and lovingly caressed her breasts as they slipped from the bra and into his palms. "You're playing with fire, girl."

"Maybe." The tickling sensation of his rough fingertips on her nipples made it difficult to speak. "But there's a cool creek right there to douse you in if things get too hot."

"Please, God, yes. Let things get too hot."

She nipped his jaw with her teeth. Then she grabbed hold of his shirt from the inside and whipped it off over his head, baring his defined muscles and artful tattoos.

"No more playing, Jake." She kissed the side of his neck, opened her mouth, and sucked in the salty flesh. A groan of appreciation caught in his throat. "No more talking. Right now I want to make you forget. To make you feel. And only feel."

"I can handle that." His hands gripped her butt harder as she worked her mouth farther down to his chest, then slowly licked her way back up to his mouth.

"And when you're deep inside me, Jake? I only want to hear one thing."

"What's that?"

He hissed in a breath as she caught his lower lip between her teeth.

"I want to hear you say *more*."

"Dammit, Annie. You drive me crazy." His arms went tight around her, and he kissed her as if nothing else in the world mattered. As if nothing else existed except her.

He kissed her deep, wet, and hot.

So hot it melted her pants and panties right off her legs. Or at least that's how she figured she'd ended up standing there naked. She'd been too lost in his kiss to care.

"It's not fair to keep a lady waiting." She reached for his belt as he filled his hands with her. Used his mouth to lick, suck, and arouse.

Unzipped, she pushed his Levi's and navy blue boxer briefs down and off. Then they were both standing there naked to the world and each other. Warm air brushed across the tips of her breasts. His mouth followed, drawing her into that warm, slick recess to tease her into mindlessness. She reached for him, and he pushed his long, thick erection into the palm of her hand. A few slow strokes from base to head quickened his breath.

"Annie? You keep that up, and we may be standing here naked for nothing."

"Well we certainly can't have that," she said, but didn't release him. Instead she continued to squeeze and stroke while she kissed her way from his mouth, to his ear, then down that incredible chest and those rippled abs. When she reached his navel, he grabbed her by the shoulders.

"Oh hell no." He leaned his head back and gave a guttural groan. "As much as I want *that*, I want this more." He kicked his clothing into a layer of protection for her back from the grass and gravel. Then he lifted her into his arms and laid her down.

"I've had about all the teasing I can stand." He gently brushed her hair away from her face. Kissed her thoroughly, then lifted his head and looked into her eyes while his fingers slipped into the hot, slick folds between her legs. His fingers worked a magic that arched her back and made her moan. "Now I want to be inside you."

"I want that too." He swirled his fingers right over her tender flesh, stroking her in such an exquisite way she nearly came undone. "Like five minutes ago."

He chuckled against her lips. Kissed her so deeply she almost forgot where his fingers were.

Almost.

Like a magician, he pulled a condom packet from behind her ear. "Showtime."

She laughed, then watched as he tore the package open with his straight white teeth. Goose bumps rippled along her skin in anticipation. Together, they rolled the latex down over his thick shaft. When it was in place, she gave him a squeeze that forced a moan from his throat.

"No guarantees how long this will last," he murmured, as his erection teased and pulsated against her slick opening. "I've been wanting for you for so long."

She inhaled his hot male scent. "If you've got more than one condom, there shouldn't be a problem," she whispered. "If you don't, I might have to kill you."

His chuckle vibrated through her breasts and warmed her heart.

She'd always wanted Jake.

Always.

"I've got more than one and all day to put them to good use." He kissed her lips. Sucked the lower one into his mouth as he rocked against her pelvis.

"Ahhhh." She arched her back as he slipped his hand between them and touched her most sensitive flesh. "I knew there was a reason I was so crazy about you."

He didn't respond. He didn't need to. His kiss stole her breath. Stole her mind. All teasing stopped as he slid deep inside her.

She tore her mouth free because she couldn't breathe. She closed her eyes to focus on the delicious sensation of having him inside, filling her more spectacularly than she'd ever imagined all those lonely nights ago.

"You feel so damned good, Annie." Her name broke from his lips in a rough groan that forced her eyes open. For a moment, he stayed still, growing more even as they caught their breath. Their heated gazes connected, and Annie knew she'd never felt closer to anyone. This was the Jake she knew. The man she admired. The man she wanted to make happy.

Reaching up, she stroked his cheek. Dipped her fingers through the side of his soft hair. Then lifted her hips and squeezed him with her inner muscles.

The man she loved.

"More, Annie." Face dark with desire, he dropped

his head back, withdrew his cock just slightly, then pushed in deeper. "More."

"Yes, Jake." She ran her fingers over his chest. Across the cross tattoo on his biceps. When he repeated the movement, he rendered her breathless. Watching him find his pleasure and lose himself in the passion heightened her sensitivity. She met him thrust for thrust. Begged for more and whimpered with need because it was impossible not to.

She raised her hips then wrapped her legs around his back to bring him in even deeper. She filled her palms with the tautness of his buttocks and felt the muscles contract and release as he pumped into her harder and faster.

"Yes, Jake." He shifted, hit her from a different angle and brought her right to the edge. She didn't bother to contain her encouragement. There was no one in the forest but the two of them. The more she encouraged, the more he gave her.

"Yes, Jake." When he shifted again, she broke. Shattered. "Yes. Yes. Yes."

With a rough groan, he pushed hard. Every muscle in his body tightened as she clenched around him, and he flew over that cliff with her. He grabbed her hands, held them above her head, and pushed into her a few more times before he collapsed.

Their hearts pounded together. Body parts throbbed with the rush of blood through their veins. He shuddered in her arms, then rolled to his side, taking her with him.

Utterly limp and gasping for air, Annie locked

her leg around his back and drew him in for one last thrust.

"I can't get enough of you," she whispered.

Panting, he lifted his fingers to her face, drew her close, and kissed her. "I wish I'd known a long time ago how good we could be together."

"Guess there's something to be said for making up for lost time."

He kissed her again. Gently stroked her face near her temple. And looked into her eyes. "Like I said, I've got all day."

"Does that make you all mine?"

"Yes." He pulled her in close and held her tight. "If you think you can handle it."

She laughed. Something she seemed to do a lot when they were together. When they weren't arguing. "I can handle *it*. Just not sure I can handle *you*."

He captured her mouth. Took complete possession. Then he lifted his head and gave her that cocky Wilder grin. "More, Annie."

"I'm glad to see you can follow instructions."

"I'm all yours." Grinning, he lay back, arms spread wide. "Do with me what you will."

Because she might never have the moment again, for the rest of the afternoon, she did exactly as he asked.

Chapter 12

"*I* should have known you'd pick a lazy, good-for-nothing dog."

"Watch what you say." Jake glared at Jackson, then put his hands over Hank's ears, which was easy since the dog sat at his feet wherever he went. Didn't matter if Jake only walked two feet away and stopped, Hank would follow and practically sit on the toes of Jake's boots. Annie had said dogs were loyal. Hank went beyond the call of duty. They'd had many private one-sided conversations, and Hank never faltered. Never judged. He'd show his love and appreciation with a lick on Jake's hand, then he'd promptly fall asleep at the foot of Jake's bed. "You'll hurt his feelings."

"Impossible." Reno picked up yet another of their mother's numerous boxes and carried it to his truck. "Before Charli and I got together, I insulted Pumpkin too many times to count. She still likes me. In fact, the way she looks at me makes me thinks she's got some kind of weird doggie crush."

"Not unusual," Jesse said. "She just sees you as one of her own kind."

"Ha-ha."

Doing his share of the heavy moving of their mother's things from the home where she'd raised her family to the new home she'd be making with Martin Lane, Jake stacked several boxes on top of each other and set them on the dolly. He hated to admit his weakness, but after hours of moving furniture and boxes filled with books and what felt like bags of concrete, his leg hurt.

Though it hadn't hurt a damn bit when he and Annie had made love. She made him feel like Superman. He chuckled.

"What's so damned funny?" Jackson asked as he pushed Jesse out of his way.

"Hey, watch it, jackass." Jesse shoved him back, and Jake waited for the usual wrestling match to break out. It didn't happen, but only because their mother stuck her head out the door and threatened bodily harm if they broke her stuff.

"You've been in an awfully good mood this past week," Jesse commented as he took the dolly and carted it over to his own truck. "What's up?"

"Am I not allowed to feel good?" Jake asked.

"Yeah. But there's got to be a reason because usually you're an asshole," Jackson said.

"I am not."

"Are too."

"Boys!"

"Sure." Jake shoved his hands onto his hips. "Get me in trouble with Mom."

"Story of your life, little brother." Reno clapped him on the back as he went to grab another batch of whatever his mom had been storing for the past nearly forty years.

"So what's put such a cheesy-ass grin on your face?" Jackson asked. "Or should I say who? Has Jessica Holt discovered some new bedroom parlor tricks?"

"I haven't seen Jessica since I've been back."

"Right." Jesse laughed. "Isn't she on your booty-call speed dial?"

"Was."

"Oh?" Reno's head snapped up. "What's changed?"

"Don't have to explain myself to you yahoos."

Jesse looked at Jackson. "You know what *that* means?"

"Yeah." Jackson gave a nod. "He's holding out on us."

"Only one way to resolve that dirty little issue."

Both of his brothers headed toward him, and he laughed. He wasn't their punching bag anymore. Yeah, they were both former Marines too. But he could hold his own. Even with a bum leg.

Unfortunately, at that moment, he thought of Annie. Not that she was his dirty little secret, it was just that they'd decided to keep things quiet for now. No need to involve anyone else or their opinions when they were both trying to figure things out on their own. But that lingering vision he had of her lying beneath him, smiling up, capturing his heart, and touching him in places that felt damn good, gave his brothers the upper hand.

Jackson grabbed him in a headlock, and Jesse grabbed him around the waist. Had he not been injured, they'd have taken him to the ground. Instead, when Hank barked his displeasure with their antics, they backed off quickly as if they suddenly remembered he was still healing. Then they both gave him a quick whack on the back of his head.

"There's nothing to tell," he insisted.

"Uh-huh." Jackson countered. "You wouldn't own up if there was."

"You're right." Jake tossed him a lightweight box. "It's nobody's damn business."

Nobody needed to know anything right now. And he had too much going on to try to figure it out in depth. For the moment, he was enjoying himself by taking the time to explore a different side of Annie than he'd ever known. He wanted to keep things quiet for as long as possible. Because the one thing he knew for sure, the minute the family found out, they'd be right up in his business. Asking questions. Pushing him toward something he wasn't ready for.

Trouble was, his mom had probably figured out what was going on the day they'd come back from the ride. Besides the fact that he and Annie were both so exhausted and boneless they had a hard time staying in the saddle on the way back, and he was probably wearing a big, stupid grin, his mom had plucked a twig from Annie's hair. Then she brushed the dirt from the back of his T-shirt.

She'd said nothing. She didn't have to. Her smirk said it all. All he could do was hope she'd hold her tongue longer than usual. But that was like asking a lifeguard to stay out of the water. Two things his mom was good at: meddling and meddling. Oh, and a third. Gossiping. Good thing she lived in a small town, where the chances to accomplish both were highly possible day or night.

The devil herself came out of the house, dragging a big green trash bag behind her.

"What's in there?" he asked when all his brothers stopped what they were doing to watch.

"You don't want to know." She kept dragging that thing toward her car.

"That's like throwing down the gauntlet, Mom. You can't do that."

She kept walking and dragging.

"Is that your secret stash?" Jesse asked, dancing up behind her, ready to snatch the bag away.

She smacked Jesse's hand and gave him the stink-eye. "You don't want to know."

"You're going about this all wrong, boys." Jackson flashed their mother a smile and held out his hand. "Please allow me to relieve you of your burden, ma'am."

She slapped his hand too and kept walking.

"Must be a dead body," Reno quipped.

"It'll be *your* dead body if you don't back off."

"All right, you guys." Jake pushed Jackson out of the way. "Leave her alone."

"Thank you, son. But it's none of your business either."

"Damn." Jake grinned. "Thought I was getting close."

She opened the door to her little white car and tossed the bag into the backseat. Then she headed back to the house.

"No worries." Jackson looked at his brothers and folded his arms across his chest. "We just have to wait for her to get in the house."

Their mother lifted her hand and clicked the lock button on her key fob.

"No fair, Mom," Jesse called out, while Reno chuckled.

"What do you think is in there?" Jake asked, as they all gathered around her car and looked in the back window.

"Sex toys." Jesse said.

"Eeew!"

"Mom doesn't have sex. She's too old."

Reno gave them all a look. "You plan on not having sex after the age of sixty?"

They threw him an "are you crazy?" look.

"Then what makes you think Mom has given it up?"

"I don't even want to go there." Jake walked away from the car, shaking his head.

"I just got the chills." Jackson went back to the stack of boxes piled up on the veranda.

Jesse grinned. "I think it's cool that Mom is still active."

Their mother came back out the door dragging another big green trash bag.

"Yep." Reno laughed. "It's a dead body."

"Who knew Mom was one of *those* kind of women?"

They teased her relentlessly, but she'd had nearly thirty-seven years to be a pro at ignoring them.

The sound of tires on gravel lifted everyone's heads and pulled their attention in another direction. Jake had to do everything he could to keep from grinning like a fool when he saw Annie's car coming up the road.

Jackson noticed too. Only the frown on his face said he wasn't happy about it because in the passenger seat sat his very pregnant wife.

"Looks like the reinforcements are here." Jesse seemed more eager because his wife was in the backseat, waving at him like he was a sailor come home from sea.

"Abby's not helping," Jackson, the stressed-out papa-to-be declared. "She can sit and point, but that's it."

"Charli said she'd be here as soon as she closed up shop and dropped Adeline off at Fiona's," Reno said by way of explanation of why his wife was absent.

"Fiona's going to have her hands full of kids by the time the day is over," Jake said. "Good thing she owns a cupcake shop to keep them satisfied."

Reno laughed. "In case you haven't noticed, Adeline hasn't moved beyond breast milk yet."

"Nope." Jake quickly shook his head. "Haven't noticed."

"Good thing, or I'd have to kick your ass." Reno hooked his arm around Jake's neck even though

Jake was a few inches taller. Reno was the oldest, and Jake gave him his due.

Silly entertainment, ridiculous arguments, and comfort from the heart. That's what his family gave him. And it was the thing he'd probably missed the most all the months he'd been away from them.

It felt good to be home.

Sadly, that small amount of joy he allowed into his soul felt like a punishment because he knew Eli had brothers too. And those brothers must miss him like hell. Jake knew that grief because he'd lost his own big brother. But he'd never felt the pain from the personal responsibility of the loss of someone's life before.

Anguish burned in his gut, and the only thing that brought his happy back was looking at Annie as she got out of her car wearing braids, boots, a pair of cutoff jeans, and a little pink tank top that read YOU'RE ONLY IN TROUBLE IF YOU GET CAUGHT.

Jake had to check his oil before he scooped her up in his arms and gave everything away. He didn't intend to get caught. He just planned to enjoy the hell out of the sexy woman before she figured out he was ten times crazy and as unsalvageable as the *Titanic*.

Jackson opened Abby's door and helped her from the car. The last thing Jake heard before Jackson helped her waddle into the house was, "I don't care if I'm having your baby. You're not the boss of me, Jackson Wilder."

Jake laughed. Seemed those words were familiar

around the Morgan women. Annie had used the
same ones on him back at the creek. Good thing he
gave in and let her take control, or they'd still be
dancing around each other. He liked things much
better the way they were. Dancing, he was no good
at. Making love was another matter.

Annie came up to him like a ray of sunshine
with a smile that surrounded his heart.

"I know we're playing it cool right now," she
said. "But if no one were around, I'd kiss the heck
out of you."

"I might be willing to blow our cover for that.
Not touching you is making me crazy."

"Me too. But we've got work to do."

He let go a sound of frustration, and she chuckled.

"Promise me one thing?"

She looked up. "What's that?"

"When we get done here, we go to your house
and make up for lost time."

"Deal." She tucked her fingers in the back pockets of her cutoffs. "I still can't believe your mom is
moving out."

Jake had to remind himself not to be obvious
about looking at her. Which was hard as hell now
that he'd finally noticed her. It might have taken
him years, but he'd rather be late to the party than
have never received an invitation at all.

Two things he loved about Annie; she gave
as good as she got, and she loved as hard as she
wanted.

Being a man who didn't have much left, he was
grateful. Because even if he didn't want to, she

made him feel alive. Even if way down deep in his heart he believed he had no right.

"It's definitely going to take some getting used to." He walked over to the boxes piled up on the edge of the veranda. "You here to pack or move?"

"Your mom asked Abby to help with the packing since she could sit down for that. Allison and I figured we'd help wherever we were needed."

"Sounds great. If Allie can work with my brother's lips all over her face. Hey," he shouted to Jesse, "cut us some slack will you?"

Jesse flipped him the middle finger.

Jake laughed. "You'd think they were still newlyweds."

"They are." Annie looked over to where Jesse and Allison stood with their arms around each other talking like they were in their own little world. "And I think it's sweet."

Yeah. Jake did too. But he wasn't about to tell anyone for fear of losing his man card.

"How about you help me put these boxes in the back of my truck? I'll let you carry the light ones."

"Gee, thanks."

He settled a couple of small boxes in her arms, grabbed a few heavier ones for himself, and followed her to his truck. Watching Annie walk was better than a bowl of your favorite ice cream on a scorching-hot summer day.

"Are you staring at my ass, Wilder?"

"Yep."

She chuckled. "Okay, but I get my turn on the way back."

"Darlin', right now?" He pulled down the tail-gate, took her boxes, and set them inside the bed. "We've got every pair of eyes on us save Miss Giddy, who's doing mama duty in the barn."

"And?" She looked up at him from beneath thick sooty lashes and a sly smile tipping the corners of her luscious lips.

"And . . . if it wasn't for that, I'd have you in the backseat with those cutoffs *off* so fast, you wouldn't know what hit you."

Laughter bubbled from her chest. "Who says I'd even let you?"

"The woman who had three orgasms the last time I took off her pants." He grinned and only barely refrained from leaning in and kissing her smiling mouth.

He studied her face, noting the slight pink to her cheeks, the tiny little blond hairs that slightly curled at her temples, and the straight line of her small nose. "Damn you make me feel good, Annie."

"You say that like it's a bad thing."

"It is."

"You're wrong, Jake. And I promise, if you keep hanging around me, I'll prove it to you." With a cute little scrunch of her nose, she walked away.

"Prove it?" He caught up to her. "How are you going to do that?"

"It's a woman's prerogative to keep a man guessing."

"I was never any good at guessing games."

"How good are you at being alone?" she asked.

"Drastic change of subject."

"Not at all." She glanced at the house, then she swung her mischief-filled gaze back to him. "Tonight will be your first night here . . . all alone."

"And?"

"Invite me over, and I'll show you what I mean."

He liked the way she thought. "You have an open invitation."

"What if *I* just want a booty call?"

"Darlin'?" He set another box in her arms. "I've always been a man who's more than happy to give a lady what she wants."

"I'd have to bring Max with me."

"Is he a deep sleeper?"

She nodded, and those loosely woven braids slipped up and down over her breasts.

"Sounds perfect to me."

"With all this moving going on, probably later is better than earlier?"

"Whatever works for you." He tried to hide his happiness but couldn't stop himself. "And don't worry about changing."

"Because you like me just the way I am?" She playfully batted her long, dark eyelashes.

"Because I'm already thinking of ten different ways to enjoy you in those shorts before I even take them off."

"Careful what you promise, cowboy."

"Lucky for you that I'm a man of action."

"That you are." She patted his chest, then turned on the heel of those worn brown boots and headed toward the house.

"Hey."

She turned around, and he was glad he'd put

a temporary halt to her disappearing into the house.

"How about you quell our curiosity by asking our sneaky mother what secret she's hiding in those green trash bags she put in her car."

Annie gave him a thumbs-up, then disappeared through the front door. Seconds later she was back.

Reno looked up and asked her, "You find out?"

"She wants to know what you boys think is in there."

Jesse piped up. "Sex toys."

"Pull your head out of the gutter," their mother shouted from inside the house.

"Then how about all those stuffed toys Jake used to protect him from the boogeyman when he was a kid."

Laughing, Jake knocked the ball cap off his brother's head. Since Jackson was still inside the house looking after Abby, or making sure she wasn't doing anything strenuous, Jake was the only one left with a guess.

"Miss Giddy's ribbons. Because Mom's taking that old goat with her when she leaves," he shouted loud enough for his mother to hear.

"No, I'm not."

Jake sighed. Looked like he was going to gain ownership of a fashion-minded goat and her kid, and that crazy-looking set of longhorns his mom had decorated with pink rhinestones.

"So who's right?" Jake asked Annie.

"I don't know." She shrugged. "She said if she told me, she'd have to kill me. And I'm too young to die, so it looks like you boys will just have to keep guessing."

Their mother's cackle from inside the house caused everyone to laugh.

Jake looked around at the boxes, pieces of furniture, and other paraphernalia making its way out of the house. The first real pang of sadness swept over him.

It was the end of an era. A new start for his mom. For him too. The house was big, and it was going to feel cavernous when he was in there all by himself. When Jackson came out the door and let the screen door slam, Jake knew all the everyday sounds he'd grown so used to would be quieted. Going from a rowdy home to the active life of the military, Jake was used to the noise and chaos of all the people around him. Isolation and tranquility weren't even a part of his vocabulary.

Now it would be just him and Hank. Not that he didn't love his new best friend, he just wasn't loud enough.

Near Jesse's truck, his three brothers argued over something stupid. Status quo.

Damn.

He was lonely already.

*N*ighttime came alive with the sounds of the crickets and cicadas in the trees that surrounded the huge house at Wilder Ranch. Annie parked near the barn and eased Max from his car seat. He'd fallen asleep on the drive over, and Annie knew he was down for the count, having spent the greater part of the afternoon playing with his cousin Izzy. At this point in his young life, Max wasn't interested in tea parties, so it was a good thing Izzy was a clever kindergartner who invented games to keep Max toddling all over the house. The result—total exhaustion.

Kissing the top of his curly, baby-fine hair, Annie carried him to the front door. Before she could knock, Jake was there, letting her in with open arms. Without hesitation, she stepped into his embrace. Why he held her and Max for so long without saying a word, Annie was unsure. But she was not about to complain.

She looked up into his face and sensed his melancholy. "Are you okay?"

"Sure." As if catching himself at doing something wrong, he dropped his arms and stepped back. "You want to put him down? Mom left a crib in one of the bedrooms."

"Could you hold him while I go get the diaper bag?" She rearranged Max in her arms to hand him off.

Jake took another step back. "Maybe you could just put him in the crib first. Or I could go get the bag for you."

Annie's heart crumpled. She wasn't offended that he didn't want to take her son, she was worried about the reason that stopped him from doing so. "How about we do both together?"

His broad shoulders lifted in a shrug. "Sure."

Together, they walked into what had once been Jared and Reno's bedroom. There were still blue stripes, various sports paraphernalia, and photos hanging on the walls. Annie had never been in this particular room before, but as a mother, she could understand why Jana had never changed a thing since the boys had grown up and moved out.

She kissed Max's forehead, then laid him down on his tummy on the clean bedding. "With your mother's love of all things antique and eclectic, I'm surprised to see such a modern, plain crib."

"This one was mine." Jake ran his hand over the smooth wood. "After Jackson ate his way around his entire crib—which was an antique—she decided to go heavy-duty and basic for me."

"Jackson *ate* his crib?"

Jake nodded and chuckled. "He gnawed his way all around the top and down the spindles. Mom said that while most kids cut their teeth on the usual frozen baby things, Jackson used his beaver instincts to seek and destroy."

Annie laughed. "Why is that so easy to picture?"

"Yeah. Guess some things never change."

Once Max pulled his little legs up beneath him and settled into his usual pill-bug position, she pulled the fuzzy blanket up over his dancing-frog footie sleepers. "I'm really going to miss these times when he gets older."

"I'm sure you'll have more babies," Jake said from right beside her.

She looked up, surprised that he'd moved so close when just moments ago he seemed so hesitant. "Not if I have to do it alone." She shook her head. "I never knew how difficult it would be. Not that I'm not happy to have him, I just worry that I'm going to do such a horrible job, I'll screw him up forever."

"Impossible." Jake gave her a smile. "No one's perfect. And you love that little boy so much, he's going to forgive whatever missteps you take."

Annie wondered if Jake had heard himself. "You're right. No one is perfect." She slipped her hand in his. "And most are willing to forgive imperfections."

"You getting at something?"

"Nope," she said but didn't miss the sadness in Jake's eyes as he glanced down at Max.

She tugged his hand and pulled him out into the hallway. "Where's that cold beer you promised me?"

"Outside." Halfway down the hall, he tugged her into his arms, slipped his hands down the backside of her blouse and jeans, then cupped her bottom in his hands. "I'm highly disappointed that you changed out of your cutoffs after I made a personal request for you to leave them on so I can take them off."

His playfulness instantly changed the mood.

"After moving all those boxes in the dirt and dust, I had to shower." She danced her hands up the front of his chest and undid the buttons at the neck of his navy blue Henley shirt. "Besides, how do you know I didn't come up with something better?"

He leaned his head back and grinned down at her. "Did you?"

"Get me that cold beer, and maybe I'll let you find out."

Instead of going to the kitchen, he turned her back to the wall and leaned in. He brushed kisses down her neck, and a flurry of tingles traveled down her spine.

"You do smell sweet." He dipped his nose against her throat, then tickled the shell of her ear with the tip of his tongue. The tingles exploded into vibrations that shot right through her middle and pooled in her core, then zipped right back up through her heart.

"Jake?" She could barely speak, with all the magic he created in her body.

"Yeah, baby?"

"I'm willing to let you see right now."

"Right now?" He swirled his tongue just below her ear, then sucked the sensitive skin into his mouth. Her knees buckled, but he caught her and leaned in more to rock his erection against her pelvis. "Are you sure? I'm kind of having fun here."

"I'm sure." She reached down where he strained against the frayed threads of his worn jeans and cupped his erection with her palm. When she gave it a firm squeeze, he moaned. "You game?"

"Fuck yes." He kissed her.

Deep.

Wet.

Hungrily.

He filled his hands with her breasts. "You're so damned beautiful, you take my breath away."

"Maybe you want to see the surprise before you form an opinion." She tore herself away from the heat of his body, stepped back, and let him look while she unzipped her jeans in her best striptease fashion.

The more he watched, the hotter his gaze grew as she revealed the sinful red see-thru lace plunge bra and thong with racy crisscross cutouts she'd bought last week. Just in case. She also left on her red high heels.

"You are full of surprises," he muttered.

"But the question is . . ." She reached out, curled her fingers in the front of his shirt, and yanked him close. "Do you like what you see?"

He didn't bother to respond with a simple yes or no. Jake had always been a man of action. He let her know what he thought by taking her head between his hands and kissing her until she couldn't breathe. His hands were all over her—touching, teasing, caressing. He kissed his way down her neck, stopping here and there to lick, suck, and gently nip. There was heated desperation in his kiss, his touch, his broken breathing.

"I need inside you." He let go of her just long enough to unzip his jeans and push them far enough down his legs to release his erection. Then he grabbed her bottom with both hands and lifted her. "Legs around me. Now."

God. He had her so turned on, she couldn't think. Couldn't do anything but what he asked. She locked her legs around his waist as he pressed her back against the hallway wall. He plunged so deliciously deep inside that he pushed the breath from her lungs, and she gasped.

"You feel so damned good, Annie. When I'm with you, there's nothing else. Just you."

Her heart flipped somersaults as he pressed his

forehead against hers and captured her lips in a hot, possessive kiss that drove her wild. Arching her back, she let him know what she wanted.

And he gave.

Long, slow strokes with passionate kisses and the murmurings of a lover's language. Touches both gentle and rough. Tender and careless.

With each push and pull of his cock inside her body, she drifted a little higher. Reached a little further. Panted a little harder. She encouraged him with words no lady would ever speak and touched him with every ounce of what was in her heart. Faster he plunged and retreated, pushing her toward the edge of the cliff. Then one slight change in motion, one small adjustment in position, and she exploded. Flew over that cliff and took him with her.

Hearts pounding together, Jake wrapped her tight in his arms and leaned all his weight into her. When she climbed down from the top of the roller coaster, she worried that the strain on his injured thigh might have been too much. Then she felt his smile against the bare slope of her shoulder. Felt his gentle laughter against her breasts.

"Are you okay?" she asked, stroking her hands up and down his back.

"No." He chuckled. "Thank God."

"Oh, Jake." She wrapped her arms around him. Wanted to tell him she loved him. But it was too soon.

"Annabelle? Anytime you want to take matters into your own hands, I'd be happy to be at your mercy."

"I'm so glad to hear that." She kissed the center of his chest. "And since you seem to like the red outfit, I can't wait to show you the black."

"You ever decide to show up in one of these lacy things in white? I might have to marry you."

She knew he'd meant it as a joke, even as she wished it wasn't. "Is that a threat or a promise?"

"You can look at it anyway you want." He kissed her again. "As long as you only look at me."

Why would she want to look anywhere else?

"Jake? We didn't use a condom."

"I know. And I'm sorry. So sorry." He kissed her three times quick. "Lack of control. Completely. Tell me you're a hell of a lot more responsible than I am."

"I'm on the pill. I learned my lesson."

"That's good. But just so you know for peace of mind, I've been poked, prodded, and put deep under the U.S. Marine's microscope. And I guarantee I'm cleaner than the window wizard on a sparkling day."

The comparison made no sense, but it made her laugh anyway. "I kind of like that I made you lose control."

"Maybe so. But I want you to know I'd never run out on you." He tilted her chin up, looked her deep into her eyes. "Never."

Nothing in the world could have prepared her for the tidal wave of emotion his words brought. Even greater still was the look of sheer determination on his face when he said them.

"Ditto."

$\mathcal{J}$ake reached across the chaise lounge and took Annie's hand. Above them, a million stars dotted the velvet sky. Between them, the light of one small candle. In front of them, his dream.

"Can you picture it?" he asked, giving her hand a squeeze, needing some kind of reassurance that he wasn't just some crazy dreamer.

"I can. And it's beautiful." She closed her eyes. "I think you have an amazing imagination. And I can't wait to see the results."

He'd spent nearly an hour walking her through every step he'd planned in his mind and on paper. He'd shown her the sketches. For whatever the reason, her approval meant everything to him.

"I don't know anything about decorating the inside of the house," he said, giving her hand a squeeze. "Might have to call Charli in for that. But this . . . this I know."

"I remember you were always building stuff when you were a kid. But the things that always got me the most were the birdhouses you made from the fallen wood you found on the hillsides. The careful details you put into the designs always inspired me."

"To build birdhouses?"

"To become a bird."

He laughed. "They were the only things I could make that didn't turn out to be a competition with the others. Jared was always good at being the peacemaker. I figured one day, he'd go into some kind of philanthropic career though he swore he wanted to be in law enforcement. Reno had the artistic talent. Jesse was the one who shone when it came to caring for the animals. Jackson always got the most attention because he was the one who'd put himself out there the most. For a long time, I didn't know where I fit."

"I never knew that bothered you," she said. "Usually, the baby of the family gets the most attention."

"I never looked for the attention. Just wanted to figure out what it was that got my mind working and my heart spinning."

"And you found that in working with things from nature?"

"I got satisfaction from that. But you . . ."

"Me?"

"Yeah. You." He pulled her close and kissed the tip of her nose. "You make my heart spin."

"Oh, Jake."

"Oh, Jake what?"

"Oh, Jake . . ." She leaned her head on his shoulder. "If I'm not careful, you'll completely steal my heart."

"I'm a bad risk, Annie." Even as he said it, he tightened his arms around her. "You'd be smart to run fast in the opposite direction."

"Maybe." She smoothed her hand in little circles right over his heart. "But I've never been very good at running. Too top-heavy for that."

He chuckled. "I'd pay to see it."

She rolled over on the chaise and ended up on top of him. His dick instantly grew hard. He'd had women, and he'd wanted women. But he'd never wanted a woman as much as he wanted her.

Her hands stroked through his hair as the plump lusciousness of her breasts pushed into his chest. "I ran once . . . all the way to Seattle," she said. "It was a stupid thing to do, and it brought me nothing but heartache. So if you don't mind, I'll stay right here and take my chances."

Relief eased through his veins like slow, melted honey. "Are you sure?"

"Mmm-hmm." She kissed his mouth, slipping her tongue inside and tasting him like he was one of those watermelon candies she favored. "Just tell me one thing."

"What's that?" He smoothed his hands down her back and squeezed her sweet ass.

"What are you running from? I mean . . . I know what happened. And I understand—the best I can. But that day I walked up and you were holding Max and Adeline in your arms, I could tell something was really wrong. And then you rode off and—"

"I know."

"Talk to me, Jake." She kissed him. "It's important that you talk."

He nodded, then rolled them both so they were lying on their sides looking at each other. Annie meant a lot to him. And he knew, eventually he'd have to tell her the truth.

"I'm running from myself, I guess." He glided his hand over her shoulder and down the curve of her waist. He couldn't stop touching her if his life depended on it.

"I can't ever forget the part I played in Eli and the others getting killed or injured. Eli was my best friend. His wife is expecting their first child. Because of me, that child will never know its father. It's guilt at the highest level, Annie. I want to forget. Every damn time I look at those babies, I want to forget, so I can pick them up in my arms and love them. But it's not right. Not right for me to feel that love—that simple pleasure—when Eli is cold in the ground because of me."

"Oh, Jake."

"I made a promise to Eli. A promise that I'd look after Rebecca if anything happened. A promise that I'd make sure she was taken care of." He took a breath and closed his eyes because the pain hit him square in the chest. "I haven't contacted her once since I've been home. Not. Once."

"I'm sure she understands that it's painful for you."

"Doesn't matter. I pussed out. Eli would be so pissed at me right now. But he could never be as pissed at me as I am at myself."

She cupped his face between her hands, leaned in, and kissed him with so much heart that it almost shattered his. "I think you've got it all wrong."

"What do you mean?"

"I don't think you need to forget." Her fingers tenderly stroked his face. "I think you need forgiveness."

$\mathcal{D}$awn broke through a crack in the curtains, and Jake eased his eyes open. The first thing he noticed was the extra warmth in the bed. Then came the sweet scent of the woman curled up next to him, one arm across his chest, one leg thrown over his thigh. That it was his injured thigh didn't matter. The extra weight added comfort. Still, with the effects of helping move all those boxes and furniture yesterday, then the sexual acrobatics he and Annie seemed to favor, it would take him a bit to get moving.

Not that he was in any hurry.

Hank, his usual nighttime partner, had disappeared during the night. Instead of sleeping at the foot of Jake's bed, he kept watch at the foot of the crib.

Rolling to his side, Jake smiled when Annie gave a little sigh, then snuffled right back into his arms. He had to wonder how it would be waking up like this every morning. If it would always be like this. For two people who never seemed to get along, he was surprised to find how well they fit. And right now, with her so warm and enticing, he planned to take advantage.

He slid his hand down the curve of her waist and hip, then back up to cup the plump weight of her breast. He leaned in and placed featherlight kisses over the slope of her smooth shoulder. He teased the peak of her breast with a swirl of his tongue, then drew the puckered flesh into his mouth. A long moan hummed in her throat. When he looked up, she was smiling. He took one last lick and kissed his way back up to her neck before he rolled her beneath him.

"Mmmm. I hope you're not going to stop there."

He chuckled. "Not unless someone breaks through the door with a shotgun."

"There's one over the front door, but I can't think of a single soul who'd be brave enough to interrupt." She slid her hand between them, curled her fingers around his erection, and gave him a long stroke with such perfect pressure it nearly crossed his eyes. Then she guided him to her slick, moist entrance, and he pushed inside.

For thirty-one years, he'd woken alone in a bed, except for the times he and his brothers would watch a horror flick that left them all too scared to sleep alone, and they'd pile up in the middle of the living room floor. Or the times after Reno came to live with them, and he'd have a nightmare. They'd all pile up together in the middle of the bedroom floor. Jake had slept in women's beds, but he'd never woken up with one in his arms come morning.

Annie was his first.

In many ways.

Unlike last night's frantic mating, he made love to her sweet and slow. And when they came together, he knew he'd probably look far and wide before he found anything or anyone to compare.

They'd barely finished when Max began to stir in the bedroom next door.

Annie chuckled. "Right on cue."

"He an early-morning riser?"

She nodded. "He's only just started to sleep until the sun comes up. Before that, he was as nocturnal as a bat."

"Mamamamama."

"Annnnd . . . there's the clincher." She pushed the covers off her legs to go to her son.

Jake pushed the covers back over her legs and got out of bed. "I'll get him."

The look on Annie's face was priceless. "Are you sure? Last night you—"

"Last night made everything different." He pulled on his jeans and leaned in for a quick kiss. "I'll get him."

"Okay." She leaned back on the pillows.

It felt good that she trusted him.

Now he just had to trust himself.

When he went into the bedroom and turned on the light, Max was obviously surprised to see Jake and not his mommy. Hank was less surprised as he stood up and stretched, then instantly found another spot on the floor to lie. Max stood up in the crib, gripped the rails with his chubby little hands, and gave Jake a smile. He'd been so taken with waking to find Annie in his arms and wondering how that would feel every morning. And now, he wondered how it would feel to be a part of Max's life too. To watch and help him grow. To teach him the things a boy needed to know—like realizing that a good woman didn't just fall into your lap every day.

"Hey, little man. I'll bet you're ready for a diaper change." Inhaling a "you can do this" breath, Jake reached into the crib and lifted Max into his arms. A rush of emotion clogged his chest when Max patted his cheeks and grinned. He cupped the back of the boy's sweaty little head and pressed his cheek against the unruly blond curls. Guilt swarmed him like he'd stepped into a hive of wasps that stung him deep.

He took another breath, felt the beat of Max's little heart, and emotion overwhelmed him in a completely different way.

With Max snuggled in his arms, Jake felt love. And protectiveness. And hope.

"I'm not that experienced with all this," he said to Max. "So bear with me. Okay?"

Max guffawed and eased Jake's pain to a degree. He laid the boy down on the floor and unzipped the diaper bag to pull out a fresh diaper and wipes. Max escaped Jake's single handhold like Houdini. Before he could crawl away, Jake grabbed him and pulled him back. Max giggled. When Jake reached for the bag, Max escaped again. He crawled farther this time and, grinning, looked over his shoulder at Jake. Game on, he seemed to say. Jake laughed, grabbed Max's chunky ankles, and pulled him back again. "So that's the way you want to play this?"

Max chortled.

"Dude, you're messing with a Marine. There's no way you're going to win."

Max slapped his little hands against his belly and continued to laugh, while Jake managed to get the sleepers unzipped and off one foot before he escaped again.

Female amusement came from the doorway. "How's it going, Lieutenant?"

"The target is restless."

"You need some help?"

"Nope. I got this." Jake pushed away the pain and allowed himself to enjoy the fun and games. "I'm all in, Annie."

"I can see that." She crossed the room, leaned down, and kissed the top of his head. "How about while you wrestle with Hulk Hogan, I go wrestle us up something to eat?"

"Sounds good."

She turned to leave the room.

"Hey, Annie?"

"Yeah?"

He looked up, caught her smile, and returned it. "Thanks."

"For?"

"Not giving up on me."

She came back into the room, tucked her hand beneath his chin, and kissed him again. "No problem, Jake. I'm all in too."

Chapter 13

Grocery shopping before a busy lunch shift at Bud's wasn't Annie's preferred way to spend the morning. But after she'd dropped Max off at the sitter's, she had to deal with the Old Mother Hubbard syndrome and admit her cupboards were bare. Normally, she didn't allow things to become so depleted, but for the past two weeks, she and Max had spent more time at Wilder Ranch than her own house. Which worked out just fine for her. Because spending more time with the man she loved and being able to help him put together his house in a fashion that made it feel more like a home than an empty shell was Annie's own version of heaven.

As she pushed the wobbling cart with the wiggly wheel down the pasta and soup aisle of the Touch and Go Market she dodged the oncoming cart of Pauline Purdy. Pauline and her husband Paul owned the T&G. Pauline, in a very 1960s way, had hair that nearly reached to the overhead lights and enough food storage going on beneath her girdle to see her through several winters. In Annie's eyes, Pauline wasn't a nice person. Not just because the woman liked to throw her ample weight around town to try and make everyone feel inferior but because the overly made-up biddy had once falsely accused Abby of having an affair with her husband Paul.

Paul was the other half of his wife. There was plenty of him to go around too. Except at the top of his head. There, one would find a gnarly comb-over that could star in its own *Saturday Night Live* skit. Annie knew that no matter how desperate her sister might have been at any point in her life, she'd never be desperate enough to give Roly-Poly-Paul a roll in the hay. Not even if she'd been starving. Still, he'd never come to her sister's defense when Pauline had fired her. For that, Annie was sorry there was only one grocery store in town where she could shop.

"Why, Annie Morgan." Pauline pressed a hand to the side of her overly lacquered hair. "Imagine seeing you here."

"It's a surprise that I need groceries?"

Pauline's cart was filled to overflowing whereas Annie had to carefully pick and choose after doing price comparisons.

"It was just an expression, dear."

"Was it?"

"I see you're stocking up on diapers. Did you know the most popular brand keeps a baby drier?"

Yes. And the most popular brand cost two dollars more a box. That was two dollars she could use on food for his tummy.

"Thanks, I'll keep that in mind."

"And how is your little one?"

Was it Annie's imagination that the woman's lip lifted in a sneer? And why was Pauline talking to her anyway? On any given day, the woman would tip up her nose and keep walking.

"He's fine." Annie eased her cart by and tried to keep moving.

"Oh. By the way."

Annie rolled her eyes. Nothing good ever came from a *by-the-way*.

"I heard Jana Wilder moved out of her house and is living in sin with that good-looking Mr. Lane now."

"Is that a question? Or are you trying to make a point?"

"Just making note, dear. No need to get in a tiff."

"I don't discuss Jana's life with anyone. If she wants people to know her business, she'll tell them."

"Of course." Pauline waved a hand weighted down with gaudy diamond rings. "I understand. At least she's more secretive than that youngest son of hers."

The hair on the back of Annie's hackles snapped to attention.

"I mean, really," Pruneilla continued. "Both he and that veterinarian brother of his prowl like cats in heat around this town."

And why didn't this beeotch call them by name?

"*Jesse* is a respected member of the community,

a former Marine, and a happily married man. And *Jake* is a military hero. I'm sure they have better things to do than prowl."

"Really? And you know this how?"

"Not that you deserve any kind of explanation." Annie gritted her teeth. "But I know *this* because I know *them*."

"Well, apparently you don't know the youngest very well if you haven't heard that he's knocked up poor Jessica Holt. I don't imagine he'll marry her. Those kinds of men never do the right thing. And the poor thing will surely be kicked out of the church choir for being an unwed mother. Not that I would blame Pastor Jeff for doing so. She'd be a horrible influence to the younger girls."

As an unwed mother herself who'd been abandoned by the father of her child, Annie took offense to the slam. But the mention of Jake, Jessica Holt, and pregnancy in the same sentence rammed a wallop to her gut she hadn't seen coming.

"Who says Jake is the father?" Especially since Jessica wasn't the purest of individuals.

"I overheard her mother talking to Gertie West the other day in the frozen foods aisle."

Instantly, Annie's mouth went dry. And she was pretty sure that was a heart-stopping cramp in the center of her chest.

Several things went through her mind. First, the night she'd turned him away. He'd been primed and ready for action when she'd shoved him out the door. Could he have gone to Jessica to relieve the ache? It wouldn't have been the first time. Or the second. He'd not mentioned Jessica to her, but why would he? What if he'd been getting it from both of them? What if he was really a dog disguised in a Southern gentleman's clothing?

The more she thought, the more her stomach churned.

They'd had sex without a condom. Yes, she was on birth control, so there was no chance to repeat her mistakes, and he'd let her know he was clean. But what if he'd done the same with Jessica? She knew better than most how one *oops* made a baby. Had Jake gotten carried away with Jessica and forgotten a condom? Was Jessica now carrying an *oops*?

Jake had told Annie he'd never run out on her. Maybe he'd told Jessica the same thing. Still, it had been only a few weeks ago. Too soon to know about a pregnancy if Jake was involved. Or was it?

It wasn't old-time rivalry that threw Annie in a tailspin or caused sweat to bead at her hairline, it was the fear that she'd been played for a fool again.

"It's been fascinating talking to you, Mrs. Purdy. But I have to get to work."

"Take care, dear. And please tell your sister hello."

Annie refrained from saying that would be a cold day in hell and pushed her cart farther down the aisle. With each step, Pauline's words rang through her head.

Poor Jessica Holt.

Knocked up.

Jake's the father.

The deep breath Annie took lasted until she got in the checkout line. While she scanned the tabloid headlines and waited for the woman in front of her to be checked out, the conversation started all over again between the woman and the cashier.

"Did you hear about poor Jessica Holt?"

"Shame on that devil Jake Wilder."

Annie looked at the shopping cart she'd just spent half an hour filling. She looked up as the two women continued to gossip about the man she loved. A heavy sigh filled her lungs as she grabbed her purse and walked away, leaving the cart filled and mouths open.

Accomplishment made a man feel good. Great even. Jake pulled open the door to Bud's Diner and laughed, even as Jackson flicked the back of his head like they were twelve-year-old boys. He was looking forward to seeing his girl and devouring a big, juicy Diablo burger. No more meat-loaf sandwiches for him. Annie knew what he liked, what he wanted. And for some crazy-ass reason, that made him feel ten feet tall.

He scanned the restaurant but didn't see her as he and Jackson sat down at their favorite booth.

"So tell me this grandiose plan of yours," his brother said while he leaned against the red vinyl seat and spread both arms along the back.

"I finished the deck over the creek this morning. Tomorrow, I'm starting on building the borders and planter areas."

"Why not build the pool first?"

"Because we're heading into winter. Not that Texas gets freezing cold or anything, but it's not likely to get used until spring. I'd rather put my energy into something I can enjoy now."

Jackson grinned. "Planning on having some wild-ass bachelor parties, are you?"

"No. It's just hard to stop seeing the place through the eyes of the kid who grew up there. Just trying to make the place my own now that Mom's moved out."

"This wouldn't have anything to do with my sister-in-law, would it?"

"Why would you bring up Annie?"

"Because, jackass, you've been looking for her since we walked in."

Jake wished for a cup of coffee, a glass of water, or anything that he could use to divert the discussion.

"So what's going on between you and her?"

Jake shrugged. He and Annie wanted to keep things quiet while they figured it out. But the facts were they'd spent almost every waking moment together for the past couple of weeks. They'd somehow seamlessly meshed their lives together. And though he didn't want to move too fast, he'd allowed himself to sink into the goodness of being with Annie and her little boy.

They felt like a family.

It was only when he was alone that the guilt snuck up and devoured him.

"I don't know," he said to his brother's impatiently tapping fingers. "Probably nothing. We'll see."

"That look in your eye doesn't say it's nothing."

Jake looked around again and finally spied Annie coming out of the kitchen holding a tray filled with tall, frosty milk shakes. They locked eyes. He smiled. She didn't.

"Jake?"

He swung his gaze back to his brother.

"Don't hurt her."

"I wouldn't do that."

"Maybe not intentionally." Jackson shook his head. "But sometimes shit happens. She's a good girl."

He watched her deliver the milk shakes to the corner booth with a smile. "I know that."

"Just be careful."

"Yes, Dad."

Finally, Annie made her way over to their table. He smiled again. And again she failed to return the gesture.

"Coffee?" She tossed the menus in front of them.

"Bad mood?" Jackson asked.

"You have no idea," she said, and away she went, without waiting for them to respond to her question.

Jake looked at Jackson and shrugged. "Must be a busy day."

A minute later, she was back, tossing their napkins and silverware on the table and setting two cups of coffee in front of them. Then away she went again.

"You order coffee?" Jackson asked.

"Nope." Jake opened up a packet of sugar and dumped it in as he watched Annie bustle about the diner—delivering, ordering, and ignoring him.

"Think she's avoiding us?" Jake asked.

"Appears so. She's definitely got a bee in her bonnet about something."

A few minutes later, she dumped his usual order in front of him and the same for Jackson in front of him. Then she scooped up the menus and started to walk away.

"Sugar?" Jackson caught her arm before she ran. "We didn't order yet."

"Well . . . eat it anyway." She spun on the heel of her tennis shoe and headed back to the kitchen.

Jake and Jackson just looked at each other.

"Definitely pissed," Jackson said.

"Ya think?"

A few minutes later, Sarah Randall, Deputy Brady Bennett's girl came to their table to see if they needed any ketchup or mustard.

"Where'd Annie go?" Jake asked.

"I don't know. She came into the back and told Bud she had to leave."

"She's gone?"

"Yep. Burned rubber pulling out of the lot just a minute ago."

A million worries ran through Jake's head. What if there was something wrong with Max? What if she was sick? What if Doug had come back?

He slid from the booth.

"Hey, what about your lunch?" Jackson asked.

"You eat it." As Jake headed toward the door, he heard his brother mutter something about how the damned Wilder men weren't ever able to get things right.

*A*nnie knew better than to walk off the job unless she was dying of some kind of incurable disease. She wasn't that irresponsible. She had a baby to take care of. Rent to pay. A small business to support. Bailing out at the first sign of trouble wasn't her style. But the moment Jake had walked through the door, she knew she couldn't deal with him. Not when her emotions were running on the spin cycle. So she'd scampered like a big coward. Not only had she abandoned her much-needed job but also her much-needed groceries back at the store. Like her sister, she'd let Pauline Purdy get the best of her.

Gossipy old biddy.

The speed limit was twenty-five. She was doing well over that as she headed . . . where? Home? To hide?

Stupid.

She forced herself to take a breath. Then another as she turned off Main Street and onto Highway 46. Maybe she'd just go for a drive to calm down. Then she'd have to pull up her big-girl panties and face the music like a real adult. She drove for miles with no radio for distraction. Only her wickedly racing thoughts kept her company.

Maybe the rumor was true. Maybe Jake had left her house that night and gone to Jessica Holt and gotten her pregnant. But again, that had been only a few weeks ago. So maybe he'd paid Jessica a visit before then. Maybe he'd gone to Jessica the minute he came home. Or maybe the rumor was just vicious gossip. And maybe, instead of torturing herself by trying to guess, she'd be a whole lot better off if she knew the truth.

Did she trust Jake?

Yes.

Did she believe in him?

Absolutely.

Did she love him with all her heart and then some.

Without question.

If all that was true, she had to give him a chance to tell his side of the story. She might not like his answer, but she had to know what she was dealing with. Because it was really hard to believe in the fairy tale when you dove headfirst into hysteria.

At the next pullout, she made a U-turn and headed back toward town, but not before stopping at Howdy's Gas It Up Mart for a giant soda for herself and a box of animal cookies for Max. When she pulled back onto Main Street, a big black truck with an enormous chrome deer guard rode up on her bumper. She snuck a look in the rearview mirror and caught the look on Jake's face. Oh good. He looked mad. What the heck did he have to be mad about?

She swung her eyes back to the road. He honked. She ignored him. As she turned onto Bluebonnet Lane, he honked again. She flipped him the middle finger. His eyes narrowed.

Like it was any other day, and her heart wasn't trying to pound through the wall of her chest, she pulled into her driveway and got out as casually as her wobbling legs allowed. The big black truck pulled in behind her and the door was flung open as she reached her porch.

"What the hell, Annie?"

"Keep your voice down." She stuck the key in the lock. "You don't want Arlene Potter getting herself hurt by falling out the window while she's trying to eavesdrop." Her neighbor was a sweet old lady, but not in the typical fashion. And Annie never forgot that while the woman and her BFF, Gladys Lewis, might look like two innocent senior citizens, they headed up gossip central. And Annie had no desire to become front-page news.

Jake was up on the porch beside her in a few long strides, glaring at her as if she'd kicked his dog. "What's wrong?" he asked, as she pushed open the door. He followed her inside. "Is Max okay? Are you sick?"

"He's fine. I'm fine. Everybody's fine."

"You don't sound fine. You sound, look, and are acting pissed off."

Tossing her keys and purse on the table by the door, Annie walked into the living room, untied her Bud's Diner apron, and tossed it on a chair. Then she propped her hands on her hips, took a breath, and turned.

Time to meet the issue head-on.

"Did you know Jessica Holt is pregnant?"

"How would I know that?" His hands went to his hips in a mirror of her defensive stance.

"She hasn't called you?"

"Why would she call you?"

"You haven't been over to *see* her?"

"When would I have found time or reason to do that?"

Annie gritted her teeth. "Why are you responding to my questions with a question?"

"Why are you asking such weird questions?"

"There you go again!"

He tossed his hands up. "Apparently, you know something that I don't, Annie. So please, feel free to share so we can get on the same page. I've been worried sick since you left the diner in such a hurry. I thought something was wrong with Max. Or you. Now you're hitting me with all these questions about Jessica Holt?"

Annie folded her arms. Shifted her weight to one hip. And watched as realization opened his eyes.

"Shit. You think Jessica is pregnant, and it's mine?"

"That night I turned you away. Did you go to Jessica's afterward?"

"Hell no."

"Have you been with her since we've been . . . together?"

"I'd be offended," he said. "But I suppose I have a track record where she's concerned. So I won't walk over there and smack you upside the head."

"You wouldn't do that anyway."

"Maybe not. But what I will do is this." He crossed the room, grabbed her, and planted a kiss on her lips that made them tingle.

When he lifted his head, she said, "That's not really a form of confirmation or denial."

"No. It's not." He held her by the arms like he

expected her to try and escape. "But it is a way to get you to stop asking stupid questions. And to stop you from thinking of more for just a second."

"If you're not going to answer . . ." She tried to pull away.

"I am. I was just waiting for you to stop seeing red long enough to hear what I have to say. And stop rolling your eyes at me."

"Fine."

"The last time I saw Jessica Holt was when I was home on leave. That was over a year and a half ago. Since I've been back, I have not seen her, and she has not seen me. Naked or otherwise." He tipped her chin up so she had to look at him. "The only woman I've been interested in seeing is *you*. Naked or otherwise."

The boulder moved off the center of her chest, and Annie swallowed her relief.

"I know I'm a big, fucked-up mess," he said. "And you'd be smart to kick my sorry ass out the door right now. But I'm hoping you won't. Because the only time I feel right, like everything might eventually be okay, is when I'm with you. I hate to put that kind of responsibility on your pretty shoulders, but that's the truth of it."

"I'm not kicking your sorry ass out the door."

"I'm glad to hear that." A smile brushed his lips and he kissed her forehead. "Because I'm pretty crazy about you. And Max."

"We're pretty crazy about you too." She hugged him close, held his strong back with the palms of her hands, and laid her head against his broad chest. His heart beat steady beneath her ear. "And I apologize. I shouldn't have gone into a tizzy before I talked to you."

"In a weird way, I understand. God knows none of us Wilder brothers have walked the straight-and-narrow path." His low chuckle tickled her cheek. "So who was trying to fry my bacon?"

"Pauline Purdy."

"Ah. Guess I'll have to pay a visit to the old T&G and convince her to spew her vile gossip in another direction."

"I wouldn't waste my energy. You'll just give her more ammunition."

"True." He held her tight as they rocked together slowly in the middle of the room. "I'm sorry she upset you."

"Me too. I had to leave my groceries in the cart."

"I'll take you shopping."

"I don't want to go there. I'd rather drive all the way to San Antonio for groceries."

"I'll drive you."

She chuckled. "Stop being so amenable."

"I just don't like seeing you upset."

Two minutes in his arms took away all her anger, her worry, and her doubt. "You know what *wouldn't* make me upset?" she asked.

"What's that?"

"If you decided to take all your clothes off."

"And what would you do with me then?"

She pulled back and smiled up at him. "Anything I wanted?"

"Hmmm." He kissed her forehead. "We all good here now?"

"Mmm-hmmm."

"Sweet." He flashed her that famous Wilder grin. "Then how about you take off that hot little skirt, we go upstairs, and I let you lose count?"

"Of?"

He picked her up, tossed her over his shoulder, and carried her upstairs. There he tossed her on the bed. "Of how many times you say 'Oh, Jake, please do that again.'"

Laughter tickled her chest as he leaned forward, shoved his hands up her thighs beneath the skirt, and grabbed hold of her underwear. "Jake, don't tear—"

"Oops." He laughed as he pulled the torn undies off. "Too late. And look," he said, holding up the plain cotton French cuts. "They're the industrial kind this time."

"You really don't expect me to wear a thong at work under this short skirt, do you?"

"Doesn't matter." He stuck the panties in the back pocket of his jeans. "I picture you naked under there anyway."

"Are you starting a collection with those, or what?"

"Or what." He began to unbuckle his belt. "How about we add mine to the stash?"

Of course, everyone knew it was nearly impossible to tear a pair of black stretchy boxer briefs with your bare hands. So all Annie managed to do was tear them off his magnificent body.

The rest, as they say, was history.

Chapter 14

Late afternoon burned hot in the sky as Jake rolled up to the house and parked by the barn. The first thing he noticed was his mother sitting in the red rocker on the front veranda, holding a cardboard box. The second thing he noticed was Miss Giddy and her kid playing on the grass beneath the shade of the largest oak tree next to the barn. Hank was in attendance and refereeing the festivities with a bark whenever the kid bounced out of line.

Jake got out of his truck and walked over to the melee to give them all a little attention. For his efforts, he received a tail wag by Hank, a bleat by Miss Giddy, and a misguided head butt to the leg by the little kid, which toppled her onto the grass. She popped up and hopped across the lawn. Then she was back with another head butt to his leg.

Jake chuckled, still feeling good from his afternoon spent in Annie's arms. "Better learn your strength before you pick on someone bigger than you."

"She'll learn. But at this point, even Wee Man can take her down," his mother called from the porch. "Won't be long before she'll have him on the run."

Allison's Jack Russell terrier had springs on his feet and could take anything smaller than a rabbit down with one hop.

Jake helped the little kid to her hooves.

"You need to name her."

"Me?" Jake laughed, watching the baby goat hop around Hank. "She's your goat."

"That's questionable."

"Well, based on watching her right now, I think I have the perfect name for her."

"And that is?"

"Popcorn."

The baby goat hopped in a circle around Hank again.

"Perfect." His mother chuckled her approval.

"It fits."

"Indeed it does."

Jake gave Popcorn, Hank, and Miss Giddy pats on their heads before he joined his mother on the veranda. "How come you're sitting out here?"

"I was waiting for you to get home."

"You could have waited inside."

She looked up at him. "This is your house now, son. In fact, I want you to get the locks changed so your brothers don't charge in on you at inopportune moments."

"The locks changed? That's pretty harsh. Why can't I just tell them to stay the hell out?"

"Really?" She gave him a look. "You think that will work?"

"No."

"Then get the locks changed."

"I don't want to keep *you* out. Just in case."

She stood and set the box in his hands.

"What's in here?"

"Miss Giddy's ribbons. It's your turn to keep her in style."

"Mom. I'm not playing dress-up with a goat."

Playfully, she smacked his arm. "Oh, don't be such a Mr. Stuffypants. You'll hurt her feelings if you don't dress her up. And I promise I won't tell anyone you're doing it."

"You know, if the brothers ever find out, I'll never live it down."

She held up two fingers and made an X across her heart.

"Okay," he said. "But if you spill the beans, I'm dressing that goat in camo."

"I won't tell." She laughed. "And don't worry, there won't be any *just in case*."

He cocked his head, not for the first time losing the train of her thoughts. "What?"

"There's no worry about me needing to move back in," she clarified. "Martin and I are doing great. We really do love each other. And we're looking forward to the next chapter in our lives. Together. So don't you worry."

"I do worry, Mom. And you can't stop me."

Melancholy shadowed her face. "You know, I remember when you were a little boy. You'd run around making sure everything was going okay.

Especially when your brothers would get into a big wrestling match. Your daddy and I used to call you the worrywart."

"Nice to be related to a skin fungus."

A bark of laughter danced between them. "You know what I mean. Which is why, I guess, I'm never surprised when you take such a big weight onto your shoulders."

"They're pretty broad. So I don't mind."

"I'm glad you've found someone to share a little of that burden with."

"There you go being all mysterious and assuming again."

"Mmmhmm. Well, this mother's got great eyesight even if you and your brothers did manage to pull one over on me once in a while. And I know when I see you smiling like you were when you pulled up in your truck just now, there's a reason behind it."

"You're imagining things."

"And does this *thing* happen to have beautiful blond hair, stand about five-foot-four, and have a darling little boy named Max?"

"Maybe."

"I'll take maybe." She reached up and patted his cheek. "Especially when you have lipstick on the side of your neck."

His hand shot to the telltale sign of where he'd spent the afternoon. His mother's hand stopped him.

"Leave it," she said. "It looks good on you."

"You sure you don't have eyes in the back of your head?"

"I have eyes everywhere, son. But just so you know, it helps when your brother calls to fink you out."

He laughed. "I'd kill him, but then I'd have no one to beat up."

"So the cat's pretty much out of the bag about you and Annie. No use hiding things now."

"I really wasn't sure until now."

"What changed?"

"Among other things, she got jealous."

"Of?"

"Pauline Purdy told her that Jessica Holt is pregnant and that I'm the father."

"Are you?"

His head went back. "Hell no."

"How can you be sure?"

"Because I haven't been within a mile of her since I came home. Because as soon as I came home, I noticed Annie. And for me, that's it. That's all there is. It's Annie. And Max."

"They do come as a package deal."

"Yeah. And I'm glad." Jake inhaled the realization. "He's a great little kid."

"She's an awesome mom."

He couldn't have stopped the grin that spread across his face if he tried. "She's all that and more."

"Are you in love, son?"

"I've never been before, so I'm not sure." He lifted his shoulders. "How do you know?"

"Most folks would tell you it's when your heart beats fast and you can't wait to see that person again. But it's more."

"Well, spill it, Yoda."

She laughed. When she sat back down in the red rocker, he knew it was going to be a long conversation, so he joined her, choosing the blue rocker and setting the box of ribbons down.

"It's when being with that person is the best part of your day," she said. "When they're the first person you think about when you wake up and the last person you think of at the end of the day."

He definitely thought about Annie at the end of the day. Thinking of her was the only way he could forget about the bad stuff enough to get to sleep.

"It's when you make their needs a priority over your own."

He was pretty sure his mom didn't mean *those* needs. But he was definitely seeing himself starting to do that with Annie. And Max. Letting himself get attached to her little boy when his heart was so guarded was a huge step for him. A good step.

"It's when you love their imperfections." Her chuckle sent a wave of tenderness though his heart. "I know you boys have always idolized your dad, and I'm glad of that. But he was as flawed as anyone else. He snored loud, his feet stunk after a long day, and he tended to grumble when he woke up in the mornings. And I loved every loud, stinky, grumbly moment with him."

Jake shook his head. "Annie likes to argue."

"So do you." She nudged him with her elbow. "But then there's all the goodness of making up, right?"

"So far." He leaned back. His mom was batting

a thousand with the way he felt. "How else do you know?"

"Well . . . I'd say that they make you a better person and that your feelings for them are unconditional."

"Annie drives me crazy, but she still makes me smile."

"Oh, then you've got it bad."

"You think?"

She nodded, but her big blond hairdo barely stirred. "Are you thinking long-term?"

Yes. He shrugged. "Maybe."

"Can you talk to her easier than anyone else?"

"Most of the time." When he wasn't trying to tear off her pretty little panties.

"Well, that all sounds real good as long as you remember something."

"I'm afraid to ask."

"I'm not offended that you are." Her smile turned nostalgic. "Remember that life has its ups and downs. You'll have perfect days and days you don't want to lift the covers off your head. You'll have arguments that will make your head spin and making up that will heal your heart. Just always remember to be the man she wants to wake up next to forever. Not just the man she wants to sleep with for a night."

"That makes sense. But I've got a whole lot of—"

"Healing inside to do first?"

He nodded.

"Don't you worry, sugarplum." She reached across and gave his hand a motherly pat. "There's an old Sinatra song that puts things in perspective."

"What's that?"

"The best is yet to come."

Morning came with a cold snap, and Jake woke early to take advantage. The deck he'd built over the creek offered a special place to sit near the cool running water. But he'd decided the platform looked unfinished, so he chose to add a pergola and a small copper fire bowl filled with blue fire glass. The fire reflection on the water would give a special effect and add a little extra enjoyment. He'd just have to watch Max carefully because the little boy's favorite thing to do was stuff objects into his mouth that didn't belong there.

He knew he was putting a lot of features into the backyard that might strike fear in Max's sexy mommy. But Jake had it figured out. Anything with any element of danger would be fenced off with wrought-iron, heavy-duty latches, and locks. No sense taking chances. Max had a pretty good grip on his heart—just like his mama. And that suited Jake just fine.

Beside him, Hank gave a wide yawn.

"Yeah. I know. Who'd have ever imagined I'd be thinking along these lines? Ever."

Hank responded with a groan before he stretched all four paws and laid his head down. Jake guessed all of that was dog talk for, "Yeah, who'da thunk it."

He stopped drilling the posts briefly to sip his coffee and enjoy the crisp, clear morning. In the distance, he heard the honk of a car horn. A signal the mailman was dropping off either a load of bills or the latest wad of junk mail. Jake carried his travel mug with him to the front of the house. For years, the mail had been delivered to a box out on the main road. About ten years ago, his mother had made a deal with the devil to get the post office to deliver directly to the house and not out on the main road. Quite an accomplishment on her part.

He gave a wave to the departing mail truck and pulled open the hatch on the big metal box.

Discount pizza coupons. A new local window-washing business announcement. A catalog for the New Braunfels Smokehouse. And a letter from the Headquarters of the United States Marine Corps.

The temptation to rip open the envelope was huge. But Jake refrained. He hadn't achieved the status of lieutenant in the Marines by jumping at the first indication of his blood speeding through his veins. Then again, he'd been stripped of the lieutenant status and callously removed from the Marines owing to his ineffective leadership. They could blame it on his injury all day long, but he knew the truth. He'd heal.

They just didn't want him anymore.

He shoved the envelope into his jeans pocket and continued toward the backyard, focusing instead on the five-dollar-off pizza coupons.

Anything the military had to say to him could wait.

Bud's Diner had been busier than usual with city-council meetings, garden-diva coffee klatches, and an impromptu assembly of the PTA at the corner table. Annie stuck her hand in the pocket of her apron as she walked toward Jake's front door. Fortunately for her, whenever large groups gathered and consumed copious amounts of caffeine, they were usually generous tippers. She wrapped her fingers around the wad of bills. Their generosity had just afforded her the ability to buy the cute little push buggy for Max. His love of cars was already apparent, and since the buggy looked like a little blue sports car, she knew he'd be thrilled.

Knocking on the front door, she was greeted on the veranda by Miss Giddy and Popcorn. The usual formalities were exchanged, but Annie couldn't help pick up the cute baby goat and give it a nose nuzzle. Growing up, she'd never had pets. Her parents hadn't allowed it. Her sister was making up for lost time taking in strays and neglected pets to her rescue center. And Annie hoped that one day she could give Max the kitten or puppy of his dreams. Maybe even two or three. In the meantime, the baby-goat nuzzle would have to do.

When no one answered the door, Annie looked around. Jake's truck was parked near the barn, so he must be home. At that moment, Hank skidded around the corner of the house and barked in a "Hey, how's it going, what's up, good to see you," tail-wagging way. And then he took off back from where he'd come. Annie followed. Wherever Jake was, Hank was never far behind.

The goats followed her to the back of the house, where she saw Jake in the distance, shirt off, muscled, tanned skin gleaming with sweat beneath the sunshine. Tight, thick muscles flexed, and she had to take a breath to still her racing heart. The man was magnificent—clothed or not.

Especially not.

She watched as he cautiously climbed up the ladder and set the huge piece of lumber in place, then screwed it into the posts. When he came down the ladder, she made her presence known.

After all, that climbing up and down had to be making his leg ache. Maybe he needed a break. "That's looking really beautiful."

He turned, and his face lit up with pleasure. "I'd tell you to get over here for a hug but I'm all sweaty and stinky."

"Oooh." She grinned and headed his way. "I love sweaty and stinky." When she wrapped her arms around him, she discovered that indeed he was. But that didn't stop her. Didn't stop her from kissing him either even though he had sweaty streaks of dirt across his face.

"You've been working hard," she said.

"Just trying to keep out of trouble." He reached into the ice chest, pulled out a bottle of water, and guzzled it about half-empty.

"I think it will take more than building a patio to keep you free and clear. But if you insist on pushing the envelope, I can put Max to bed early tonight."

"I'd be happy to take you up on that offer." He leaned in, gave her a quick, salty kiss, then picked up the plans and construction dimensions he'd sketched out.

When he leaned over, she tore her gaze away

from his delicious muscles and noticed the paper sticking out of his back pocket.

"Speaking of envelopes, whatcha got going there in your back pocket?"

"A letter from the Marines."

She squinted against the sun and noticed the immediate frown on his face. "What's it say?"

"Don't know." His broad, bare shoulders lifted. "Haven't looked."

"But you've been carrying it in your back pocket all day?"

"Yep."

"What if it's important?"

"They said everything they had to say to me when they gave me my discharge papers."

"Jake"— she laid a hand on his back—"you were injured."

"But I'm better now." He stood up straight as if to prove it. "Look at me. I'm climbing ladders, riding horses, and carrying my girl up the stairs. There's no reason I couldn't have fulfilled the rest of my contract."

"So you feel like they kicked you to the curb because you took a bullet to the thigh, and you still had more to offer?"

"Yes."

"And you'd rather have left on your own terms."

"Yes."

A breath pushed from her lungs. She didn't quite know how to deal with this. She'd never had to face such a sensitive subject. She knew Jake had his pride, and it had been damaged. But the truth of the matter was she was glad they'd given him an honorable discharge. His oldest brother had been killed in action. Jake had taken a bullet that nearly killed him when it barely missed his femoral artery.

She was done with the damn war.

All she wanted was for those she loved to be safe at night.

Yet she knew if she said those exact words to Jake, he'd tell her that's exactly why he and his brothers had fought. To keep their loved ones safe. The men and women of the military never ceased to amaze her. She respected them, and honored them, and prayed for their safety. But she was still glad Jake was home.

So . . . how to handle a man with wounded pride and a heart burdened with guilt?

"Stop stalling," she said.

"I'm not stalling."

"Okay." She held out her hand. "Then give it to me to read. Because I'm curious as hell."

He pulled it from his pocket and slapped it into the palm of her hand.

Carefully, she slid her thumb under the flap and removed the paper. The seal at the corner of the document was the sign of an important correspondence. "Do you want me to read it out loud?"

"No."

She sighed. When she read the words a chill ran up her back. "Jake?"

"What?" He'd turned back to his work as if a letter from the branch of the military he'd respected and dedicated years of his life to meant nothing.

"This says this is a second attempt to contact you regarding awarding you the Purple Heart."

His eyes narrowed. "Not interested."

No hesitation in his response whatsoever. No anger either. Just an indifferent response that held no emotion.

"What do you mean *not interested*?"

"I mean I don't want it.

"You can't say no."

"I just did." He picked up a wooden post and began measuring.

"Jake."

"Annie." He exhaled a frustrated breath of air, and from where she stood, she could see every muscle in his neck and shoulders tense.

"This is an honor." She held up the paper and rattled it to make her point.

"For who? I got shot. Big fucking deal. I got shot because I was stupid. What about Eli? What about my brother? Jared has been dead for years. Where's his fucking medal? I got a bullet in my leg. He died. Eli died. I deserve nothing. They're the heroes. Purple Heart, Silver Star, Medal of Honor, they deserve it all."

"But—"

"Annie? I could never, with a clean conscience, accept an award for something I don't deserve. Especially when those who do deserve it have been forgotten." He turned back to the post and slammed it onto the table saw.

"Is that the end of this discussion?" she asked.

"Not much else to say."

She stood there and watched him work. Tears

filled her heart, but she refused to let them fall from her eyes. She had to be strong. She had to say what needed to be said, regardless of the outcome.

"Jake?"

A hard breath of frustration pushed from his lungs before he turned to look at her.

"You may not think what you did was heroic. Your mother does. Your brothers do. And I do. I admire you. And I love you. But you have got to find that forgiveness you so desperately need. Whether it comes from yourself, or Eli's wife, or somewhere else. It's impossible for you to move on with your life if you keep going like you are."

A long silence floated between them. In that moment, an entire spectrum of emotions crossed his face. His jaw clenched and unclenched. And because his chest was bare, she could see the hard pulse of his heart.

"If what you say is true," he said, "that you love me . . . you'll understand."

"Oh, Jake." The tears finally fell. "I do love you. And I understand as much as I possibly can. But this isn't about me understanding. This is about your life. You keep taking two steps forward and one step back. Baby, for your own good, you need to keep moving forward."

"I can't." He shook his head. "I just . . . can't."

She moved to where he stood with his gloved hands fisted and his broken heart laid bare. "You have to figure this out. Trying to push it back isn't working." She touched his face. Kissed his lips. Then turned away. Simply because there wasn't anything more she could say or do.

"Annie?"

The desperation in his voice caused her to stop and turn.

"Do you think I should go see Eli's wife and family? Maybe the families of the others who died and were injured too?"

"Whatever it is you promised your friend you would do, you need to make that happen. For your own sake, you need to go wherever your heart takes you, so you can find a way to heal." Annie gave him her bravest smile. "As for me? I'm not going anywhere. When you come back, I'll be right here waiting for you."

Leaving her heart behind, she walked away, leaving him to figure things out. The old saying that you could lead a horse to water but you couldn't make him drink was true. Jake was stubborn. And he was broken. If there was a chance for him to ever find happiness, he had to face his demons head-on.

Grief was such an individual process. Annie had suffered loss in her lifetime. Not always from a death. She'd lost the love of her parents although she and Abby were never sure they'd had it in the first place. She'd lost the man who'd fathered her little boy, a man she thought she'd loved. Loss could take its toll on a person.

There was no right way to grieve, just as there was no way to anticipate exactly how the feelings of sadness, anger, and loss would be resolved. From what she'd lived through in her own life, the process could be like a roller-coaster ride with extreme highs and tremendous lows.

Jake was a perfect example of the effects of that rough ride. One part of him thought he had to be tough and never show his fear. Another part of him seemed to want to crawl up in a ball and cease to exist.

A good cry always made her feel better. But she knew Jake would see tears as a sign of weakness. In her mind, a man who allowed his tears to fall was far stronger than someone trying to fake it in order to hold it all together. Right now, Jake was walking on the thin edge of a blade that one day would cut him deep if he didn't get off.

And if he wouldn't cry for himself, she'd do it for him.

Jake watched Annie walk away.

Because he had to. He had to force himself to watch the possibility of losing the very best thing in his life. He pressed a hand to his chest, but it didn't relieve the ache.

As she got farther and farther away, the emptiness overwhelmed him. He'd been trying to get lost in the present, but the past kept catching up with him. The tragedy had taken place not that long ago. Only a few months actually. He'd barely had time to catch his breath with all that had happened since they'd flown his bleeding body and that of his brothers in arms out of that sandpit of hell. He could still taste the dirt in his mouth as he'd hit the ground. Could still smell the blood and smoke. Could still hear the repeat of rapid gunfire.

The shouts. The profanities that tore through the air when they'd come under attack.

In his mind, he could still see every movement made.

Except his own.

He could hear every voice.

Except his own.

He'd failed because he'd tried to get them to safety, and he'd done just the opposite. He'd ordered them straight into danger. The minute details of the mission began to get foggier with each passing day. All that remained was the gritty truth.

He wasn't just devastated, he was angry.

Perhaps this might be the first time he realized that.

In the beginning, everything happened so fast there hadn't been time to think other than to get his men the hell out of there. Then there was the injury, the recovery process, the inquest into the incident, the funerals he'd missed, the injured troops who'd been taken to other areas for treatment. None of them had spoken since that day.

Why?

Maybe if they'd all bonded together, they could have avoided the aftermath that bred anger, confusion, guilt, and loneliness. But maybe not. Everyone had to deal with things their own way. He was the perfect pathetic example of *not* dealing.

He sat down on the edge of the deck as Annie disappeared around the corner of the house. Hank laid down next to him and settled his big black head on Jake's thigh.

"She said she loves me."

Hank looked up with his big, brown, under-standing eyes and whined.

"She deserves better."

Apparently, Hank took offense to that. He jumped up and began to bark and growl at Jake like he completely disagreed. He pawed at Jake's leg, then reared back and pushed at Jake's chest with both front paws and such force he knocked Jake back to the deck. The sun blinded him as Hank jumped on top of him and lay down, set-tling his front legs on Jake's chest and giving Jake a canine version of the stink-eye.

If his heart didn't ache so damn bad, Jake would have laughed. Instead, he laid his head back on the smooth wood deck and looked up at the blue sky and vibrant treetops. He inhaled a long breath of clean air as Hank settled his moist nose beneath Jake's chin.

"If I don't do something—if I don't figure it out—she won't love me for long." He stroked Hank's head again and was rewarded with another low growl. "I know, buddy. I can't let that happen."

Maybe like with alcoholism and drug addiction, the first sign of healing was realizing you had a problem.

He'd been through enough battles to know you had to go through it to get to the other side. So before he started sounding too much like a girl, he had to get this shit figured out.

He blinked against the bright sunlight.

He was ready.

Whatever it took.

He was ready to fulfill his duty and keep the promise he'd made to his fallen brother, then pull himself back together.

He was ready.

Chapter 15

Visiting Jana at Martin Lane's house instead of Wilder Ranch seemed strange. But two days after she'd left Jake wallowing in his guilt, that's where Annie headed. In her hand, she had a list of names and numbers. In her heart, she bore determination.

He'd called her before he and Hank drove out of town in his big black truck to say good-bye. He'd made arrangements with the brothers to feed the cattle and Miss Giddy, but he'd decided to take his four-legged best friend for company on the long drive to Arizona. She'd wished him the best and asked him to drive carefully, but she'd stopped short at telling him she loved him again. Not because he hadn't returned the sentiment but because she felt he didn't need any added pressure to do so. If he loved her, he'd realize that, and he'd say it in his own good time. If he didn't love her, she wouldn't regret letting him know how she felt. She'd hidden it for way too long. And no matter what happened down this rocky road, she'd always love him.

After Annie parked her car in Martin and Jana's driveway, she heard Frank Sinatra music and laughter floating out from the house. Maybe she should have called first. Who knew what the soon-to-be-marrieds were up to. Knowing the business at hand was important, she knocked on the door anyway.

"Sugarplum!" Jana opened the screen door and pulled her into a hug. "What a surprise to see you. Come on in."

Annie followed her inside the ranch-style home and immediately saw that Jana had been putting her own stamp on the interior. Both Jana and Martin wore paint-splattered clothes and broad smiles. The walls in the living room had a fresh coat of khaki-tinted paint, and the furniture was covered with drop cloths.

"I'm sorry to interrupt. I know I should have called first, but . . ."

"Nonsense. I can see you've got worried all over your pretty face," Martin said. "How about I go make us a fresh pot of coffee and we all sit down at the kitchen table. Unless this is private?"

"There's no such thing." Jana waved a hand at her fiancé. "You've got a ring on my finger, so that makes you a big part of whatever mess we get ourselves into. Unless you're planning on running."

"In for a dollar." Martin laughed and kissed the top of Jana's head. "I'll go get the coffee started." He disappeared into the kitchen, and Annie took a deep breath of, unfortunately, paint fumes.

"I hope Jake called you and let you know he was going out of town," she said.

"He did." Jana nodded. "Though he didn't fill me in on the specifics. Just said not to worry. And you know, when a child says that, a parent worries."

"Luckily, those days are way ahead of me." Annie fidgeted with the papers in her hand. "I know you've figured out that Jake and I have been getting . . . closer lately."

"I figured." Jana gave her hand a squeeze. "So try not to look like I'm about to take a bite out of you. I couldn't be happier that you two finally figured out what most of us have seen coming for a long time."

"A long time? Wish I'd have known that. Maybe I could have saved myself some sleepless nights." Annie sighed. "I'm not going to beat around the bush. I love him, Jana. I've always loved him. Even when there were times I wanted to rip him to shreds because of his sheer orneriness or his stubbornness. But right now I don't think he's telling you the whole story. And I think you need to know. Plus, I need your help."

"Just tell me what you need, sugarplum."

Martin poked his head out of the kitchen. "Coffee's on."

"How about we go sit down. Looks like you've got a lot to say."

"I do." She followed Jana into the kitchen, which was in as much disarray as the rest of the house. Martin had cleared a space on the table, and they all sat down. "Jake will probably fry me in oil when he finds out I've come to you, but I can't do this on my own."

"Do I need to call in the troops?"

Annie nodded. "You might."

For the next few minutes, Annie explained why Jake was headed to Arizona. She showed Jana the notification letter she'd taken with her when she left his house that day. And though she didn't have the right to take such an important correspondence, she'd feared he'd only have destroyed it out of misplaced anger. He hadn't asked for it back, and she figured the names and numbers would help her mission.

For two days, she'd struggled with the decision of whether to intervene or not. But the overwhelming love in her heart pointed her in Jana's direction.

"Oh, that rascal." Jana smoothed her thumb over the letter. "I knew he'd gotten the first notice that the Marines planned to give him the Purple Heart. He didn't say much after he got the letter, so I thought he contacted them. The award is a done deal. The Marines just want to know a date, time, and place they can present it to him. I had no idea he'd refused because Jared hadn't received his awards."

She smoothed her hands down her paint-splattered blouse. "I wish that boy would have shared more with me. I received a letter from the military some time ago about Jared's honors. I hadn't responded either. Looks like my boy and I are two of a kind."

"Miscommunications are common." Annie

could swear someone lifted a Mack truck off her shoulders. "Especially when you're dealing with something of this nature."

"Ain't that the truth." Jana patted Martin's hand when it slipped over the top of her shoulder. "I'm so glad Jake has you. And that you understand each other's needs. That's the way it should be between couples. You share the good, the bad, and the ugly. And you just pray for a good resolution when times get tough. So let's get moving on this. I'll make some calls to the officials, and we'll make this happen. Knowing Jared will receive his awards too should make Jake happy."

A river of positive energy flowed through Annie's blood. Coming to Jana had been the right thing to do. And since she was his next of kin, she was the one who could make things happen.

By the time Annie went to bed that night, she lay there alone, thinking of Jake, and hoping he would find a way to ease his torment. After what he'd been through, no one deserved to carry so much guilt and pain when all they'd been trying to do was the right thing. Jake certainly had his faults, but he was one of the most honorable men she'd ever known. And even while he struggled, she knew there was no way she'd give up on him.

Not now.

Not ever.

For ten minutes, Jake sat in front of the typical subdivision house on a typical street in Yuma, Arizona. The tan house matched the xeriscaped yard and the cactus accents. The sky above was a hazy blue and the weather unusually cool for the desert community.

Realizing he might possibly go inside the house, he wondered about leaving Hank in the truck with the windows down. But the Lab gave him a look of promise that he'd be good and not take off after the first cat that might cross his path. Still, that wasn't what kept Jake belted in behind the steering wheel. It seemed the manners he'd been raised with had vanished. Walking up unannounced and unexpected to someone's door was discourteous. Walking up to the door of someone you knew would most likely not be happy to see you went beyond impolite.

Not to mention it was scary as hell.

He double-checked the address even though he knew he was in front of the right house because there was a homey little sign that read HARRIS. He took a breath, grabbed the keys from the ignition, and opened the truck door. As he closed it, he said to Hank, "Might be back in two seconds if Rebecca slams the door in my face."

Hank gave him another one of his all-knowing, growly dog barks.

Jake briskly rubbed the top of the Hank's head through the open window. "You think you know so much." He strode to the front door and rang the bell.

It wasn't Eli's wife who answered. Instead, a woman with the same electric shade of red hair but in an older version stood in the doorway.

"Can I help you?"

"I'm looking for Rebecca Harris."

A roadblock of frown lines crossed the woman's forehead. "And you are?"

"Jake Wilder. From Texas."

He waited for the door to slam.

It didn't.

"Lieutenant Wilder?"

"Former lieutenant, ma'am."

"I'm so sorry, Mr. Wilder. Rebecca's not here right now."

"Do you know when she'll be back?"

"I'm afraid not for some time. She's staying at a hotel near Yuma Regional."

The woman immediately understood that he didn't know why Rebecca would be at the hospital. From what he remembered, her baby wasn't due for another month or so.

"I'm her mother." She extended her hand and they shook. "The baby was born premature. He's in NICU. Our family got her a room so she could at least get a shower and a few hours of sleep between sitting and worrying. In fact, I'm headed that way soon to temporarily relieve her of worry duty."

Eli's son had been born premature.

He was fighting for his life.

Jake's heart cramped, stole his breath, and draped him with guilt.

Everyone knew high levels of stress could cause a premature birth. Having your husband shot and killed, leaving you alone to plan a funeral, and figure out how to wake up every day without feeling like your world has ended was the ultimate trauma.

"Do you think she'd mind if I stopped by to see her?"

For a moment, the woman's green eyes searched his face. During this tedious process, she kept tight-lipped. Jake envisioned a forthcoming rejection.

Then she surprised him.

"Actually, I think that might be a good idea. You were close to Eli."

"Yes ma'am. Outside of my brothers, he was my best friend."

"Then I think she might like to talk to you. This has all been very difficult for her."

"She isn't alone in that, ma'am. Which is why I'd like to talk with her." At last.

In his heart, Jake knew the conversation with Rebecca could go two ways. She could rip him for letting her husband get killed, or she could forgive him for letting her husband get killed.

Though Annie believed he needed it, he could never ask for her forgiveness. Still, he needed Rebecca and her family to understand how much Eli meant to him. How sorry he was. And that from now on, Jake would be there if they needed anything.

Eli had tried to save another soldier's life. He had died a hero. His family needed to know that. It wouldn't change the outcome, but Eli hadn't even thought twice that day about trying to save someone else's life. He'd just done the right thing. Because that's who he was. He was a damned good man.

"Thank you, ma'am." He waited while she scribbled down the address of the hospital, then accepted the piece of paper. "Just so you know, Eli was not only one of the best soldiers I ever served with, he was one of the best men I ever knew."

"I'm sure he'd be pleased to hear you say that."

"I doubt it." A smile trembled on his lips. "I told him that plenty of times. Next thing I knew, he'd have me in a headlock."

"Well, Eli was quite a spirited young man."

Was.

"Yes, ma'am." He held up the piece of paper. "Thank you." He turned to go.

"Lieutenant?"

He stopped. "It's just Jake now, ma'am."

"If I remember correctly, you also lost your brother in the war."

"Yes, ma'am. My big brother. He was the best of us."

"I'm so sorry for your loss."

"Thank you. And you also."

On the way back to his truck, Jake heard nothing but the pounding of his heart and the rhythm of his boots on the concrete path. When he got inside, he started the engine, kicked the air conditioner on to full blast, and leaned his head back.

"Fuuuuuuuck."

Hank whined and belly-crawled over onto his lap. Stroking the dog's smooth head lowered Jake's blood pressure but did nothing to absolve his guilt. If anything, he felt more now than before he'd knocked on that door.

Eli's son was fighting for his life.

Jesus H. Christ.

With the exceptions of the sounds of beeps and low murmurs, hospitals were notoriously quiet. The halls he walked through now were no different. The pungent scent of cleaners, medicines, and illness clung to the air as he punched the floor number inside the elevator.

An elderly woman next to him with a bouquet of homegrown roses smiled. "Maternity floor. You a new daddy?"

"No ma'am. Just visiting . . . a friend's wife." He eyed the vivid orange and yellow buds wrapped in a holder made from aluminum foil. "Pretty flowers."

"Thank you. I'm on my way to see my husband, George. These are his favorites from the few bushes I've been able to keep alive. We've been married for fifty-eight years. He's leaving me now though. Guess that time comes for all of us."

"I'm sorry, ma'am."

"Me too. I'm gonna miss the old coot." Her expression wavered. "Even gonna miss the way he snores at night and grunts while he's reading the paper. Wouldn't change a minute though. It's been a good fifty-eight years. Even if right now all I feel like is crying."

Jake completely understood.

"What's your friend's name?" the woman asked.

"Rebecca Harris. I served with her husband in the Marines."

"Well, I thank you both for your service."

"I'll pass that along."

Thin gray brows pulled together. "Your friend didn't make it back?"

"No, ma'am."

"Makes your heart hurt real bad. I can tell."

"Yes, ma'am."

"Can you take a bit of advice from a strange old lady?"

He chuckled. Hell, he'd been taking advice from his mother for years. And sometimes it didn't get much stranger than her. "Yes, ma'am."

"Some days you got to dig down deep to push past the trouble life hands us. But if you keep digging long enough, you'll get there. And so will your friend's wife. All you need is a good shovel and some strong determination."

The elevator doors whooshed open, and the woman stepped out. She put her hand on the door so it didn't close too quickly. "Only thing that really keeps us going, young man, is holding on to those memories. The good ones. Keeps them alive." She pulled her hand back and gave him a nod before the doors closed.

Jake leaned back in the empty elevator and sucked in a breath.

The memories of Jared and Eli—of his dad— had been too painful, so he'd pushed them away. It had been the only way he could get up every day and face the world without them.

And then along came Annie.

He didn't know at what moment he'd started to see her in a different light. When she'd stopped being such a pain in the ass and had become the one person he wanted—needed—to see every day.

There were moments when he was wrapped in her arms, buried deep in her body, that he'd forget the ugliness life doled out. She'd had her own share of heartbreak when Doug had left her high and dry and pregnant. And yet she still faced the world head-on. With a smile. And, as the old woman just now had said, with strong determination.

Damned if Annie wasn't a better soldier than he.

He didn't know what would happen if Doug ever changed his mind about wanting Annie and his little boy and decided to show up at her door. Jake didn't know how Annie would react. He also didn't know if he'd punch Doug in the face and let the idiot explain later, or if he'd step back and take a chance that Annie might throw him aside for the father of her baby.

All he knew was, Annie meant everything to him. Without her he'd be lost. Nothing.

Less than nothing.

He loved her, he realized. He loved Max too. And when he got home, he planned to do whatever it took to keep both of them in his life forever.

The elevator opened again on the next floor. He stepped out and headed to the nurses' station. There he found a young woman in a bright pink pair of scrubs with hearts and ribbons on the top. He gave her Rebecca's name and waited while she made a call. Several minutes later, Eli's wife came around the corner. Her red hair was pulled up in a bun, and dark circles dimmed the light in her green eyes.

"Jake?" As she looked up at him, she rubbed her forehead as if she'd forgotten something. And then she hugged him. The gesture was completely un-expected, and it took him back a notch.

"What are you doing here?"

"I needed to talk to you," he said. "I know this is probably a bad time but—"

"No. It's okay."

He scanned the hallway. "Is there somewhere private?"

"Probably. But I'd rather you come meet Elijah."

"Oh. No." He took a physical step back. "I don't think that's a good idea."

"Why not?" Rebecca folded her arms, and he saw that same spark of stubbornness that Annie possessed.

"I know this must be a really hard time for you, and, honestly, I didn't mean to interrupt."

"So you *don't* want to meet Eli's son?"

He knew the darkness that lived in his heart. And so he just spoke the truth. "I don't deserve to meet him."

"God." Rebecca shook her head. "You are so much like Eli. No wonder you were best friends."

Before he could protest, she reached down and took his hand. "What was it the two of you used to say? *No pussies allowed?*" She gave his hand a tug. "Come on, scaredy cat. Elijah's too little to bite."

Jake let her tug him down the hallway until they came to a big glass window. Inside, there were a row of little beds and incubators, rocking chairs, and two nurses in yellow masks and scrubs busily taking care of the three tiny patients in their care. Jake had been in combat—in the direct line of fire—but his heart had never pumped blood through his veins quite this hard before.

"He's too little to hold," Rebecca said, "but I can stroke his arms and back with my finger. It seems to comfort him."

"Which . . ." Jake swallowed, unsure he could do this. "Which one is he?"

"The one in the middle. Do you want to go in? See him up close?"

"No." *Hell no.* He could barely stand seeing the tiny life from this side of the window.

"You do?" Rebecca grabbed his arm and tugged him toward a room past the window. "Wonderful. I know that would make Eli happy."

He really wished people would stop saying that. Eli would *not* be happy with him.

Ever.

He'd gotten the man killed with his badly-thought-out orders.

"Rebecca. I don't think—"

She opened the door and pushed him inside. "Of course they'll have a size to fit you. Don't be silly."

"I don't think you're hearing what I'm trying to say."

"That's because I'm not going to let you say it." She opened a cupboard and pulled out the same kind of paper-thin scrubs and booties she wore, then shoved them in his arms. "Put these on and come meet Eli's son."

"Rebecca?" Unable to meet the seriousness in her eyes, Jake looked down at the bundle of protective clothing. "I came here to say I'm sorry. Although now that I say it, it sounds . . . inadequate."

"Sorry?" Her head tilted slightly.

"It's my fault you're here alone, facing all of this by yourself. I gave the order to move. The move that cost Eli his life. The order that made you a widow and probably sent you into labor early because of the stress. And now you're facing the possibility of losing your son. I know *sorry* doesn't cut it, Rebecca. But I am. And if I could trade places with Eli right now, I would. I swear to God I would."

She stepped back, and he couldn't blame her. He probably looked like a big fucking mess right now because he was shaking. Physically shaking, and he couldn't stop himself. If he was a hard-drinking man, he'd run out of this hospital and drown himself in a bottle. But he wasn't, and he had to face this like a man. Even if he might rattle right out of his boots.

Rebecca looked up at him and her eyes narrowed. "How dare you."

Not what he expected her to say.

Then she gave his chest an angry shove. "How dare you give up when that little boy in there is fighting for every breath, every second that will keep him in this world long enough to survive. He's a fighter. Just like his daddy. Just like *you*, Jake."

"Rebecca, I know you're trying to be nice, because you *are* nice, but—"

"I'm not trying to be anything. As gut-wrenching as it was, Eli's death didn't cause me to go into premature labor. I developed gestational diabetes. It wasn't something I had any control over. I did everything the doctors said. But Elijah was born early. End of story. Just like you didn't plan for your troops to be ambushed. It was something you had no control over, you just had to deal with the situation the best you could. You made a decision in a risky environment that could have gone either way. But when most men would freeze and be unable to know what to do, you trudged forward."

"I made the wrong decision. It got men killed. My best friend died because of my poor assessment of the situation."

"Wrong. Your best friend died because the enemy fired a mortar that blew up right where he was trying to rescue someone else."

Jake's chest constricted so tight he couldn't breathe. Nausea rolled through his stomach, and he could swear his heart might stop at any second. "I don't deserve your empathy."

She reached out and grabbed his arm. "I'm not blaming you for what happened, Jake. So stop blaming yourself. When Eli joined the Marines, I knew what could happen. But I wanted him for as long as I could have him. So don't you give up. Damn it. *You fight.* And you go on and enjoy your life to the fullest. That's what Eli fought for. The right for others to enjoy freedom and a happy life. That's what he would want for you. Just as you would want for him."

Tears rolled down her face. "If you give up now, you'll destroy everything Eli fought for and believed in."

The turmoil in his head and heart made it impossible to think. He felt like he was drowning under the pressure of what had happened that day. Rebecca's words were powerful, but he didn't know if he could ever forgive himself.

"Don't you remember what happened that day, Jake?"

"I remember." The break in his voice did not surprise him.

"I don't think you do. I think you're so focused on the order you gave that you're missing everything else you did." Her fingers tightened around his arm. "I read the report. You risked your own life to pull your men to safety. Repeatedly. Even after you'd been shot. Even after the bullet that tore through you barely missed hitting your femoral artery, you aided those who needed you. War is ugly, Jake. It's unpredictable. But as soldiers, you all knew the chances you were taking every time you put on the uniform. Didn't you?"

He nodded.

"Eli knew too. And if he were here right now, he'd knock you on your ass for blaming yourself. So please . . ." She wrapped her arms around him. "Please don't blame yourself. I know you guys like to think of yourselves as invincible, but you're only human."

The compassion in her embrace allowed the bricks around his heart to tumble down.

"Please forgive yourself, Jake. Because I forgive you. And Eli would too."

And there it was.

The words he needed to hear but couldn't bear to request.

In that closet-sized room, Jake knew that once again, Annie had been right. He'd needed forgiveness. It was just going to take some time to fathom the magnitude of the gesture Rebecca had just bestowed on him.

Could he ever really forgive himself?

Rebecca backed away. "Now, how about you put on those scrubs and come meet Elijah?"

Jake nodded because at the moment he doubted he could speak. He slipped on the protective layer of clothing and followed Rebecca into the NICU. His stomach tightened when her smile blossomed as she looked into the plastic isolette at the fragile life that was her son.

Eli's son.

The baby wore a little blue knit cap on his head. He was hooked up to tubes and lines, and he looked small enough to fit in one of Jake's hands.

Jake swallowed down the frantic thump of his heart.

"This is Elijah Matthew Harris," Rebecca said. "In all ways that mattered, Jake, you were Eli's brother. He loved you. Admired you. And he trusted you. In the end, Eli always made his own decisions. It was his decision to go back after that fallen soldier that day. Not yours. So do your *brother* a favor and say hello to his son."

His heart pounded like it meant to leap from his chest as Rebecca showed him how to reach through the portals in the side of the isolette and touch this tiny life that had been created by one of the best men he'd ever known.

The baby had dark hair like his dad and long fingers and toes. Jake thought of Max and how healthy Annie's little boy was. How big and solid he felt in Jake's arms when he picked him up. He wondered if Eli's little boy would ever be able to put his arms around his mother's neck and hold on while she carried him off to bed. If he'd ever hold those arms up so his mother could lift him and tell him stories of his brave father.

"He's gained almost two pounds," Rebecca said proudly.

Jake gave her a shaky smile. When he placed his finger beneath Elijah's little hand, he finally found his voice. "Hey, little man. I'm a friend of your dad's. He'd sure be happy to see you fighting so hard." Tangled up with emotion, his words caught in his throat. "So you keep gaining weight and keep growing. Don't give up. Okay? And I promise . . . I won't either. I'll be right here to tell you stories about what a fine soldier and a great man your daddy was. I've got a feeling you might be a lot like him."

The baby curled his tiny hand around the tip of Jake's finger and gave a featherlight squeeze. That almost imperceptible gesture was like Eli's saying, "No worries, buddy. I got your back. It's all going to be okay."

That's when the dam holding back all the stored-up guilt and brittle emotion shattered.

And Jake finally cried.

Chapter 16

On a normal day, Annie preferred to leave flying to the experts like the flying monkeys from the *Wizard of Oz* or Sully, the pilot who miraculously landed a crippled jetliner safely in the Hudson River. Today, however, wasn't a normal day. So Annie was happy to join the league of those who strapped on wings of happiness.

Jana had finally heard back from the Marines regarding the honors for Jared, and Annie couldn't wait for Jake to hear the news.

Not that the prospect of hearing from him anytime soon was likely. She hadn't heard a word since he'd taken off for Arizona over a week ago. So she didn't actually know when she or his mother would be able to share that information. Her worry meter had peaked the moment he'd driven away, but she knew he needed this time to sort things out. To find whatever it was he sought so he could move forward—one step at a time.

Grief and guilt didn't make for good partners, and Jake had spent a lot of time in their company. She hoped this mission would give him some peace of mind. She hoped he'd come home to her, able to breathe a little easier, and maybe even to see part of the heroics he'd played that fateful day. And she hoped the news would add to the inner peace he so desperately needed.

In the meantime, she waited for a call, a text, anything to tell her he was doing okay. That Hank was being a good travel companion. And that he'd be coming home soon. To her. But as she put Max to bed, took her shower, and slipped into her most comfortable sleep tank set, the only thing her phone registered were several attempts from an anonymous caller with an area code from the Seattle area.

She didn't know who or why anyone from there would be calling her. Scratch that. She might know who, but she didn't want to know the why. So she'd ignored the calls. Pushed away the niggling at the back of her conscience and carried on after deleting the number from her list of recent calls.

Though it was barely eight o'clock, exhaustion from the long day washed over her, and she flipped on the TV to unwind. Bad news, sitcom reruns, and the duck dudes weren't going to help. She turned off the boob tube and turned on her collection of sexy country tunes. While Rascal Flatts made her melt, she lay down on the sofa, opened the historical romance novel she'd picked up just yesterday, and got lost between the pages.

A noise startled her, and she realized she'd fallen asleep on the sofa with the book in her hands. For a moment, she thought maybe she was dreaming that Lord Ambersley was breaking down her door to ravish her. Two long blinks and a knock on the door helped her realize she remained in the modern world, and the rakish lord would remain within the book covers without her.

She ran a hand through her hair, then stood on tiptoe to peer through the peephole. The tremulous smile and hesitant wave that greeted her stole her breath. Quickly, she unlatched the dead bolt, and threw open the door.

"You're home!"

Instead of a verbal response, Jake pulled her into his arms and crushed her against his big, strong body. His mouth covered hers in a searing kiss hot with desperation and passion. His hands slipped down her backside and his fingers snuck beneath her short pajamas, digging into her bottom and lifting her until she wrapped her legs around him. He came inside the house, kicked the door shut behind them, and turned her so that her back pressed against the wall.

"God, I missed you," he whispered against her ear as he trailed hot, moist kisses down the side of her neck. "Is Max asleep?"

"Yes." The single word came out on a rush of air. "I missed you too."

She felt his smile against the curve of her shoulder.

"Then you won't mind if I do this?" His thumbs hooked in the straps of her stretchy cotton top and pulled it down to her waist. "Or this?" While she hung on to his broad shoulders, he lowered his head and licked her pebbled nipple before he slowly sucked it into his mouth.

A lusty moan was her response to the slick heat of his tongue circling and his mouth gently tugging one nipple before he moved onto the other.

"And damn but I've been dreaming of this." He moved back so that she had to drop her legs from around his waist. When her feet touched the floor, he whipped off her shorts, dropped to his knees, and parted her eager flesh with his tongue. One touch was all it took to have her begging. But he took more than one taste. He took two. Three. And then she was mindless. Still, coming without him was unthinkable.

"I need you, Jake," she moaned as he did something amazing with his tongue and fingers. "I need you inside me. Now." He licked her again. "Please."

Like that was the magic word, he came up her body using his hands and mouth until her hands could reach for his belt buckle. The downward slide of the zipper on his jeans was a rhythmic accent to Billy Currington's "Don't" on the stereo. Her hands captured the waistband of those worn jeans and boxer briefs and pulled them down. His erection sprang free into her hands, and she stroked him slowly, with pressure, from base to head. He pushed into her hand and groaned his approval.

"Put your legs around me again." His deep, sexy request rumbled against her chest and tickled her deep inside.

She did as he asked, and, in one smooth motion, he was inside her, hot and throbbing. His favorite word slipped from his mouth on a long, lusty groan as he buried his face in the curve of her neck. Instead of withdrawing and plunging inside her again, he held completely still.

"Annie?"

"Yes?"

He lifted his head and looked straight into her eyes. "I love you."

"Oh, Jake." Her chest clogged with emotion as she captured his face between her hands and kissed the mouth that had just said the three most wonderful words she'd ever heard. "I love you so much."

A happy spark ignited in his dark blue eyes. He gave her that devilish Wilder grin as he withdrew his erection and slowly thrust inside her again. "Show me."

Of course, she did.

$\mathcal{A}$ man always had good intentions when he made love to the woman he loved. He wanted her to feel good, be satisfied, and cry out for more. All that might have happened, but for Jake, it went too fast. He'd wanted to last all night. Regrettably, he'd been too happy to see her. Too eager. And now their reunion required a round two.

Maybe that wasn't so bad.

"You smell so damned good." He kissed her neck and inhaled deeply. "Like frosting on a cupcake."

"And hot sex?" She chuckled.

"Yeah." He grinned "That too."

They kissed again, and Jake knew his heart had never been so glad. So content. It hadn't taken a trip to Arizona for him to realize his feelings, but it had taken that trip for him to be able to set them free.

"Are you hungry?" she asked, pulling her little cotton shorts back on while he managed to tuck himself back into his jeans.

"Nope. I just got what I've been starving for."

Her smile made him feel so damn good.

"But if you've got something in the fridge that can be warmed up quick, I'd be happy to make it go away."

"How does a bowl of beef stew and some homemade corn-bread muffins sound?"

"Not half as delicious as tasting you all over again. But it sounds pretty good. I haven't eaten since I left Yuma."

"Where's Hank?" She ran a hand through her hair to untangle the muss he'd created.

"Dropped him off at home. Gave him a big bowl of food, but he was out and snoring before I even left the house. He was a pretty good travel buddy except for the time I gave him a burger from Mickey D's that gave him gas."

She laughed. "I'm sure he's sorry."

"Yeah. He gave me those sad eyes every time he tooted. I figured that was his form of apology."

For anyone listening to their easy banter, they'd figure this was any other day in an otherwise normal life. Jake realized Annie wasn't asking about the trip or what had happened there. In her untypical fashion, she was giving him enough time to bring up the subject when he felt comfortable.

"You want something to drink? A beer maybe?" she asked, heading toward the kitchen.

He caught her hand, drew her into his arms, and kissed the back of her fingers. "I want *you*." He gently touched the side of her face and tucked a lock of hair behind her ear. "I love you, Annie. I just want you to know that I mean it, and I wasn't just saying it earlier in the heat of the moment."

"I know." Her eyes searched his face. "I can feel it."

"Good. And I promise not to let you forget."

Her cheeks dimpled, and her quiet understanding soothed away all the anxiety he'd suffered those long, last fifty miles coming home.

"I just need one favor," he said, "and then I'd like to tell you what happened in Arizona. If you want to know."

"Anything for you. And yes. Absolutely I want to know."

"Can I see Max?"

In response, she took him by the hand and led him into her son's room. She didn't turn on the light, but the room was aglow enough from the hall light to see the little boy sleeping in the spindle-post crib.

Peaceful.

Not a care in the world.

That's what Jake saw when he looked down to the chubby tot in the dancing-frog sleepers. Jake touched his soft blond curls and huffed out a chuckle when he found the little guy a bit sweaty.

Settled against the mattress, his plump cheek pushed out his bottom lip, and his long lashes lay like dark feathers against his cheeks. He looked like a cherub you'd see on a Valentine's Day card. In Jake's heart, he felt sure Eli's son would look like this soon—healthy and sleeping soundly. Elijah—like Max—had angels watching over him.

"Will he wake up if I hold him?" Jake asked Annie.

"If he does, he'll go right back to sleep." She gestured. "Go ahead."

Jake reached into the crib and lifted the boy into his arms. Max sighed, snuggled against Jake's chest, but didn't wake up.

"No worries, little man. I'm going to watch over you and your mama." He stroked his fingers over baby-soft hair and kissed the top of Max's sweaty little head. "I love you."

Beside him, Annie audibly sighed. "He has your name, you know."

Surprised, Jake looked up. "What?"

"You never asked, but his full name is Maxwell Jacob Morgan."

To know that Annie had gifted him with that honor did something crazy to his heart that made him feel like crying all over again.

"I promise I'll do right by him, Annie. I'll do right by you."

"I know." She leaned in and pressed her lips to his. "I didn't give him your name because I thought anything would ever happen between the two of us. I gave it because you've always been one of the most decent men I've ever known. And in some way, I wanted my son to bear that dignity."

"I'm grateful, Annie. I truly am."

"And hungry?"

He chuckled. "Very."

"Then how about we put the tornado back down, and I'll serve you up that soup."

"Okay." Reluctantly, he turned back toward the crib. Before he laid Max back down with the fuzzy yellow blanket and plush Scooby-Doo, Jake kissed his sweaty forehead again. The love that filled his heart was unexpected, but he embraced it. Because the alternative was too hard to bear.

Once Max was settled back in, Jake turned to Annie and voiced the one thing he never expected to say. "I wish he was mine."

Her smile wobbled. Just a little. "He's more yours than anyone's."

Not true, Jake thought. Until recently, he'd barely been able to hold him without falling apart. But he appreciated the sentiment. And in the future he planned to play an important role in little Max's life. He'd earn that right—whatever it took.

"Come on." Annie took his hand and led him into the kitchen. "Let's get you something to eat."

While she warmed up a big bowl of stew and several corn-bread muffins, he sat at the table and told her of his visit with Rebecca Harris. And while he ate, he told her of Eli's son. Tears filled her eyes.

"Is there anything we can do to help?" she asked, blotting her tears with a tissue. If he hadn't been stuffing his face, he would have kissed them away. Annie had so much spirit, and she tried to be so tough, but deep down she was just a sweet little marshmallow with a heart so warm she'd dared to let him inside.

"I thought about that on the way home." He slathered a muffin with butter. "All this time I've been trying to decide what to do with my life beyond feeding cattle and digging up the backyard. I think I finally have it figured out."

"That's wonderful."

He nodded. "It feels right."

"What did you come up with?"

"I want to go back to college and get my degree in horticulture. Eventually, I'd like to open a landscape-and-design business."

"That sounds perfect."

"But first I want to put together an organization in honor of fallen soldiers that will assist their children with financial aid for medical issues like Eli's son, or help them with their educational endeavors. Jared was always the smartest of all of us. I think that might be a good way to thank him and to honor him."

Annie set down the dish towel, crawled onto his lap, and wrapped her arms around his neck. "There's my hero."

"I just want to pay tribute to the men and women who gave their all." He rubbed her back, enjoying the feel of her and the closeness they shared. "I'm no hero."

"That's not what the Marines believe."

"Annie, I don't—"

"And you know what else they believe?"

"I really don't care."

"They believe . . ." she continued, obviously not listening to him. "That your brother, Eli, and the other men in your group that day are heroes too. And that they *all* deserve proper honor. I went to your mother and explained the situation. She said that the Marines had already contacted her about Jared's honors. But like you, she'd pushed it aside and *forgotten* to respond."

"What?"

"When you're awarded the Purple Heart, you will also be accepting Jared's honors." A little smile tipped her lips. "Do you care now?"

"How . . ." He took a breath, but it did nothing to slow the excited leap of his heart. "I don't know what to say."

He really didn't. So he just wrapped his arms around her. "Thank you. Again. For not giving up on me."

"Don't thank me." A suggestive look darkened her eyes as she trailed her fingers down his chest. "Unless you want to do it *my way*."

He stopped chuckling when her hands reached his belt buckle.

God, he loved this woman.

Prepared to do things *her way* right there on top of the kitchen table, he pushed his bowl aside and began to lift her up onto the surface.

A knock on the front door stopped the action.

Annie looked up at the clock. "Who the heck can that be this late at night?"

"I don't know." He kissed the frustrated groan from her lips. "But hold that previous naked thought. I'll be right back."

"That's okay. You finish eating. I'll get it. It's probably just snoopy Arlene wondering why your truck is parked in my driveway."

Annie flipped on the outside light and opened the door. When she saw the person standing on her porch, her eyes widened. The guy could easily be taken for a vagrant. Holey jeans, a wrinkled flannel shirt, and a slouch knit cap that did not hide long, dark, curly hair that looked like it hadn't been washed in some time.

"Doug!" Shock infiltrated every cell in her body, and she battled the urge to slam the door and lock it tight.

"Hey." He gave her a casual nod. "How's it going?"

"How's it going? *Seriously?* After almost two years, you show up, and you want to know how it's going? What the hell are you doing here?"

"My band and I are heading to Austin for a gig, and we need a place to crash." He gestured toward the beat-up white van parked in front of her house. "I thought since you lived close, you wouldn't mind putting us up for a few days."

She'd heard the expression "words escaped me" before, and now she knew how it felt. For the life of her, her mouth would not form anything further than a gasp of disbelief. Her fingers curled into fists. She went numb, and the buzz in her ears became deafening. Like a tower of strength, she felt Jake come up behind her. He settled a warm hand on the small of her back as he stepped forward and with him, brought the support she hadn't realized she'd ever really need.

"Who are you?" Jake asked, glaring down at a much shorter Doug.

"Doug Patterson."

Jake looked at her and obviously took note of her stunned silence. Either that, or it was the collision of frown lines pulled taut between her eyes. "*The* Doug?" he asked her.

She managed to nod, while the numbness dissolved, and the burn of anger took flight through her chest. "The one and only."

"Who are *you*?" Doug asked Jake.

Instead of a frown, Jake grinned. "The man who's doing everything in his power not to step out there and kick your ass."

"Hey, man." Doug's eyes widened as he took two steps back and held up his hands. "I'm not looking for trouble. Just a place to crash for a couple days. That's all."

"Really?" Jake's fingers tightened against her back. "That's all? You didn't come for any other reason? Because I'm having a hard time wondering why you suddenly show up after so long and don't ask to see your son."

"I don't really have a place in my life for a kid. Or a steady girlfriend." Doug glanced at Annie, then shrugged. "Sorry. I just need a place to crash."

A cry burst from Annie's lips that came out like a maniacal laugh. "It's always about *you*, isn't it, Doug? *You* need a place to crash. *You* need some cash. *You* need some space so you can *create*. *You* need a new surround-sound for the TV you charged in my name without my permission. Well guess what, *Doug*, it's not about *you* anymore. How dare you show up at my door after walking out on me and my baby?"

"Darlin'?" Jake curled his arm around her shoulders and kissed her forehead. "Take a breath. I've got this."

Jake stepped out onto the porch, and Doug took another step back. "Got a question for you." Jake crossed his arms across his chest and spread his feet just enough to make him look a little more like the Marine he used to be.

"Sure, man."

"Are you high?"

Doug shrugged. "Smoked a doobie a couple hours ago, but it's probably worn off by now. So can we crash here? We won't smoke anything in the house if that's what you're worried about."

Jake looked over his shoulder and tossed Annie a *were you seriously with this guy?* look. She shrugged. Because, yeah, this wasn't her first moment in recognizing she'd hooked up with a total loser.

"Smoking isn't my concern," Jake said. "I just want to know if you're of a clear mind when I ask if you're willing to sign away your rights to Max."

"Max?"

"You don't even know his name?" Jake's favorite four-letter word leaped from his mouth. "And do *not* shrug, or I might have to hurt you."

"Don't know his name."

"I never contacted him after Max was born," Annie rushed to explain.

"Doesn't matter. The asshole should have made yours and Max's well-being his first concern."

"Hey, dude. No need for name-calling."

Annie almost laughed at the total panic on Doug's face.

"Okay. Then how about this, *dude.*" Jake's shoulders came up, and he stood even taller, looked even more threatening. "You've made your intent pretty clear. And the way I see it? No one like *you* deserves to be called a father. Especially not when we're talking about a special little boy like Max. So, if Annie decides she wants to legally cut you out of his life, I want you to tell her right now that you won't object. That you'll quietly sign the papers and go away."

"What's in it for you?" Doug asked.

"Nice to see you finally show some interest, my friend. But it's too little, too late. What's in it for me is that I love Annie. She's an amazing woman and an incredible mother. And I love that little boy in there too. They're *my* family now."

Annie gasped, and pride blossomed in her heart. She'd never had anyone take a stand for her before. Other than Abby, she'd never known anyone to completely have her back and be ready to go to war in her honor. Jake had staked his claim. He loved her and her son, and he wasn't afraid to let the world know. He'd protect her no matter what. He'd be her soft place to land, but he'd also step up and take down anyone who tried to hurt her or Max.

If she thought she'd been crazy in love with Jake

before, there were no words to describe the absolute love and devotion that spun through her heart now.

"Wow, dude," Doug exclaimed. "That's a little caveman."

"It's better than being a selfish, ignorant prick."

Once again, Doug shrugged, and Annie could tell Jake had to hold himself back from picking the weasel up by those skinny shoulders and tossing him on his ass.

"It's cool, man." Doug looked at Annie completely emotionless. "Whatever. Send the papers. I'll sign."

Jake looked at Annie, reached out, and took her hand. He gave her a reassuring squeeze then stepped back to the doorway to be by her side. Concern darkened his eyes. "You okay?"

She nodded. "As long as I've got you, I'm perfect."

"You've got me. Forever." He grinned, then he turned back toward Doug. "It will be good to know someone as self-centered as you won't be able to change his mind someday and try to come back and screw up a kid's life. Annie and Max deserve better."

"If you say so." Doug gave a *whatever* toss of his dirty hair.

For Max's sake, it hurt Annie to know this person really had no emotion at all. None.

"So . . . can we crash here or what?" he asked.

"Darlin'?" Jake turned to Annie. "What are your thoughts on this? It's your call."

"You want a place to crash?" She speared Doug with a glare, released the leftover anger and hurt she'd held inside for almost two years, then she completely washed him from her heart. "Sorry. Not here. Not now. Not ever." She took extreme pleasure in closing the door in his face.

"Someday, he'll regret his stupidity," Jake said, while Annie clicked the dead bolt in place.

"It's probably going to take a couple of decades or more. But I can live with that because I'm not going to sit around and wait. I've got better things to do."

Jake caught the huge grin on her face just before she pushed him up against the door.

"Darlin', what are you doing?"

She responded by kissing him like there was no tomorrow. Not that he minded. When they came up for air, she touched his face with gentle fingers.

"We're *your* family now?" •

"Yeah, Annie. You are. I hope you want that too."

"More than anything." Next thing he knew, her hands were unbuckling his belt, and her grin had turned seductive temptress. "You are so getting laid. Right. Now."

It was his turn to grin. "So you're saying I handled that okay?"

"Like a man who truly cares." She hummed her approval. "And now it's my turn to handle *you*."

At the slide of his zipper, Jake reaped the rewards of loving an incredibly sexy woman who didn't seem to mind if he occasionally went a little alpha crazy. Or got a little possessive. After all, he was a man who was just learning how to let all the love he had inside finally break free.

And it felt damned good.

Chapter 17

$\mathcal{A}$ month had passed since Doug's surprise visit, and life had definitely taken a turn for the better. Now that Jared and Eli were both to receive the appropriate honors, Jake felt he could finally breathe.

When everyone hadn't been sitting at the old kitchen table helping put together their mother and Martin's wedding, they'd been gathered together working on the nonprofit to memorialize Jared and Eli, and to benefit Elijah. They'd come up with an idea for a fund-raiser that held a lot of appeal for the community of Sweet and the surrounding towns. A spectacular affair they'd created to allow adults to be kids for a night was being planned for their first event. Not surprisingly, all his sisters-in-law had a lot of experience with fund-raisers, so Jake had welcomed them on board as chairpersons alongside Annie to organize the event.

He'd completed the pergola over the creek but

hadn't yet shown it to anyone. The pool would come last, but the backyard was taking shape with the new stone flooring, patio roof, and landscaping he'd put in place. Still, there was a lot of work to be done.

Even so, his mother had decided to have a Thanksgiving-themed wedding in the barn, with decorations of straw bales and pumpkins. She'd also decided to keep it a semiprivate affair, with only family and close friends in attendance. For a woman who provided the town with a big summer blowout barbecue, her choice was a bit surprising. That she'd chosen to be married on the property she and their father had built together was just as unexpected. Until she explained that it was her way of letting go of the past.

Letting go of the past and grabbing onto the future was a concept Jake was learning to embrace. Baby steps, Annie had told him, were better than no steps at all. Today he planned to kick off his training wheels and take one of the biggest steps of his life. Yes, it was his mother's wedding day. But it was also Thanksgiving, and Jake was so damn thankful for all he'd been given, he wanted to celebrate in a big way.

With the entire family inside his house waiting for the minister and getting ready for the nuptials, the sound level was close to deafening. Jake looked around at the hustle and bustle and grinned. The family had grown by leaps and bounds with the arrival of Jackson and Abby's baby girl Lily just two weeks ago. Jake chuckled as he watched his brother hold his new daughter as if he might break her. Reno, now an expert at handling Adeline, who was a little over four months old, was trying to give suggestions. It seemed odd seeing the two brothers who had a strong, tough side, be so gentle with their offspring.

While Annie helped in the kitchen with the reception dinner, Jake volunteered to be in charge of keeping an eye on Max, who seemed to have learned how to run in recent days. Either that, or Jake had just grown slow.

His mother rushed by with curlers in her hair and her dress half-zipped, followed closely by Arlene Potter, who held a can of hair spray in her hand, and Gladys Lewis, who held a tube of red lipstick while tugging at the waistband of her orthopedic stockings through the bright orange muumuu she'd chosen for the festivities.

Nearby, Martin, his mother's fiancé, straightened his tie and tried not to look nervous as hell. Jake couldn't blame him. The man had led a quiet life until he'd gotten tangled up with the Wilders. And since the poor man had escaped bodily harm when the brothers discovered he was seeing their mom on the sly a couple years ago, Jake figured they should all go easy on him today.

"Chaos." Jesse chuckled, watching his wife Allison trying to zip up the wedding gown on a moving target.

"Status quo." Jake laughed. "So when are you and Allie adding to the Wilder brood?"

"We were going to wait."

"*Were?*"

"Yep." Jesse nodded. "Past tense."

"So that means . . ."

"We'll probably make an announcement tonight after the wedding."

"Allie's pregnant?"

"Three months."

"Unplanned?"

Jesse grinned. "Not really. At least not with all the practicing we've been doing."

"Congratulations." Jake extended his hand, and they shook.

"So when are you going to make an honest woman out of Annie?"

"Truthfully?" Jake said, as she came into the room, hands full of autumn-colored cloth napkins, and he couldn't stop the jolt of happiness that shot through his heart. The yellow dress she wore was perfect. Formfitting yet still soft and flirty. He couldn't wait to take it off her. "I can't believe she'd want to be stuck with me for the rest of her life."

"Bullshit." Jesse grinned again, something he did frequently these days. "She's crazy about you."

"Hard to know why."

"Well, maybe she's just crazy."

"She'd have to be to put up with me."

"You know what they say, real love is when you know the worst thing about someone, and it doesn't matter."

"Yeah, well, she's sure had to wade through a lot of worst."

"Doesn't look like she's running off."

"Nope. I'm pretty damned lucky."

Jesse patted him on the back. "That you are, little brother."

Jake glanced into the kitchen, where Annie stood next to Fiona, Jackson's ex, putting the finishing touches on the wedding cake. Fireman Mike, Fiona's new husband, held up Izzy so she could help. The entire family was here.

Everyone except his father and his brother.

Not for the first time that day did Jake feel a pang of sadness in his heart. Of course, if his dad were alive, there'd be no reason for his mom to be putting on a wedding dress.

His dad and brother had loved when the entire family got together. They'd be even more thrilled with all the girls now in the family. And they'd love little Max.

Jake caught sight of the toddler heading toward the front door and ran to scoop him up before he escaped the next time someone came into the house. He made a big deal of catching Max and lifting him into the air, and was rewarded with the little guy's giggles. Just as he settled Max on his hip, someone knocked on the door. Jake opened it to find a blond-haired man standing there wearing a nice suit and a wary expression as he glanced over Jake's shoulder to all the activity in the house.

"I hope I'm in the right place," he said. "I'm looking for Jana Wilder."

"You the minister?" Jake asked.

"No. I'm . . . uh . . . a friend. Hopefully."

"And your name is?"

"Peter Castlewood." He offered his hand and Jake shook it. When Max stuck his chubby little hand out too, the man named Peter smiled and shook it also.

"I think all the guests are supposed to meet in the barn for the ceremony."

Peter looked at him like he didn't understand.

"Aren't you here for the wedding?"

"I apologize." He stepped back. "It looks like I've come at a bad time."

Jesse joined them at the door. "How can we help you?"

The man was taking another step backward, and Jake's curiosity grew.

"I just wanted to say hello to Mrs. Wilder."

"Well, you've got about another thirty minutes to do that."

"I'm sorry I interrupted. I'll come back another time."

Jesse looked at Jake and shrugged. Then enlightenment dawned and Jake grabbed Jesse's arm. "Holy shit."

The man was halfway down the steps.

"Hold up." Holding Max, he stepped out onto the veranda, dragging Jesse with him. "How do you know our mother?"

"I don't actually. Except for what I've been told."

"You're him."

Perplexed, Jesse asked, "Him?"

"*Him.*"

Jesse's eyes widened and his head whipped around to where the man stood on the bottom step, looking like he was about to make a run for it. "You were Jared's partner."

The man's chest lifted on a sigh. "Yes."

"Oh my God."

Both Jake and Jesse pulled him into an embrace

that included a lot of backslapping and laughter. Max squealed like it was Christmas morning. Before the poor guy could think they were all crazy and try to escape, they pulled him into the house and shouted for their mother. She came running from the bedroom, with half her hair down and half still in curlers. Her dress was still halfway unzipped, and she was trailed by an entourage of ladies in orange muumuus.

"What in blazes is going on?" Her wedding-day nerves were showing in the tension at the corners of her eyes.

The rest of the family gathered, also waiting to see what the commotion was all about. Max continued to squeal happily in Jake's arms.

"This is Peter Castlewood," Jake said.

"*Jared's* Peter Castlewood," Jesse announced.

A collective sigh floated about the room, and their mother's eyes instantly began to water. In an instant, Martin was at her side, holding her hand, and bringing her forward.

Both her smile and her hand trembled as she lifted it to Peter's cheek. "Sugarplum, we've been waiting for you for so long."

Jake glanced across the room to where Annie stood with her hand to her mouth and tears in her eyes. The emotional impact of meeting the love of their brother's life grabbed Jake by the heart. Life was precious. And short. And you had to make the most of it before it slipped away.

He never expected Annie to be anything more than a pain in his backside and someone to argue with. But she'd become so much more.

She'd become everything.

He kissed the top of Max's little head as joy rippled through him and his mother embraced Peter Castlewood.

"Welcome to the family, sugarplum. Welcome to the family."

Peter looked relieved, and maybe a little teary.

As Peter returned the embrace Jake noticed something in the man's eyes that formed a lump in his throat. Peter seemed truly happy to be there, to be accepted by the family who were now all pushing their way forward to meet and welcome him. But for all that mattered, the man Peter had loved was not there. Would never be there. And that made Jake's heart hurt in too many ways to count.

Yes, life was way too short.

And Jake had no intention of living another day without making the most of it.

Their mother had finally gotten the curlers out of her hair and her dress zipped up in time to say her I do's. The wedding went off without a hitch and was made even more special with the arrival of Jared's partner, who seemed to fit in with their loud and rowdy family just fine. The man had a ready smile and quick wit. Jake could understand how his brother would find Peter Castlewood special. Then again, in Jake's mind, Jared had been the special one. And in his mind, he could also see his big brother and his dad, watching over the festivities and nodding their approval.

In general, weddings were happy affairs. Oh

sure, there was always someone who tipped the champagne bottle a little too hard. And someone who thought the dance floor was a great place to show off their dirty dancing skills. And someone who bowled everyone else down to get at the bridal bouquet or the garter. All things considered, Jake never expected for BFFs Gladys Lewis in her orthopedic shoes and Arlene Potter in her matching orange muumuu to fight over the bridal bouquet and end up on the ground wrestling like Hulk Hogan and Stone Cold Steve Austin.

He did expect eighty-year-old playboy Chester Banks to tip back an adequate amount of George Dickel, but he didn't expect the bowlegged old cowboy to monopolize Jake's time with his woman. From Jake's count, Chester and his giant schnozzola were on dance number three with Annie. Ironically the tune was "Drunk on You," and Jake didn't like the idea of anybody else being drunk on Annie except him.

As the hour grew late, it was time for the babies to be put to bed. Jake carried Max—who'd laid his weary little head on Jake's shoulder—over to Annie to get her help in taking the little boy into the house and putting him in the crib. Abby, exhausted from having a newborn, had offered to sit inside with all the little ones until the reception was over. Jake, looking for some one-on-one time with the woman he loved, took Abby up on the offer.

Annie smiled as he approached.

"I think it's time this little man got some sleep," he shouted over the loud music. "How about you?"

"When I'm done dancing with Chester."

"Yeah." Chester poked an arthritic finger in Jake's chest. "Don't be such a party pooper. It ain't fair you Wilder boys get all the pretty girls anyway."

Annie mouthed "*sorry*," and kept dancing.

Rather than upset the old man and have to listen to his inarguable complaints, Jake made his rounds to have everyone say good night to Max. When he got around to his beaming mother, she held out her arms and embraced them both.

"Thank you, sugarplum, for making this night so special."

"I didn't do anything."

"You smoked the turkeys perfectly. And you built the altar. And you even made sure Miss Giddy and Popcorn had ribbons to match my dress."

"For God's sake, Mom. I didn't buy special ribbons for your goats."

She laughed. "I suppose they just suddenly appeared in the box I gave you."

"Geez. No. Annie bought them."

"Well, I'll make sure to thank her. Unless you'd like to do it for me."

"Can't seem to get her away from Chester long enough to get anything said."

"Oh?" She cocked her head, but that Texas-sized hairdo didn't budge. "Is there something special you want to say to her? Maybe something you'd like to share with your mother?"

"Mom. I didn't know you were so pervy."

"Oh, you." She playfully slapped his arm, then pulled him in for another hug. "Did you hear Allison's expecting?"

"Yeah. Jess told me just before Peter showed up."

"Our family is really growing."

"It sure is."

"Maybe you'd like to add to it?"

"I brought Hank into the family," he said, giving a nod to the black Lab sitting on the toes of Izzy's satin shoes while his niece struggled to keep her eyes open.

"And he's a very special dog. But I was thinking more along the lines of someone like this precious little boy."

"If you take him into the house and put him to bed, you might get your wish."

His mother gasped. Grinned. And said, "Hand that baby over right now."

He chuckled as he handed her the now-sound-asleep toddler, then watched her and her ivory satin gown disappear through the crowd.

The band changed songs again, and Jake took his cue. Unfortunately, by the time he got back to the dance floor, Annie was dancing with Peter. Jake stood on the perimeter and tried to catch her eye, but she was too busy teaching Peter the Texas Two-Step to notice. With a sigh, Jake left the barn and took care of some things in preparation for what he hoped would happen tonight.

When he got back to the barn, Annie was dancing with Chester again. Jake felt his irritation rise. If he didn't know better, he'd think everyone was trying to interfere with his plans. All he wanted was Annie. All to himself. Right now.

Finally, the band took a break and Jake jumped into action. Much to Chester's red-nosed disappointment, Jake snagged Annie by the hand and hauled her away to the tune of Chester's complaints.

"Where's Max?" Annie asked, a little out of breath from all the dancing as Jake pulled her toward the barn door.

"He went out for a horseback ride with Izzy, Adeline, and Lily."

"Funny." Sensing his irritation, she tugged her hand from his and planted her feet in the gravel just outside the door. "Where's Max? Where are you going in such a hurry? And was that an eye roll?"

"Max is in bed. Abby's tired and offered to watch the kids. And yes. That was an eye roll." He caught her hand up again and kissed her fingers. "I've been trying to get five minutes alone with you. I saw my chance, and I'm taking it before anyone else asks you to dance."

A funny little tingle danced in her heart. "Are you jealous?"

"Yes. I've had to share you all night, and I don't like it."

"Awww." She touched his face. "That's so sweet."

"It's not sweet. Because now I'm cranky."

He was. She could see that. She also knew how to unravel his tension quickly. But his mother's wedding reception wasn't really a good place.

"Come on." He took her by the hand she had settled on his cheek and tugged her off into the darkness.

"To where?"

"It's a surprise."

"It's not very polite to just disappear from the reception without saying good night."

"We can tell them tomorrow."

"By then it will be too late, and we'll look rude."

He stopped and pulled her against him. "Why are you giving me such a hard time?"

"Why are you being such a butthead?"

"Because you're giving me a hard time."

She sighed. "Are we fighting?"

"No." He sighed.

"Seems like we are."

"We're not."

"Okay. Can you at least slow down a little? These high heels aren't the easiest to maneuver in."

"Fine. I'll carry you."

"No need—" Without warning, he lifted her into his arms and kept walking. "Ack! Jake, this isn't good for your leg."

"Don't you worry about my leg. I'm fine."

"You're limping."

"That's going to happen the rest of my life. So let's just pretend it's not happening."

"But, Jake—"

"Annie." He stopped, dropped his mouth to hers, and kissed her into silence.

When he lifted his head, she sighed and surrendered. "Okay. Lead the way."

"Thank you."

Jake and the rest of the Wilder men were a tenacious bunch. When they got something in their heads, it didn't creep away on silent feet. It clanged loud like an iron bell until they either got what they wanted or . . . got what they wanted. One of these days, Annie knew she'd probably get used to his dogged determination. Right now, he just had her curiosity up.

Across the backyard they went, and Annie vaguely caught the lovely changes he'd made since they'd made love outside beneath the moonlight.

"Close your eyes," he said.

"Why?"

His chest expanded on a sigh. "Please?"

"Okay." She shut them tight. In the distance, she heard the gurgling of the creek. "Are you planning to drown me in the creek or something?"

"Or something."

The sound of water falling over rocks grew louder, and the scent of damp earth and warm man filled her head. Then Jake stepped up, and the sound of his boots on wood took over her senses and piqued her curiosity. Finally, he set her on her feet, held her by the shoulders, and turned her around.

"Okay. You can open your eyes now."

When she did, she gasped. Somehow, she'd been transported to a fantasyland far, far, away. The deck that crossed the creek made her feel like she was floating downstream on a raft. A copper fire bowl was alive with blue ice and hot flames. The pergola that towered over the deck came complete with soft, white, billowing curtains that fluttered with the breeze. The tree branches overhead and nearby bushes twinkled with fairy lights. And all around the deck were glass votives lit by white candles.

She took a deep breath to contain the happiness in her heart and was surprised when she found the air scented with jasmine. The setting was so romantic, she couldn't help but be utterly charmed.

"Jake, this is beautiful." She turned a full circle to see everything again. "When did you finish it?"

"A couple of weeks ago."

"And you're just now letting me get a look?"

"I wanted to wait for something special."

"Well, your mom's wedding is definitely a special moment."

"I'm not talking about that. I'm talking about this." He eased down to one knee and took her hand, which immediately started to tremble.

"What . . . what are you doing?"

"You want to know why I've been so uptight tonight?" he asked.

"Yes."

"It's because *this* has been burning a hole in my pocket." He pulled out a stylish princess-cut diamond ring set in white gold, then held it up so that the candle and firelight flashed against it and sent sparks flying.

Annie gasped.

"I've been trying to get you alone for hours, so I could tell you how much I love you. And though I don't understand why you put up with me, I'm grateful. I'm sorry we wasted so many years sniping at each other when I could have been kissing you, but I'm glad we finally figured it out."

"Me too." Annie felt like her heart might burst at any moment.

"You're home for me, Annie. You're the one I can

count on to light up my life. You stand by me. You make my life better. And you make me want to be a better man." He gently squeezed her fingers. "You make my heart happy, and I can't see a forever without you and Max in it. I love you, Annie. And I want to have babies with you. Lots of babies. I want to argue with you, then have great makeup sex for the rest of our lives. But more than anything, I want to know if you'll do me the honor of becoming my wife. Because without you . . . I'm nothing. You make me whole, Annie. And I love you. So much."

"Are you serious?"

The smooth skin between his brows puckered. "Please don't make me ask again. It was scary enough the first time."

She laughed to release all the bubbly happiness floating around her heart. Then she kicked off her heels, got to her knees, and cupped his handsome face in her hands. "There's nothing I've ever wanted more in my life. I've loved you since the moment we met. And I've wanted you since you walked naked through your house in the middle of the night."

His head tilted. "So you're saying yes?"

"No." She let that word linger for a split second. Then she kissed the firm, masculine lips that gave her so much pleasure—especially when they smiled like they were doing right now. "I'm saying, hell yeah."

Some things in life were worth waiting for. Some were worth fighting for. And some were worth their weight in gold.

Jake Wilder was all of the above.

Epilogue

All her babies were settled.

And happy.

While a perfect summer night came alive around them, Jana Wilder Lane sat at the beautifully decorated table next to her husband and watched her baby boy dance with his brand-new wife and little Max cuddled securely between them.

Jake had told her just this morning that he'd already filed the papers to legally become Max's daddy. Not that he wasn't already. No one needed a stack of legal papers to know Jake adored the little boy and thought of him as his own.

When Annie looked up and gave Jake that special smile reserved only for those deeply in love, Jana knew everything was going to be all right for her son.

Also enjoying the wedding reception and dancing on Jake's newly finished patio with their little ones were Jackson and Abby with a wiggly six-month-old, Lily, who looked just like her father and appeared to have his fiery temperament as well. And Reno and Charli with their nearly one-year-old, Adeline. Looking as happy as the day they married, Fiona and Mike had included Izzy as they danced about the floor. Sitting out the romantic song were Jesse and Allison, who were too busy cooing over their newborn son, Jared Joseph Wilder.

With the ever-present competition among brothers, as the one who'd delivered the first boy—by blood—into the family, Jesse took delight in using both his brother and father's names. Jana knew deep down her boy had gifted his son with the names out of love though the others would swear it was pure orneriness just to beat them to the punch.

Peter, the newest member of the Wilder boys, laughed as he led the overly amorous Arlene Potter into a wobbly two-step, while Arlene's male counterpart, Chester Banks, got his old bowed legs rocking with Gladys Lewis and her ever-present smear of bright red lipstick.

Just last week, they received word that Eli's son was not only thriving but was growing big and strong with each passing day.

"Our family is really expanding." Martin slipped his arm around Jana's shoulder. "Hard to believe Jake and Annie's wedding will be the last for a while."

"But it all feels so right. Doesn't it?" Jana looked up at the handsome man who'd supported her through some tough moments her sons never knew she'd had. Martin had done it all with quiet reserve and an abiding love she never thought she'd find again.

He kissed her cheek. "As long as you're beside me, it feels perfect."

"We're lucky, you know." She curled her fingers over the top of his hand. "To have found each other in this big old world."

Martin smiled. "I know you must miss them at times like this."

Them.

Her husband, Joe, and her firstborn son, Jared.

"I'll always miss them. But at moments like this . . ." She glanced around the patio, where those she loved were gathered. "At moments like this, I feel closer to them than ever. I know Joe and Jared are here. I can feel them in my soul. And I know they're both smiling."

"You're an amazing woman, Jana."

"No. But I am very blessed. Because right now, life at Wilder Ranch is truly sweet."

Heart full of happiness, she laid her head on Martin's shoulder, and sighed.

Next spring, join Candis Terry
for a sparkling new series . . .
Welcome to Sunshine Valley,
deep in the heart of the Washington wine country.
Prepare to fall in love with the Kincade Brothers
as they attempt to rescue their beloved
Sunshine Creek Vineyards,
restore their family name,
and tackle a chance at happily ever after.

Coming 2016

From Avon Books

Indulge in all of Candis Terry's Sweet, Texas books!

Anything But Sweet

A Sweet, Texas Novel, Book 1

For years Ex-Marine Reno Wilder managed to uphold his end of the Wilder Boys' wild reputation. But the scars of war and the deaths of those he loved have flipped the switch on his point of view. Now, to keep tradition and memories alive, he'll settle for a staid life of wash, rinse, repeat.

When the senior citizens of Sweet, Texas believe it's time for their little town to become a destination for tourists, they contact a new TV makeover show. Their community is chosen to participate and everyone is pleased—except Reno.

Beneath her headstrong desire to upend Reno's peace and quiet, makeover show host and designer Charlotte Brooks has something to offer that has nothing to do with changing drapes and everything to do with showing him that change can be sexy, hot, and very, very sweet.

Neither of them saw it coming. Who will stand their ground? Who will find common ground? And who will let go of their past and grab hold of a future full of promise?

Sweetest Mistake

A Sweet, Texas Novel, Book 2

From the moment he became her toddler-sized sandbox knight in shining armor to the day he went off to war, Jackson Wilder has secretly been in love with Abigail Morgan. She's his best friend and the first girl he ever made love to. With the sands of war at the bottom of his hourglass, he heads home to surprise Abby and finally profess his love. But as everyone knows surprises can backfire, and upon his return, Jackson discovers that his news comes way too late.

Abby has made some mistakes in her life, but none as monumental as marrying a man she barely knew and sinking into a loveless marriage. When she hits the age of thirty her job as a trophy wife comes to an abrupt end and there's no place for her to go but home. Abby thinks she's learned her lesson the hard way until she returns to Sweet. And a homecoming just wouldn't be complete without coming face-to-face with her biggest (and sexiest) mistake.

Home Sweet Home

A Sweet, Texas Novella

Lieutenant Aiden Marshall returns to Sweet, Texas after facing the devastation of war. With the help of the entire town—and a tail-wagging companion—the woman he's always loved makes her hero's homecoming all the more sweet.

Something Sweeter

A Sweet, Texas Novel, Book 3

A dream come true . . .

To the single women of Sweet, Texas former Marine Jesse Wilder is hot, hunky perfection with six-pack abs and a heart of gold. He's a veterinarian who loves animals, kids, is devoted to his family, and is financially stable.

The best part? No woman has yet snagged him or put a ring on his finger.

The problem? Jesse's been down a long, bumpy road and isn't the least bit interested in setting his boots on the path to matrimony.

Comes heart-to-heart with a wedding planner and her big secret . . .

Sure, Allison Lane makes a living helping others plan their big day, but that doesn't mean she has to actually believe in matrimonial bliss. Her family's broken track record proves she just doesn't have the settle-down gene swimming in her DNA. And though she finds Jesse fantasy material, why should she take the word of this confirmed playboy that all roads lead to "I do?"

In their battle for a happily-ever-after

Sweet Fortune

A Sweet, Texas Novella

Sarah Randall has lost her job, her apartment, and her patience hoping for her own Mr. Right. Tired of being invisible to the opposite sex, a leap of faith sends her straight to Sweet, Texas. There she encounters sexy Deputy Brady Bennett. To catch his eye, Sarah needs to face her fears and become a woman interesting enough to pique his curiosity.

Deputy Brady Bennett thought he had his life all tied up in a pretty package, but she married someone else. Determined not to suffer another heartbreak, he finds he can't resist the fascination attached to the gifts that mysteriously turn up in his mailbox. Will his secret admirer ever reveal herself? And if she does, will he be ready to let love in?

Sweet Cowboy Christmas

A Sweet, Texas Novella

Mistletoe, holly, and cowboys. Oh my! Christmas in Texas has never been sweeter.

Years ago, Chase Morgan traded in his dusty cowboy boots for the shimmering lights of New York City and a fast track up the corporate ladder. But when his shiny life is turned on end just in time for Christmas, Chase knows he needs to reevaluate, even if that means going home to Texas to endure his least favorite holiday.

When Mr. Tall, Dark, and Smoking Hot walks through her door at the Magic Box Guest Ranch, Faith Walker sees just another handsome, rich exec looking to play cowboy for a week—at her expense. She's sure the grumpy, but sexy-as-hell Scrooge will put a crimp in her holly-jolly plans. Until a sizzling kiss has her seeing him in a new light.

Chase is haunted by secrets, and even though it goes entirely against her "hands off the guests" rule, Faith is tempted to help him leave the past behind. As the magic of the season swirls around them, she is determined to succeed, because now she is certain one sweet cowboy Christmas will never be enough.

Sweet Surprise

A Sweet, Texas Novel, Book 4

Fiona Wilder knows all about falling in lust. Love? That's another story. Determined not to repeat past mistakes, the single mom and cupcake shop owner is focused on walking the straight and narrow. But trouble has a way of finding her. And this time it comes in the form of a smoking hot firefighter who knows all the delicious ways to ignite her bad-girl fuse.

Firefighter Mike Halsey learned long ago that playing with fire just gets you burned. He's put his demons behind him, and if there's one line he won't cross it's getting involved with his best friend's ex. But when fate throws him in the path of the beautiful, strong, and off-limits Fiona, will he be able to fight their attraction? Or will he willingly go down in flames?

At Avon Books, we know your passion for romance—once you finish one of our novels, you find yourself wanting more.

May we tempt you with . . .

- **Excerpts** from our upcoming releases.

- Entertaining **extras**, including authors' personal photo albums and book lists.

- Behind-the-scenes **scoop** on your favorite characters and series.

- **Sweepstakes** for the chance to win free books, romantic getaways, and other fun prizes.

- Writing **tips** from our authors and editors.

- **Blog** with our authors and find out why they love to write romance.

- **Exclusive content** that's not contained within the pages of our novels.

Join us at
www.avonbooks.com

AVON *An Imprint of* HarperCollins*Publishers*
www.avonromance.com

Available wherever books are sold or please call 1-800-331-3761 to order.

*G*ive in to your Impulses!

These unforgettable stories only take a second to buy and give you hours of reading pleasure!

Go to *www.AvonImpulse.com* and see what we have to offer.

Available wherever e-books are sold.

AVONIMPULSE